Hershey Herself

Cecilia Galante

ALADDIN MIX
New York   London   Toronto   Sydney

This book is a work of fiction. Any references to historical events, real people, or real locales are used fictitiously. Other names, characters, places, and incidents are the product of the author's imagination, and any resemblance to actual events or locales or persons, living or dead, is entirely coincidental.

ALADDIN MIX

Simon & Schuster Children's Publishing Division

1230 Avenue of the Americas, New York, NY 10020

Copyright © 2008 by Cecilia Galante

All rights reserved, including the right of reproduction in whole or in part in any form.

ALADDIN PAPERBACKS, ALADDIN MIX, and related logo

are registered trademarks of Simon & Schuster, Inc.

Designed by Jessica Sonkin

The text of this book was set in Fairfield Light.

Manufactured in the United States of America

First Aladdin Mix edition May 2008

2 4 6 8 10 9 7 5 3 1

Library of Congress Control Number 2007934386

ISBN-13: 978-1-4169-5463-7

ISBN-10: 1-4169-5463-5

ACKNOWLEDGMENTS

Writing may begin as a solitary task, but it is rarely completed without the aid of others. To this end, I would like to pay special tribute to those who believed in me throughout the process, especially my agent, Jessica Regel, whose unwavering commitment leaves me continually awed; my editor, Molly McGuire, whose enthusiasm for Hershey brought an entirely new—and brilliant—dimension to the story; and for the entire team at Simon & Schuster, who have done so much to bring this book to life.

Thank you to my readers along the way who offered sage and sensitive advice: Dr. Joseph Plummer, Theresa Plummer, Judy Plummer, Gina Marsicano, Donna Burns-Rader, Lou Rader, Aly Bartolomei, and Don McMillan, as well as my writing teachers at Goddard College, especially Rebecca Brown, Darcey Steinke, and Martha Southgate, all of whom read sections of the original manuscript and encouraged me to continue. A special thank-you to my sisters, most notably Josie Jesser, who assisted me with all the Spanish translations, and to Therese Plummer, who came up with the wonderful title.

I remain forever grateful to my husband and my children, whose infinite patience and generosity remain two of the greatest gifts I will ever receive.

And finally, I would like to thank Brighter Tomorrows, who, fourteen years ago, took me in and sheltered me from the storm. There are no words to express my gratitude. I owe you everything.

This book is dedicated to my girl,
my heartbeat,
Sarah Tate.

PROLOGUE

NOTEBOOK #3

*This notebook is the property of Hershey Hollenback.
If lost, please return IMMEDIATELY to
113 Lilac Lane, Sommersville, PA.

August 12, 2001
MY FAVORITE THINGS IN THE WORLD
(otherwise known as things I seriously couldn't live without):
   1. Cheetos—the real kind that stain your fingers
   orange, not the store brand ones.
   2. My notebooks.
   3. Mom.
   4. My new kitten, Augustus Gloop.
MY LEAST FAVORITE THINGS IN THE WORLD
(otherwise known as things I seriously could live without):
   1. Mom's boyfriend, Slade West.
   2. Slade's Job List.
   3. Andrea Wicker.

4. My bad eye.

5. Did I mention Slade West?

November 11, 2001

SOME THINGS I KNOW FOR SURE:

1. I hate Slade.

2. Cheetos taste even better if you put them in the microwave for 6.5 seconds.

3. I am fat.

4. My eye will never get better.

5. Most people I know suck.

NOTEBOOK #6

*This notebook is the property of Hershey Hollenback.
If lost, please return IMMEDIATELY to
113 Lilac Lane, Sommersville, PA.

September 3, 2003
FIRST DAY OF EIGHTH GRADE:
Positives:
    1. They put Cheetos in the lunchroom vending machine.
    2. My new homeroom teacher, Mrs. Grant, is
    pretty cool.
    3. Met a new girl named Phoebe. Kind of weird,
    but nice, too.
    4. Don't have to take gym until the second quarter.
Negatives:
    1. Got into it with Andrea, who was giving the new girl
    a hard time.
    2. Andrea is starting the fat jokes again.
    3. Science teacher picks his nose when he thinks no
    one is looking.
    4. The mashed potatoes at lunch taste like soap.

September 28, 2003
PHOEBE MILLRIGHT:
    1. Wears really weird things in her hair.

2. SUPER skinny.

3. Has like five million black rubber bracelets on both arms.

4. Always has on the same cardigan sweater, no matter how warm.

5. Wants to be a professional juggler. (Can already juggle three bags of Fritos for 24.8 seconds, and four pears for 12.2 seconds.)

6. Eats lunch with me every day.

November 3, 2003

WHY I SHOULDN'T BE FRIENDS WITH PHOEBE ANYMORE:

1. Andrea is even meaner to me now that I am friends with Phoebe.

2. She lives in a motel. (Weird!)

3. Her cardigan sweater is starting to stink.

4. She says I am too negative.

5. She saw Mom crying on the front porch yesterday.

November 15, 2003

WHY I WILL ALWAYS BE FRIENDS WITH PHOEBE:

1. She makes me laugh.

2. She asked me to be her juggling partner in the Sommersville talent show at the end of the year ($1,000.00 prize!!).

3. Andrea Wicker will probably always be a jerk to me—no matter who I'm friends with.

4. She still hasn't asked why Mom was crying on the front steps.

5. She's helping me get a plan in place to get Mom away from Slade. (For good this time.)

NOTEBOOK #7

*This notebook is the property of Hershey Hollenback.
If lost, please return IMMEDIATELY to
113 Lilac Lane, Sommersville, PA.

January 1, 2004
SLADE PLAN-WEEK ONE
1. Don't line up shoes in the hallway.
2. Leave one of Ella's dirty diapers in his closet.
3. Don't sweep under the bed.
4. Mess up the soup cans in the pantry.
5. Only clean litter box once a day-instead of three.

January 7, 2004
SLADE PLAN-WEEK TWO
1. Don't put sofa pillows back in order.
2. Sit on his bed after he makes it.
3. Leave out the butter after making grilled cheese.
4. Leave one saucepan in the sink-still dirty.
5. Leave toenail clippings on the bathroom rug.

January 14, 2004
SLADE PLAN-WEEK THREE
1. Leave wet towel on the bathroom floor after shower.

2. Put knife and fork in the wrong places when setting table.

3. Leave out peanut butter and jelly after making Ella's sandwich.

4. Forget to put caps back on shampoo and conditioner.

5. Don't fold towels in fours, the way he likes them.

I got my first notebook about three years ago, the summer I turned eleven. I had just finished fifth grade, and the only thing I was looking forward to was heading down to the local pool so that I could (finally) take the swim test that would give me my Trout badge. I already had my Minnow, Guppy, and Goldfish badges, but a Trout badge meant that I could go to the pool alone—without Mom—if I wanted to.

And I wanted to.

Mom's new boyfriend, Slade West, had moved in with us a few months earlier, and I wanted to spend as much time as possible away from the house. I wasn't sure which was worse—Slade himself, with his crazy, neurotic habits (lining up his shoes at the foot of his bed, stacking the canned goods in alphabetical order inside the pantry, popping a quarter off his bedsheets every morning) or the way Mom got whenever she was around him. She was a different person when he came into the room, all giggly and silly, running her hands through his crew cut hair, and blowing into his ear when he sat down next to her on the couch. It was gross.

To be fair, Slade wasn't all that bad in the beginning. He used to come over every Tuesday after his shift at the Coca-Cola factory and take Mom and me out to dinner at Hot Diggity, our favorite diner. I'd always order the same thing—a chicken-finger-and-french-fry platter with coleslaw and red beets. Slade laughed the first time I ordered red beets. "You're one in a million, Hershey," he said. "I've never seen a kid eat red beets without putting up a fight first." He always ordered a bowl of rice pudding for dessert, which the three of us would split. It was kind of nice. I almost didn't mind the way Mom squeezed in next to him in the booth or the way they held hands under the table.

But then he started coming over way too much. Every night, practically, including the weekends. It was hard having a third person around so much, since it had been just Mom and me for as long as I could remember. The other weird thing was how much he was *into* her. Mom's had other boyfriends, but I couldn't remember a single one who called four or five times *after* getting home from spending the whole evening with her. It started to get irritating, and one day I told her so. Mom just giggled. She said that was how people who were in love acted, and that I would understand it when I got older. Adults are always saying things like that, as if I only have half a brain now. It makes me want to barf. I guess I shouldn't have been surprised when he actually moved in two months later, since he was practically living at our place anyway. But I *was* surprised at how quickly the Job List went up. I'm getting a little ahead of myself here. Let me explain.

Before he got the job at the Coca-Cola factory, Slade spent six years in the army. It's been a long time since he was discharged, but he still looks like a soldier. The little hair he has is cut so close to his head that you can see the razor nicks on his scalp. He keeps his mustache trimmed within an inch of its life, and he has pretty big muscles. When it gets warm out, he wears tight black T-shirts to show off his chest and arms. And he is never, ever without his big, black, clompy army boots, which go up past his ankles and are tied with thick black laces. I think if there was ever an occasion for him to wear a suit somewhere, Slade wouldn't think twice about putting on his boots to go with it. I don't mind the military look so much. It's the military *attitude* that makes me crazy. Slade is wild about neatness. Like to a fault. He's obsessed with having everything in order. Mom and I, well . . . we're not. It's not the end of the world, say, if my clean laundry sits in a hamper at the foot of my bed for a day or two. Or three. And neither of us has ever gotten worked up over things like keeping the kitchen spotless or arranging the items in the refrigerator just so. But after a week of living with us, Slade decided that we were living like animals. And so he created a Job List, posting it on the front of the refrigerator door so that Mom and I would be reminded what it was that had to be done every day.

Make the beds—the army way! Fold the laundry. Sweep under the dining room table. Make sure all canned goods are facing outward and are in alphabetical order. Straighten the pillows on the couch. Empty the cat litter at least three times a day. Line up shoes in front hallway. And on and on. All of the chores had to be done by the end of every day, with a check mark after each one when it was completed. Mom put up a mild protest at first, telling Slade that she just didn't understand the necessity of it all. But Slade insisted. It was the only way to live, he said, and while it seemed like a lot at first, we would get used to it. Pretty soon, keeping the place spotless would become like second nature.

But that's not what happened. Mom and I gave it our best effort, but there was always something we hadn't done right, something Slade didn't approve of. One night he took all the dirty dishes out of the dishwasher and made Mom reload it—his way. I think that was when the giggling and tickling began to be replaced with yelling and shouting. Pretty soon their arguing turned into full-blown screaming matches, and then one night, right in the middle of one of their fights, I came into the room and said I didn't want to stack the cans in the pantry. I'll admit I don't have the best timing when it comes to certain things. And it probably wasn't the best idea to say something that would further upset an already agitated Slade. So shoot me. I was eleven.

You would have thought I'd called him a bad name or something, the way he looked at me after I said that. And then, before Mom or I could blink, Slade picked up a glass out of the kitchen sink and sent it sailing across the room. He said later that it wasn't aimed at either of us—Mom was sitting at the kitchen table and I was standing in the doorway, between the kitchen and the dining room—but it hit the wall between us with such force that when it splintered into a thousand pieces, a sliver of it shot directly into the center of my eye.

Needless to say, I did not get my Trout badge that summer. Instead, I spent four days in Sommersville Memorial Hospital, having my eye operated on, and then the rest of the summer at home, recuperating. Three years later, I still can't see very well out of my injured eye, but the doctor said it was a miracle that I regained any sight at all in it. I have to wear these horrible glasses with special lenses so that I can see the same out of both eyes. Without them, everything looks fuzzy out of my bad eye. The glasses are big with rose-colored frames and make me look like a total dork, but truthfully, when all is said and done, I guess I'd rather wear them than not be able to see.

It was in the hospital, a few days after my surgery, that I got my first notebook. I wasn't allowed to read or watch TV or do much of anything, really, since I had a bandage the size of Montana over my left eye, so Mom brought a notebook for me to doodle in. It was just an ordinary notebook, the kind you buy at the Dollar Store, with a yellow cover and a spiral edge and ninety pages of lined paper inside. Mom and I played sixteen games of hangman—which I won twelve of—and then she kissed me and went home for the night. My room felt eerily quiet with her gone, and suddenly I missed her with an intensity that is hard to explain. It was more than the absence of her physical presence; I missed *her*, just the two of us. I missed the way things had been between us before Slade came into the picture, the way I could make her laugh by squinting one of my eyes like a pirate and saying "Aarrggh." Would it—could it—ever be that way again?

My mind drifted back to a Saturday earlier in the year when Mom and I went to Sally's Thrift Store, something we did every weekend, to poke around and see what we could find. Mom always says there's nothing better than finding something you didn't even know you needed. That day, we were looking around for flowerpots because Mom wanted to start planting some flowers to put out on the front porch. But she got distracted by an old, dusty piano sitting in the corner of the store. It was covered with clothes and books and there was nothing to sit on, but she stood in front of it anyway and drew the tips of her fingers over the keys. A kind of dreamy look came over her face.

"Hey," I said. "Whatya doing?" She just smiled and shook her head. "Do you know how to play the piano?" I asked. In response, she pushed down on one of the white keys, very lightly. A small, hollow sound, like a cowbell, floated up.

"I took lessons for a while," she said. "When I was about your age. But then I stopped. I can't even remember why now." Finding things out about my mother that I had not known before never ceased to fascinate me. It was hard for me to imagine that she had been my age once, let alone that she had interests and hobbies apart from me. I glanced around the store. Aside from us there was only Sally the owner, standing behind the counter riffling through a bag of old shoes. Wisps of gray stringy hair stuck out from the sides of a scarf tied around her head.

I turned back around. "Play something, Mom. Come on."

She shook her head. "Oh, I don't think I remember . . ."

"I bet you do." I dragged a beat-up swivel stool out from behind an old dresser. "Come on. Just try."

She pushed a few keys down tentatively, as if she was

afraid of making too much noise, but then she brought her other hand down on the keys, and all at once her fingers began to move, as if with a mind of their own, running back and forth over the keys like little legs. Even better, the music she was playing was beautiful. Breathtaking. Unlike anything I had ever heard before. I stood next to her, mesmerized. And then suddenly, about a minute into the piece, she stopped short, interrupting the melody so abruptly that I gasped.

"Keep going!" I demanded. Mom looked up at me. Her cheeks were flushed pink and her blue eyes were shining.

"I don't know how," she said. "I never learned the rest."

"Was that 'Für Elise'?" said a voice behind us. Mom and I turned around. Sally was watching us, her arms crossed in front of her.

Mom nodded and smiled. "Yes," she said. "A little bit of 'Für Elise.'"

"That was one of the first pieces I learned too," Sally said. "Back about a million years ago. What is it about Beethoven? All piano teachers always start with him." I had heard of Beethoven in grade school, but just enough to know that he was a famous musician. I didn't know any of his music.

"What's 'Für Elise'?" I asked Mom as we left the store a while later, armed with three terra-cotta flowerpots and a lamp with a purple shade for my room.

"It's a song Beethoven wrote for some woman named Elise," Mom said. "It's pretty, isn't it?"

I nodded. "I liked it. A lot."

Mom winced. "I always wished I had learned the rest of it." She shrugged and then grinned, putting her arm around my shoulder. "Maybe someday I will."

Now, in the hospital, I opened my eyes again. What was it about that day that made me remember it? Was it the fact that I had found out something new about my mother? Could it have been the beauty of the song that drifted out from under her fingertips? Or was it, I realized slowly, the last time Mom and I had done anything alone together? Just the two of us. Two weeks later, she had brought Slade home to meet me for the first time. Now I couldn't even remember the last time we had gone to the thrift store.

I looked back down at my new notebook, opened like a white moth across my legs, and started writing words that had begun swirling around inside my head. I've never been much of a writer, and I *hate* English class, but for some reason I needed to do this. When I was done, I read the words out loud, each one slowly and softly, my voice barely above a whisper:

blind
scared
hurts

blood
screams
ugly
hate

Each word drifted out of my mouth and then hung in the air above me like a little storm cloud. When I was finished, I closed the notebook. I could still feel the storm cloud over my head, but at least it was outside of me instead of crammed in the center of my chest, where it was making it almost impossible to breathe.

I've filled seven more notebooks since that night. All of them are written in lists, exactly like the first one. After that first night, I just didn't feel like writing any other way. Lists are short, to the point, and only take up half a page, which is the only way I can read comfortably now with my bad eye. Everything that I think about or need to figure out is put in those notebooks. When I fill one up, I put it in a paper bag that I keep in the back of my closet and start a new one. No one knows about my bag of notebooks. They're nobody's business but mine.

Until one day, when they weren't.

ONE

"Yeah, well, what about yesterday, Daisy, when she left her toenail clippings all over the bathroom rug? Or on Monday, when she threw her shoes in the middle of the hallway again? I almost broke my neck tripping over them when I came in from work!"

I press myself flat against the crack of Baby Ella's door, watching Slade rant and rave in the kitchen. I always sneak into my baby sister's room when they start to argue, in case she wakes up and gets scared. Holding my breath, I wait for Slade to continue his tirade, but he just leans against the stove and, with his cigarette between his thumb and index finger, takes a long, restless drag. Mom is standing in front of the dishwasher, filling the top rack with dirty glasses. Her forehead is furrowed, her mouth pulled tight. I watch her closely whenever they argue. She has no clue about the Slade Plan or the reason I have concocted it in the first place. But, if everything goes the way I am hoping it will, we'll be leaving again—for good this time.

Mom left Slade once before, right after the accident

with my eye. She brought me home from the hospital, and just as I was getting ready to go into my room and go to sleep, I heard her tell Slade that she couldn't live with a man who had hurt her baby. I stopped dead in my tracks, hardly even daring to breathe. Slade wept and bawled as Mom hauled a suitcase out of the hall closet, getting down on his knees at one point, and hanging on to the bottom of her shirt like a little kid. He swore up and down that the whole thing had been an accident, and that he would spend the rest of his life making it up to me. But twenty minutes later, Mom had packed me and four suitcases into the back of her Toyota Corolla, and we were high-tailing it out of Sommersville faster than Slade could blink. Looking back now, I think that was the single best day of my life. I remember how blue the sky looked out the rear window, the same kind of blue I saw—or used to see—when I opened my eyes at the bottom of the pool. It made me hopeful, that blue, as if nothing could touch us, as long as Mom kept driving toward Manchester, where her sister Kemi lived.

But it didn't last. A week after we arrived at Aunt Kemi's, Mom began to feel strange, rushing to the bathroom every hour or so to get sick. Two days later, sitting at the dinner table, pale and trembling, she told Aunt Kemi that she was pregnant. I was sitting there too, right next to her, but it was like I was invisible. She didn't even look at me.

I remember Aunt Kemi glancing over quickly in my direction, probably to make sure I hadn't fallen off my chair or something, and then she looked away too. I knew right then, at that exact moment, that we were going to go back, but I sat there anyway, hoping something Aunt Kemi said to Mom would change her mind. It didn't. Two days later, we pulled back into our old driveway in Sommersville. I watched from my seat in the back as Slade helped Mom out of her seat and then kissed her on the lips.

"Oh, baby," he said. "I missed you so much." She buried her face into his neck and wept. I looked away, forcing myself not to cry. That night, I started eating. With a vengeance.

Now I look up as Slade's heavy black boots clomp across the kitchen floor. He waves the cigarette in front of him as he talks. "I'm telling you, Daisy, she's doing this stuff on purpose, just to drive me crazy."

"Slade, stop, okay?" Mom's using her begging voice, the one that makes my stomach turn. "You know that's not true. She's just a kid. Kids are messy, all right? That's just how it goes." I hate that she has to be the one to duke it out with him, when it's my fault that they're arguing in the first place. But since the accident, he barely even looks at me anymore, let alone argues with me. Especially when Mom's around.

"See, you're always saying stuff like that, Daisy, like

she's six years old or something. She's thirteen! And she knows the rules." He taps the Job List on the front of the refrigerator with the backs of his knuckles. "They're all spelled out, right here, just like they've always been." He bends over, scanning his handwriting. "There isn't a single check mark after any of her chores this week. Not one!" He lowers his voice to a muted growl. "I'm telling you, Daisy, that girl is playing me for a fool. She's turned into an overweight, spiteful slob, and you know it."

"I told you not to talk like that!" Mom says. Her voice is different, slightly stronger now. "It's not Hershey's fault that she's put on a little weight. It happens to lots of girls her age. She's still growing."

"A *little* weight?" Slade sneers. "What're you, blind? That girl's put on at least fifty pounds in the last three years! That ain't a little weight."

Pushing my glasses along the bridge of my nose, I glance at my reflection in Baby Ella's bureau mirror as they continue to argue. I don't know if it's as much as fifty pounds, but there's no doubt that I've gotten bigger. My cheeks are fuller, I have another chin, and the tops of my arms look and feel as wide as tree trunks. I stand up a little straighter, smoothing my T-shirt down and sucking in my stomach. The rolls don't go anywhere. I'm glad the mirror stops at my stomach. I don't even want to look at my thighs or butt. It's a funny thing, though, the extra weight. Being bigger makes me feel as if I have a kind of armor around me that no one can break through. And so while losing the weight would be nice in a way, it would also terrify me. Stripping that armor off would make me feel defenseless. And with Slade West in the house, I can't afford to feel that way—even a little bit.

Behind me, Baby Ella stirs in her sleep as Slade's voice continues to rise. The Winnie-the-Pooh night-light, plugged into the wall over her dresser, casts a yellow halo over her face. She's only two years old, but she's one of the cutest kids I've ever seen. I always feel guilty when I remember how, just after Mom went into labor, I began to wish that she wouldn't bring the baby back home with her. I guess I just saw her as something else that would come between Mom and me. Now, strange as it might sound, I can hardly remember *not* having her around. I stare at her over the bars of her crib. Her arms and legs are flung wide, as if she's getting ready to make a snow angel, and her mouth is slack from sleep. A chunk of her blond wispy hair is matted to her cheek. Every time Slade's voice drifts into the room, her little nose twitches, as if she can hear him. Which she probably can. Slade's got a voice that could wake the dead.

"And *I* can't say anything," he continues, blowing smoke out of his nose. "Oh, no! God forbid, mean, evil *Slade* say anything to the poor, tormented teenager of the house."

"*Stop* it," Mom says between gritted teeth. "Just knock it off." There is a rustle of movement beneath me as Augustus Gloop squeezes his way into the room. His tail is pointed straight in the air and his little ears are pricked forward.

"Gusty," I whisper, snapping my fingers lightly. "C'mere, boy." My cat rubs himself in and around my ankles and then sits directly on top of my sandaled foot. I know it sounds weird, but I think he likes the smell of my bare feet. He sits on them every chance he gets.

"You know I'm right, Daisy." Slade's voice is getting louder and louder. "You know I am. You just don't want to admit it because that girl's got you wrapped around her pinky finger." He shakes his little finger under Mom's nose to illustrate his point. "Ever since the accident, she's been playing me like a fiddle. She thinks she can get away with whatever she wants, and I've had it."

"Oh, Slade, you're getting paranoid. Hershey is not playing anyone like a fidd—"

"You can't *see* it!" Slade hollers, stooping over briefly to light a fresh cigarette. "You can't see it because you're not the one whose skin she's always trying to get under. *You're* not the one she hates, okay?" Mom slams the dishwasher shut. Slade starts pacing back and forth across the kitchen, rolling up the short sleeves of his black T-shirt until the tops of his shoulders are exposed. His mustache twitches under his nose. When he starts in again, his voice is much softer. "You know, all I'm askin', Daisy, is that you try to look at things through my eyes. Just a little bit." He pauses, inhaling deeply on his cigarette. "Because if you did, just once, you might see things a little differently."

"Okay, Slade." Mom leans heavily against one of the blue kitchen counters. She pulls a handful of her long brown hair over one of her shoulders and starts twirling the ends of it through her fingers. Even from where I'm standing, I can see the dark circles under her eyes. "Okay, honey. I'll try."

"I'm going out," Slade says, stubbing his cigarette out. There is a rustling sound as he shoves one arm and then the other into his nylon Windbreaker. "And I'm telling you right now, Daisy, if that girl doesn't have at least half of her chores checked off on that list before I get back, there's gonna be trouble. Keepin' the place clean isn't a lot to ask in your own home."

The door opens, slams shut.

I glance at the Big Bird clock on Baby Ella's wall. Seven thirty. Perfect. I'll have just enough time to sneak out of here, update Phoebe on things, and get back before Slade returns. Going out for him always means heading down to Petey's on the corner and griping to the guys for a few hours over some beers. I'll be back before he even realizes I've been missing.

Sliding out of Baby Ella's window always takes some maneuvering, now that I'm so big, but it's not a far drop since the ground under the left side of the house is sloped. Augustus Gloop gazes up at me with his wide hazel eyes as I tap the windowsill with my fingers. He knows the routine. After leaping up soundlessly, he surveys the ground below for a moment and then jumps. A few seconds later, he turns and looks back up at me, blinking once.

"I know, I know," I mutter, squeezing through the narrow space. "I'm coming, hotshot."

TWO

I run the whole half mile to Phoebe's, even though I hate to run and my lungs feel like they will burst. I always run after I sneak out, as if Slade or Mom will catch me if I don't. It's not quite dark yet, and the late May air is light and warm. The sky is a deep blue, with a little bit of purple along the horizon. Crickets chirp loudly in the grass, and somewhere in the distance I can hear a dog howling. Twilight is my favorite time of day, when everything starts to slow down. I pause briefly as the Dairy Queen looms into view on the corner, and consider stopping to get Phoebe and me a giant peanut-butter-crunch Blizzard to share. Peanut butter Blizzards are her favorite. But there are at least six people in line already, and waiting would eat up too much time. I pick up speed again, wishing with every step that Phoebe lived closer.

Phoebe Millright is one of the weirdest people I know, and I mean that in the best way possible. Of course, being weird can get you into a lot of trouble in eighth grade, and when Phoebe moved here last year, she was no exception.

My homeroom, which is usually complete chaos until the bell rings, fell completely silent the first time she walked into it. Forget the fact that the long black cardigan she was wearing had a hole right in the front of it, or that her blue-and-black-striped tights, tucked into a pair of red ankle-high Doc Martens, screamed "oddball." The *really* strange thing was the object in her hair, a wide white blob of something pinned just above her right ear. I'm usually sleeping in homeroom, but I sat up straight that day and watched from my seat in the back as Mrs. Grant asked Phoebe what it was.

"Oh, this?" Phoebe asked, touching it gently with her fingertips. "It's an octopus."

"A *what*?" Andrea Wicker demanded. Andrea Wicker is the leader of the prep clique at Sommersville Middle School. She's beautiful, wears the best clothes in the school, and has rich parents. She also torments me every chance she gets. I hate the very air she breathes.

Phoebe grinned. "An octopus," she said. "Rubber, of course. Don't you like the way it looks? I mean, the tentacles and everything. I think it looks like a flower."

"And I think," Andrea Wicker said, curling her glossed lips over her perfectly straight teeth, "you look like a first-class freak." The class laughed as Phoebe's face fell. Mrs. Grant rapped her desk for order, but nobody listened to her. Things took a turn for the worse at lunch, when other kids began to jump on the Andrea bandwagon. I watched as Phoebe tried to get past a group of jocks who blocked her path in the pizza line. When she turned in the opposite direction, a horde of preps knocked her books out of her hand. "Go back to your planet!" one of them yelled. Andrea howled with laughter. "Get the octopus!" she screamed. "Someone get the octopus!" Hands grabbed at Phoebe's hair and someone yanked it free. Phoebe stood mutely as her hair ornament was tossed from table to table. Her face was pink and she was chewing the inside of her cheek as if she had a piece of steak in there. Kids all over the lunchroom were screaming, "Over here! Throw it here!" And then, just as the gym teacher, Mr. Cordaro, started yelling at kids to sit down, the octopus landed on my table, right on top of my mashed potatoes and gravy. It splattered food all over the front of my shirt, and then landed in my lap, a wet, rubbery, sticky mess.

"Hershey!" Andrea hissed, keeping one eye on Mr. Cordaro, who was busy yelling at one of the Goth girls. "Give it here! Give it to me!"

Now, I've been picked on long enough by Andrea Wicker to realize that the best way to deal with her is to either give her what she wants or just ignore her altogether. If I don't, there will be a future price to pay, which is never worth the aggravation in the first place. And so I picked up the octopus, ready to toss it to Andrea. But then I looked at Phoebe, who was standing behind Andrea's table. Her hair was askew from where the boys had pulled at it, and even as her teeth worked the inside of her mouth, her lower lip trembled. I knew that look. I wore it every single day. Closing my hand around the octopus, I looked past Andrea and spoke directly to Phoebe.

"You want to sit over here?" I asked. "With me?" Phoebe looked bewildered for a moment, as if she wasn't sure I was talking to her, but then she nodded and scurried over. She could have taken a seat anywhere at the long table, since I ate by myself every day, but she sat down directly across from me and inhaled deeply.

"*Pig,*" I heard Andrea growl behind me. "Fat cow. I'll get you." She made a few oinking noises and then turned around in her seat again as Mr. Cordaro walked over in our direction.

"You okay here?" he asked, brushing his Superman swipe of brown hair out of his eyes. For a teacher, Mr. Cordaro is very good-looking. Phoebe nodded, still staring at me. She was trembling under that big ugly sweater. "Okay," Mr. Cordaro said. "You let me know if anyone gives you any more trouble. Got it?" Phoebe nodded again. She yanked up the sleeves of her sweater, exposing two rows of black rubber bracelets. Her fingernails, which were bitten down to the quick, were painted a glittery fuchsia.

I slid the octopus across the table. "Here's your . . . octopus."

Phoebe gave me a small grateful smile and put it into her pocket. I was glad to see her do that. If she had put it back in her hair, still coated with mashed potatoes and gravy, I don't think we would have hit it off as well as we did.

"Thanks," she said. We didn't say anything for a minute or two. I'm not exactly Oprah Winfrey when it comes to talking to people, and Phoebe still seemed stunned by everything that had just happened. I spooned the last of my corn into my mouth and chewed quietly. "You sit here all by yourself?" she asked finally. "Every day?"

My eyebrows narrowed. "Yeah. So?"

She held up her hands, palms out, in front of her chest. "No, no. Don't take offense. I was just wondering." She ran her hands over the front of the table. "It's nice, actually, having all this room." I kept chewing. I wasn't trying to be rude. If you want to know the truth, beads of sweat were actually breaking out on my forehead, thinking that she might become my friend. I hadn't had a real friend since third grade. But I didn't want her to know that. Phoebe glanced over my shoulder and then leaned in across the table. "That girl is still giving us dirty looks," she said.

I nodded without turning around. "That's Andrea Wicker. She's got the dirty look thing down to a science."

"She bothers you, too?" Phoebe asked. I nodded.

Phoebe grinned. "Well, maybe she'll think twice about it, now that there's two of us."

"I wouldn't bet on it," I said, pleased that she had referred to the "two of us."

Phoebe stuck out a bony hand. "I'm Phoebe Millright. And you are . . . ?"

I smiled, hoping she couldn't hear my heart banging around underneath my shirt. "Hershey Hollenback," I said, giving her hand a shake. "Nice to meet you."

The Mandarin Motel, where Phoebe has been living with her dad, Jack, for the past nine months, is set back on a scrappy-looking dirt field, like a lost kid. A lopsided NO VACANCY sign hangs down over the front door of the main office, swaying from side to side. The front steps are cracked and buckled in the middle, with a rickety handrail dangling off to one side. There are ten rooms, the front door of each marked with a number. Some doors have baskets of flowers on the front; number three still has a Christmas wreath hanging over the knocker. Still others are bare and lonely-looking. Phoebe says that her living situation is only temporary, and that when Jack saves up enough money, they'll get a regular apartment like regular people. Things have been tight since Phoebe's mother ran off on them last year, taking their savings account with her. But they were doing okay for a while, until Jack, who's a construction worker, fell off a roof in April and hurt his back. Now the apartment plan has been put on hold indefinitely.

Phoebe's sitting in her usual spot in front of door number six as Augustus Gloop and I finally arrive. Augustus pads softly up the steps. His eyes are riveted on the three rolls of toilet paper Phoebe is keeping aloft in the air before her. A red silk flower, large as a cantaloupe, flops back and forth behind her ear. Little bits of gold glitter, splashed across the petals, sparkle in the fading light.

"Heeeyyyy," Phoebe says, not moving her eyes from the middle roll of toilet paper, which, she has informed me, is the key to juggling anything. "What'd you bring him for?" Phoebe hates Augustus Gloop. She's assured me it's not personal; she thinks all cats are sneaky, creepy animals. But if you want to know the truth, I think she's just scared of them.

"Slade—and Mom—got—into—another fight," I gasp, leaning my hands on my knees. I scrunch up my nose to prevent my glasses from sliding any farther down my face. "You know he—hates it when—they—start—fighting." A roll of toilet paper hits me on the head. Startled, Augustus Gloop scurries over to a worn niche under the step where Phoebe is sitting and begins to lick his paws.

"Shoot," Phoebe says. "I knew I was gonna lose that one." I stand back up and hand her the escaped roll. "Jeez," Phoebe says, "sit *down*, why don'tcha? You look like you're gonna fall over. What, did you *run* all the way over here again?" I nod, still breathing hard. Phoebe pats the empty space next to her. The rotting floorboards make a groaning sound as I sit down. "So what happened this time?" she asks, tossing the toilet paper up into the air again. "And remind me again what part of the Slade Plan we're up to."

The Slade Plan was originally Phoebe's idea. Well, sort of. She was the one who told me that I had to figure out a way to get Slade mad enough—without him realizing it—so that he would freak out again the way he did when he threw that glass all those years ago. I was the one who came up with the idea of bucking his Job List, and then the two of us created the Slade Plan one night on Phoebe's front porch. "We're on week two," I say, leaning my elbows back on the rough wood. "Mess up the sofa pillows, sit on his bed . . ."

"Ooooo, did you sit on his bed yet?" Phoebe asks, picking the toilet paper up again. "An army guy like Slade would *wig* if someone sat on his bed. I can just see it. Is that what happened tonight?"

I shake my head. "No, I didn't get around to doing that yet. But I don't think I'm going to have to. He's already starting to lose it about some of the other stuff."

"Like what?" Phoebe asks. All three of her rolls are back up in the air.

"Oh, he freaked tonight about the toenail clippings I left on the bathroom rug. . . ."

"Ha!" Phoebe chortles. "Actually, that is pretty gross. What else?"

"Um . . . my shoes, I think. Yeah, I left my shoes in the hallway. He almost tripped over them when he came in from work." I stretch out my legs, which have started to throb. "Anyway, I think we're close. He threatened me tonight just before he left for Petey's."

Phoebe drops her hands. One by one, the toilet paper plunks on the dirt lawn like fat, heavy snowballs. "He *threatened* you?" she repeats.

"Well, not to my face. Just to my mom."

"What'd he say?"

"He said . . ." I straighten up and stick my chin out, imitating Slade in a deep voice. "She better have at least half of those chores done by the time I get back, Daisy, or there's gonna be trouble." I lean back against the porch again. "Or something like that." Phoebe stares at me. A purple bug zapper hanging from the porch ceiling makes a sudden zzzzz noise. "*What?*" I ask. "Why do you look so worried all of a sudden? This is what we want."

Phoebe shakes her head. "I don't know, Hershey. Maybe this wasn't such a good idea after all. I don't know . . ."

"Don't know what?" I press. "What are you talking about? We want to get him mad, remember? We want him to freak out."

"But not on you!" Phoebe says. "Or your mom!"

I sit back up. "He would never touch my mom. He's crazy about her. Trust me. It's like a sickness or something.

And he's not gonna lay a finger on me. Not after the accident. It's like we said. All we need is for him to throw a chair or something. You know, act like an even bigger idiot than he already is. He's not going to hurt anybody."

Phoebe stands up and walks down the steps. I watch as she leans over, collecting the toilet paper rolls and tucking them under her arms. "Still," she says slowly, "I'm getting a little worried, Hersh. For him to say something like 'There's gonna be trouble' gives me the creeps. Almost like he's planning something."

"*Plan*ning something? What would he be planning?"

"I don't know. Maybe I'm being paranoid." Phoebe tosses the rolls up into the air again. The sleeves of her cardigan sweater droop down past her wrists, but she doesn't seem to notice. The sweater, which Phoebe wears every day, with every outfit, used to belong to her mother. "Just be careful, okay? And maybe we should go a little more slowly with the Slade Plan. Just do one or two things a week instead of all of them." Her hands look like tiny windmills as they fly from side to side under the toilet paper. "Guys like Slade can be pretty unpredictable, you know?"

"Well," I say, trying not to show my disappointment, "maybe you're right."

Augustus Gloop jumps suddenly from his place under the porch and scampers into the field facing the motel. The field is loaded with mice and other little rodents. He'll have a great time in there. Phoebe is standing directly in front of me now, completely absorbed with her juggling. The toilet paper spins faster and faster, until the only thing I can see is a blurred circle of white.

"You're totally going to win the Sommersville talent show this summer," I say. "I bet no one's ever seen someone juggle the things you can."

"I *better* win," Phoebe says. "That thousand-dollar first prize would put a ginormous chunk in my circus fund." Phoebe's saving up to go to a real circus camp next summer. She wants to join the Ringling Bros. when she turns eighteen.

"And guess what else?" Phoebe says, a huge smile on her face.

"What?"

"Jack said that if I raise half the money in another year, he'll put in the other half so that I can go to camp a year early."

I blink. "How's he gonna do *that*?"

Phoebe lets the toilet paper fall again. "What do you mean?"

"I mean, isn't he still hurt? From falling off the roof last month?"

Phoebe nods. "Yeah," she says. "The doctor says he won't be able to get out of bed for at least another week or so either."

"So if he can't work, then where would he get the money?" I ask carefully, thinking about all the empty Miller Lite bottles I saw on the floor by Jack's bed the last time I came over.

"Well, he's gonna start working eventually, Hershey. We're living off his workers' compensation money now, but he'll get another job. Besides, Jack wouldn't make a promise like that to me unless he meant it. He'll find a way."

I nod. "Okay."

Phoebe pulls at a strand of her hair. "What, you don't believe me?"

"I didn't say I didn't be*lieve* you."

"So what're you thinking, then?"

I don't like it when Phoebe and I argue. It scares me. She's the best friend I've ever had anywhere, and it scares me to think that I might do something to lose her. I stand up and put my arm around her. "I'm thinking you have a really cool dad to believe in you like that."

Phoebe's thin shoulders relax under my arm. She smiles. "Yeah?"

"Yeah." Phoebe picks up the toilet paper again. "*And* you're going to win the talent show," I add. "Sommersville hasn't ever seen anything like Phoebe Millright."

"Phoebe Millright and Hershey Hollenback," Phoebe corrects me. "We're a two-woman act, remember?" She walks over to the center of the yard. "I just wish I could do something with fire, you know? Flaming sticks or hoops or something. To make me really stand out from everyone else."

"Fire?" I repeat. "What're you, crazy? Do you know how long you have to train to throw fire in the air and be able to catch it without burning yourself to death?"

Phoebe shrugs. "I bet I could do it. That's what the kids at Camp Lohikan were doing. But Jack won't let me. He's even hidden all his lighters, because he thinks I might try." She throws the rolls at me one by one. I catch them awkwardly. "Come on, Hersh, let's start from the beginning. And don't forget to use my stage name this time."

I arrange myself several feet away from Phoebe, as she has instructed me so many times before, and raise my arms in a dramatic flourish.

"Ladies and gentleman!" I yell out in a loud voice. "May I introduce to you the great and awesome, the wonderful and amazing, the one and only juggling extraordinaire . . . Midnight Slim!"

We're interrupted by the sound of Phoebe's name being called from inside the motel room.

"Just go ahead," Phoebe says, glancing back at her window. "He's fine." But her father calls again.

"Phoebe! I know you can hear me! Get in here now!" Phoebe rolls her eyes and runs for the door.

"Just gimme a sec," she says over her shoulder. "He probably lost the remote again or something. I'll be right back out." I sit down on the front steps and wait, trying to blot out the sound of Jack's angry voice behind me. I have only been inside the motel room once or twice since Jack got hurt. Phoebe says Jack doesn't like anyone seeing him lying there in bed, but I think it's also because he's gotten kind of ornery. He was pretty cool when I first met him, taking Phoebe and me out for ice cream a few times, and staying up late, playing backgammon with us when I slept over. But something changed when he fell off that roof. Maybe he hit his head as well as his back. Who knows? I *do* know Phoebe does a lot for Jack since his accident. She told me she makes dinner most nights and runs to the store all the time for his pain medication. I hope he appreciates it.

After a few minutes Phoebe opens the front door. Her face is scrunched up, like she might cry.

"What's wrong?" I ask, getting up from the steps.

"Nothing." She closes the door softly behind her and pinches her nose with her first two fingers. Her cuticles are bleeding. "He just gets mean when he drinks that stupid beer." We both stare at her rubber bracelets as she spins them around her wrist.

"Yeah," I say. "I know."

"I have to go," Phoebe says after a minute. "I shouldn't leave him alone in there."

"Okay." The crickets' singing in the night air sounds incredibly loud all of a sudden. I clear my throat. "Well, I'll come back tomorrow and we'll run through it again, okay?"

Phoebe nods. "That'd be great."

I head toward Route 11, whistling for Augustus Gloop as I go. He comes tearing out from the tall grass, a brown mouse dangling from his mouth.

"Hersh?" Phoebe calls out.

"Yeah?"

"You got the cat, right?"

"He's right here!" I yell. "Don't worry!" I can hear Phoebe giggle a little in the dark.

"Okay," she says. "Good night, Hershey."

"Night, Phoebe."

THREE

I take the long way home, kicking an empty can of Sprite ahead of me for Augustus Gloop to play with. I wish that I had some kind of talent, like Phoebe and her juggling. I know she works hard at it, but she picked it up right away, like she was born to juggle. At least that's what she told me. She was in fourth grade when she went to her first circus and saw the clowns juggling hoops and balls in the middle ring. When she got home that night, she tried it with three oranges. It took her a while, but she had them all up in the air before she went to sleep. And she's been doing it ever since. I'd give anything to have a gift like that, something inside of me that needs a little work but is already there, waiting for me to find it. Something big. Something that would make people sit up and take notice.

The Sprite can clatters loudly along the sidewalk as Augustus Gloop pounces on it again. He must think it's a very large metal mouse. I sigh heavily at the thought of going home. Hanging around Mom aggravates me. It's not like I hate her now or anything. I love her more than anyone else in the world, but things are different. So much has happened. So much has changed. I don't feel like I can trust her, and things just aren't as easy between us as they used to be. Sometimes I even feel like I have to work at it.

I take a detour at the corner of Rigby Avenue and turn right instead of left. Piggy's Place is halfway down the block. My pace quickens as the familiar smell of doughnuts fills the air. Walking into Piggy's Place is one of the most spectacular experiences ever. It feels as if you've walked inside an actual doughnut, because everything is so warm and sweet and sugary-smelling. My knees get weak sometimes, just thinking about it.

"Hey, Hershey!" Mavis says, looking up as I walk through the front door. "Whatchou doing out so late?" Mavis Miller is my favorite waitress at Piggy's Place, and not because she gives me free doughnuts all the time. She always smiles when I come in, and acts like she is genuinely interested in me. I can never leave until I've told her all about school and how Baby Ella is doing.

"Just practicing our talent show act over at Phoebe's," I reply, giving the back wall of doughnuts a quick once-over. It looks like there's a fresh batch on the top row, right behind the sugared bear claws. Mavis stops rubbing the top of the counter.

"You know, I'ma be in that talent show too." She raises an eyebrow. "I play the saxophone."

"Oh, yeah?" I sit down on one of the pink swivel stools. Taking a napkin out of one of the dispensers, I start cleaning my glasses. Augustus Gloop arranges himself neatly around my feet. "I didn't know that, Mavis. That's cool." Mavis reaches up and gives the left side of her wig a yank. It's a different color today, not quite as blond as it usually is. Last year Mavis got sick and lost all her hair. On her first day back to work, she came in with a bright red curly wig. She looked like a middle-aged Little Orphan Annie. She wears a regular wig now, cut into a short, modest shape, but she's always changing the color.

"Cool or not, I need that money," she says. "My car's just about had it, and I got my eye on a used Oldsmobile I seen over in Grant Perkins's lot." I stare again at the doughnuts on the back wall.

"Are those new doughnuts?" I ask. "They look different."

"Yep," Mavis answers. "Lemon Meringue Miracles. Piggy just made 'em about an hour ago. I think they're still warm." I dig down into my front pocket. I've got a dollar and twenty cents in loose change.

"I'll take two." I push the money across the counter and pretend not to notice as Mavis slips four of the lemon doughnuts into a paper bag. She slides the money across the counter and drops it into the front of her apron.

"You and Phoebe the Phenomenal better keep practicing,

you hear? Ol' Mavis here's gonna give you two a run for your money."

"I'm gonna tell Phoebe we've got some competition." I get up off the stool and whistle once for Augustus Gloop. He scampers out from under the stool and sits at my feet, waiting.

"That darn cat's in love with you," Mavis says.

I laugh. "He's just hungry. Thanks for the doughnuts, Mavis."

"Anytime, love," Mavis says. "See you around."

The Lemon Meringue Miracles are amazing. The cake part is dense and flaky at the same time, and the tart lemon filling is just warm enough to be gooey. I eat the first two in three large bites and let Augustus Gloop lick the sugar off my fingers. I am heading down Lilac Lane, just about to bite into my third, when I stop short. One of the potted geraniums, which Mom always keeps on the front porch, is in a heap on the sidewalk. The orange clay pot is cracked down the middle and chunks of black dirt are splayed everywhere. I peek around the side of the house for Slade's car. Nothing but tire tracks in the driveway. A sour taste fills my mouth. Dumping the bag of doughnuts into the garbage on the side of the house, I walk up the back steps as quietly as I can, and then stand there, waiting for the goose bumps on my arms to go away. They don't. I just know that something awful is waiting for me on the other side. I almost don't go in. But then I think of Baby Ella. And Mom. I push open the door.

Augustus Gloop scampers over to his food bowl in the kitchen and starts eating. I scan the inside of the house. Empty. Opening Baby Ella's door as quietly as I can, I peek in. She is on her belly, her little legs curled under her, sound asleep. The stuffed starfish I bought for her last Christmas is tucked under one arm. I close the door again and walk toward Mom's bedroom. The door is closed.

"Mom!" I whisper loudly. "Mom?"

"Hershey!" Mom hisses. "Get in here now!" I open the door. Mom is throwing clothes from her dresser drawers into a black garbage bag on her bed. "Where've you been?" she asks, not looking at me. Her hair is hanging down loosely, obscuring her face from view.

"I went over to Phoebe's," I say. "What's going on?"

"Why can't you ever *tell* me you're going to Phoebe's?" Mom asks behind her hair. "Why does it always have to be this big *se*cret all the time?" She grabs a handful of underwear from her top drawer and throws them into the bag.

"I don't know," I say, picking my fingernails. "You guys were fighting again. And I had to go. We had to practice for the talent show."

"Well, you're not going to have to worry about Slade and me fighting anymore," Mom mutters, pulling open another drawer. She flings a handful of shorts into the bag.

"Why?"

"We're leaving."

I almost stop breathing. "We're *leaving*?" I repeat. "For good?"

"For good," Mom says. "You, me, and Ella."

Even though I am watching Mom toss her clothes all around, and I can hear the shaky determination in her voice, I still don't believe her. I can't. It happened just like this before and we went back. I cross my arms. "I don't believe you." Mom stops throwing her clothes into the garbage bag and looks up at me for the first time, her hair settling back on either side of her face. I run to her when I see the way her lip, split down the middle, is beginning to swell. It looks enormous against the delicate features of her face. I am nearly as tall as she is, and when she holds me tight, I can smell the honey-lemon shampoo she uses. Up close I can see a red mark on her pale cheek, and another cut high on her forehead, small and dark red, like a raspberry.

"Oh, Mom, what *happened*?"

She sits down on the bed and begins to shake her head, like she can't quite believe it either. Reaching up with two fingers, she touches the puffiest part of her lip. I wince with her. "I'm going to get ice," I say, getting up. But Mom pulls me back.

"We don't have time, Hershey. I've already called a cab. We've gotta get out of here before Slade comes back."

She looks so serious that for the first time I am genuinely scared.

"Okay. But what happened? You've got to tell me what happened, Mom."

She raises her hands and then lets them fall again. A whimper comes out between her swollen lips. "I thought, you know, that Slade had left for Petey's," she says. "I knew he was coming back, but not for at least a few hours." She stares off into space.

"And?" I push.

Mom shrugs. "And I was going to get everything straightened up the way he likes it, but I just decided to lie down for a few minutes." She looks down at her hands. The gold and blue promise ring Slade gave her on their first anniversary is tarnished and dirty. "Just to rest, you know? I was so tired, Hershey."

Why did I leave? And how could I have left my mess for Mom to clean up? Why didn't I come back sooner?

"And he came back?" I guess.

Mom nods. "He forgot something. I can't even remember what it was now. His wallet, maybe? Or maybe it was his driver's license." She scratches the side of her head. I am getting impatient. Why isn't she getting to the point? She sounds like she is talking in her sleep or something.

"So he came in and saw you lying down?" I ask. "And so he beat you up?"

Mom looks at me quickly. "Oh, Hershey," she says. "Don't say that, honey. He didn't *beat me up*. He hit me. Once." She looks down at the floor. "Maybe twice. You know, we had been arguing earlier, and I guess he was still angry."

"Guys like Slade can be pretty unpredictable." Even Phoebe knew. I pushed him too far and he took it out on Mom this time, not me. It wasn't supposed to happen this way. Why did I leave? What have I done?

"Oh, Mom," I say, collapsing against her. "Oh, Mom, I'm so sorry!" The tears come fast, rolling out from behind my glasses. My bad eye stings and pulses under the strain.

Mom holds me tight. "You don't have to apologize, sweetheart. It's not your fault."

Oh, Mom. If you only knew. I cry harder, struggling to breathe as my nose gets blocked. Mom rocks me back and forth. "Shhh . . . ," she says. "It's okay, Hershey. It was just an argument and he lost his temper. That's all."

I push myself away from her. "That's *all*?" I stand up. "Mom, have you looked at your face in the mirror?" Mom tilts her head. She puts her hands on her hips.

"Let's not make this any more dramatic than it has to be, Hershey." She's all business all of a sudden, the sleep-walking side of her gone, like smoke evaporating into the air. "I've already decided we're leaving. I don't want to be here if and when he comes back."

"Why do you keep saying that?" I ask. "Did he say something?" Mom nods. That vacant look is still in her eyes, as if she is not quite here. "Mom!" I say loudly, resisting the urge to grab her around the shoulders and shake the pee-willy out of her. "What did he *say*?" She clears her throat, begins to speak in a hoarse voice.

"He said, 'Get out of my house, Daisy, because if you or anyone else is here when I get back, I'm not going to be responsible for what happens next.'"

"That was a threat," I say. "A real one."

"I think it was," Mom whispers, pressing her fingertips against her forehead. Her eyes look like blue cornflowers against her pale skin. She shakes her head. "And for the first time in all these years, I'm really afraid of what he might do, Hershey." I glance away when she says that, because she has the same fearful look in her eyes that Baby Ella gets when she knows she is going to get in trouble. It makes me sick to my stomach.

"So we definitely have to get out of here," I say. "He could come back any minute." It is like I have turned a light switch. Mom is back again, all fury and responsibility.

"Exactly. The guy at the cab station said he'd give me twenty minutes. You're going to need to take as many clothes as you can, Hershey. Just throw them into one of those big plastic garbage bags. I've already packed most of Ella's things, and I'm just finishing up mine. Do you need any help?"

I shake my head. "No, I can do it. Don't worry."

"All right." Mom starts tossing clothes again. "Let's go." I am halfway down the hall when I think of something.

"Mom?" I ask, standing in her doorway once more. "Are we going to Aunt Kemi's again?"

"No, sweetheart."

"Where, then?"

The muscles in Mom's neck flex again and her hands squeeze into fists. "We're going to a battered women's shelter, Hershey."

"A *what*?"

"A battered women's shelter," Mom repeats. "I called right after Slade left and told the woman there what happened . . . what Slade said . . . and she said to come right away. Slade won't be able to find us there."

"Where is it?"

"Just across town, honey. Behind the new Wal-Mart."

"Is Baby Ella coming?"

Mom steps toward me. "Oh, Hershey. Of course she is. I wouldn't leave either of you behind. Ever." I let Mom hold me for a minute. Her heart is beating wildly under her T-shirt, like a little mouse scurrying around. I step back and look up at her uncertainly.

"Well," I say, "as long as you and Baby Ella and Augustus Gloop are there, I guess it'll be okay." Mom smoothes my hair and kisses the top of my head.

"We can't take Augustus Gloop," she says.

I take a step back. "Why not?"

"They have a policy there, honey. No animals. I told them about Augustus Gloop, but they said they couldn't make any exceptions."

"Well, we can't leave him *here*!" I say. Panic is rising within me like water.

"I know you'll miss him, sweetheart, but he'll be fine here with Slade. He'll take—"

"No!" I cut her off. "No way, Mom! We are not leaving Augustus Gloop here alone with Slade!"

Mom looks at me helplessly. "Hershey. What do you want me to do? I already told—"

"We'll take him somewhere," I say. My brain feels numb. "Can't we take him to a kennel or something? Just until we leave the shelter?"

Mom puts her hands on my shoulders. "Sweetie. We might have to stay in the shelter for a while. I have just enough money right now to pay our cabdriver. There is no way I can pay a kennel to keep the cat." She shakes her head sadly. "There's just no way. You'll have to leave him here. He'll be warm, he'll have food, he'll be safe—"

"He *won't* be safe!" I yell, wrenching myself out from under Mom's hands. "No one's safe around that monster! Look at us, Mom! *We're* leaving because we're not safe!" Mom stands there as if nailed to the floor. Her bottom lip is trembling. And then, all at once, it comes to me. "Phoebe," I say. "We'll take him to Phoebe's."

"I thought you said Phoebe didn't like cats," Mom says.

"It'll be okay. She'll do this for me."

"Well, the motel is on the way," Mom says, running her hands through her hair. "I guess I can ask the driver to stop for a few minutes." She looks at me hard. "But just for a few minutes, Hershey. We can't afford any extra time right now. I want you to understand that."

"I know," I say, running out to the kitchen to retrieve Augustus Gloop and his food bowl, which, when all is said and done, is all he really needs to go anywhere. "Don't worry, Mom. I'll take care of everything. It'll be fine."

FOUR

But nothing feels fine when Mom, Baby Ella, Augustus Gloop, and I are squeezed into the backseat of Jerry's 24-Hour Taxi, zooming through the dark streets of Sommersville like a bowling ball shot out of a cannon. The heat inside the car, combined with the sickeningly sweet smell of a vanilla-scented air freshener dangling from the front mirror, makes me feel like I might throw up. To make matters even worse, Baby Ella is screaming at the top of her lungs and has been ever since we woke her up. Mom keeps bouncing her up and down on her knee, saying, "Shhhh, Ella. Shhhhh, sweetheart," but nothing is working. I try to roll down a window, but Mom snaps at me.

"It's too much wind on the baby, Hershey. Roll it back up."

I look at her, aghast. "It's like five million degrees in here, Mom!" She shakes her head. I roll the window back up, catching the cabdriver's eye in the rearview mirror as I do.

"I got the air on," he says, pointing toward the air conditioner. He's an older guy, with bushy eyebrows, a tweed cap, and a greasy little ponytail sticking out the back of his head. He gives me one of those looks adults give you when they think you're being rude to your parents: a combination of disgust and annoyance. I glare at him and he looks back out toward the street, which is where he should be looking in the first place, if you ask me.

"Did you tell him to go to the motel first?" I ask Mom. She leans in closer.

"Yes, but he's not happy about it," she murmurs into my ear. "His shift ends in an hour. So make sure you're quick, Hershey. And I mean it."

"Okay," I say. "I will."

There's not much room to move, since the three garbage bags Mom and I managed to pack with our stuff are now sitting on the floor of the cab, along with Augustus Gloop, who is crammed into his travel box like a hot dog in a bun. He mews frightenedly every few minutes, staring at my legs. I tap the top of the box with my fingers and lean over so that he can see my face.

"It's okay, Gusty. You're going to stay with Phoebe for a while at the motel. You like it there, remember? There's lots of mice and things in the field. Don't worry. You'll have a good time. And I'll be back for you soon." He mews again, pitifully. I wish I could put him on my feet so that he could calm down a little, but my feet are squished under Mom's; her knees are bent at an angle, trying not to squish mine. It's so hot that I can feel my back sticking to my shirt. Little pools of sweat are starting to collect inside the folds of my belly. The dampness under my arms feels—and smells—like a swamp.

"Did you pack deodorant?" I ask Mom.

She gives me a strange look. "De*odo*rant?"

I nod. "I'm going to need it."

Mom sighs. "I can't remember, Hershey. But if it's not in the bags, I'll get you some."

"Do you think they'll have some at the shelter?"

"I don't *know*, Hershey. But if there isn't, I'm sure someone will be able to get us some." I can tell Mom's almost at the end of her rope, so I close my mouth and stare out the window again. The lights from the oncoming traffic zoom past us like enormous shooting stars. My eyes burn, thinking about Slade coming back from wherever it is he ran off to, only to find an empty apartment and "his girls" gone. Again. *He'll never find us*, I think. *And even if he does, we'll never go back*. Not after hitting Mom like he did. My head pounds, thinking about it. I try to push out the ugly pictures that are filling my head, and I press my forehead against the dirty window glass. I'd give anything for another Lemon Meringue Miracle.

Five minutes later we are pulling up in front of the Mandarin Motel.

I grab the handle of Augustus Gloop's travel box and turn it around so that Baby Ella can see him through the little wire bars. "You wanna say good-bye to the kitty, Ella?" I ask. Baby Ella's face is nearly blue from screaming so hard at this point. The taxi driver is drumming his thumbs on the steering wheel and staring straight ahead.

"Hershey, go!" Mom says. "Come on, honey! You're wasting time."

"All right," I mutter. "I just thought it would get her to stop crying." I withdraw the cat box from the car and shut the door. Baby Ella's screams are muffled momentarily behind the thick glass as I head toward Phoebe's steps. She's already standing in her doorway, her eyes winking with sleep.

"Hershey?" she asks. "Is that you?"

Jack's voice drifts out from inside. "Phoebe! Who is it?"

"It's Hershey," Phoebe answers.

"What's wrong?" Jack asks. "What time is it?"

"Hold on," Phoebe says. "I don't know yet." She's wearing a turban on her head and her mom's red Chinese silk robe with a blue dragon splashed across the back. The hem is dragging on the ground.

"What's wrong?" Phoebe asks, gathering the robe up around her knees. "What happened?"

"We have to go," I say, setting Augustus Gloop down on the porch.

Phoebe gives the cat a fearful glance. "Go where?"

"We're going to a battered women's shelter," I answer. "Slade got all psycho on my mom and hit her and then threatened to do something to all of us when he comes back."

Phoebe covers her mouth with her hands. "Oh my God, Hershey. Is your mom okay? Does she have to go to the hospital?"

"Phoebe!" Jack bellows. "*What* is going on out there?"

"I'll tell you in a minute!" Phoebe yells. "Just hold on!"

"No, she doesn't have to go to a hospital," I say. "But we have to go to the shelter, Phoebe. My mom doesn't feel safe staying with Slade anymore." We don't say anything for a second.

"Man," Phoebe says. "And I was just telling you . . . I *knew*—"

"I know, I know," I say, cutting her off. "Listen, I don't have time right now to get into all of it. But, Phoebe, we're not allowed to have animals in the shelter. And there's no way I'm leaving Augustus Gloop alone with Slade."

Phoebe takes a step backward. "Oh, Hershey . . ."

I reach out and take her hand. "*Please*, Phoebe. Please take him. It's just for a little while. I'll get you money for food and stuff and give it to you in school. It won't be for long. I promise. Please."

"It's not the money," Phoebe says, pulling at her bottom

lip. She looks at the cat out of the corner of her eye. "It's just that . . . Oh, man, he'd have to come out of that box, wouldn't he?"

"Well, yeah . . ."

"Let's go!" the taxi driver yells, leaning out the front window. "I don't got all night!"

I close my eyes. "Please, Phoebe. I know it's a lot to ask, but he's such a good cat. I swear. He won't scratch or bite or anything. You won't even have to play with him. And he can go outside at night, if you're afraid to sleep with him."

"*Sleep* with him?" Phoebe recoils in horror. "You *sleep* with him?"

I nod, kneading my fingers into my palm. "But you don't have to. He likes to go out at night too. You can just put him out and he'll do his thing, and then he'll come back in the morning for breakfast."

"What does 'do his thing' mean?" Phoebe asks warily. There is a loud growling sound as the taxi driver revs the engine. Mom is tapping frantically on the glass, beckoning for me to come, and Baby Ella is still screaming. I gulp hard, trying to push back whatever is rising inside of me. I feel like I am going to lose it.

"Okay," Phoebe says suddenly, miraculously. "I'll do it." Her voice is hesitant, frightened even, but she has said yes, and I am going to get the heck out of here before she changes her mind.

I lean forward and hug her tightly. "You're the best. It'll be fine, don't worry. I'll see you in school on Monday, okay?" Phoebe nods, pulling hard on her lower lip. "I have to go," I say. "That guy is going to freak out if I don't get back in the car."

"Wait, you're going to a *shelter*?" Phoebe asks, as if she has just realized the entirety of the situation.

"Yeah," I say. "Across town, behind the new Wal-Mart. We're probably going to have to stay there for a while, until my mom figures out what she's going to do next. But I'll be in school on Monday."

"Can you call me?"

"I don't know yet. I'll try." The taxi driver honks his horn.

"Hey, kid!" he yells. "I'm outta here!" I take a couple steps backward.

"I gotta go," I say, waving. Then I remember Augustus Gloop. There's no time to take him out of his cage and give him a proper good-bye, so I kneel down in front of the little wire door and touch the tip of his nose. "You be a good boy, Gusty. I have to go now." His tiny sandpaper tongue comes out and licks the edges of my fingers. I fight back tears.

"It'll be okay," Phoebe says. "You better go." I stand back up.

"Thanks, Phoebe." I run down the steps so that I don't start to cry for real.

The taxi driver shakes his head as I get back into my seat, and mutters something under his breath. He steps on the gas so hard that Mom's head snaps back and the wheels make a squealing sound underneath us. I look out the back window as we tear down the dirt road toward Route 11. Phoebe is still standing in the doorway in her silk robe, with Augustus Gloop at her feet. I wave frantically. She reaches up with a skinny arm, the robe slipping down to her shoulder, and waves back. She waves and waves until I can't see her at all anymore.

Mom is rummaging around frantically inside one of the bags, her face getting pinker by the second.

"What are you looking for?" I yell above Baby Ella, who by now is starting to turn a slight shade of purple.

"Her green binky!" Mom shouts.

Baby Ella can't get to sleep without her green pacifier. Sometimes, if Mom or I hold her and rock her back and forth in the rocking chair, she'll accept the pink one, but most nights if she doesn't have her green one, we're in for a night of inconsolable shrieking.

"God." Mom sighs. "I've probably left a ton of stuff behind."

Everything stops for a pinpoint of a second as I remember my notebooks. I can't feel the car moving, or feel the heat under my shirt, or hear Baby Ella's screams, because all I can think about is the paper bag in my closet, all the way in the back. In the rush and clamor of leaving the apartment, I completely forgot about it. And now, with Slade there, alone in the place . . .

"Mom!" I grab her arm. "I left something really, really important behind at the apartment. We have to go back."

Mom looks at me like I'm crazy. "Don't be ridiculous, Hershey." Suddenly, her eyes get wide and she withdraws her arm from the garbage bag, holding the green binky. "Aha!" she says, popping it into Baby Ella's mouth, who immediately begins sucking and then conks out against Mom's chest. Mom sags against the backseat. Her shirt is damp with sweat too. She lifts a hand and rests it on her forehead, just above her raspberry cut. "Oh thank God," she says, closing her eyes.

"Mom. I can't leave it behind with Slade there in the apartment. What if he destroys it or something?"

Mom opens her eyes and turns her head. "Destroys it? What are you talking about? What did you leave behind?"

"My notebooks," I say in a whisper. "They're all in a paper bag in the back of my closet."

Mom closes her eyes again. "Hershey. For crying out loud, honey. Slade is not going to destroy a bunch of notebooks that are hidden all the way in the back of a closet."

My face gets hot. "They're not just a bunch of notebooks, Mom. They have personal things in them. Stuff that I've been writing down and saving for years."

Mom looks at me again. Her blue eyes have a glassy appearance and the cut on her lip is starting to crust over. It looks gross, like a fuzzy caterpillar. "Hershey, why do you think Slade would even go looking for something like that?"

I shake my head. Sometimes I don't think my mother knows anything. "Because we *left*, Mom! He'll want to get back at us! He'll want to do something to make us pay for leaving! Why do you think I didn't want to leave Augustus Gloop behind?"

Mom blinks a few times. "What are you talking about, Hershey? Slade is not going to do anything like that." She sits up a little straighter, rearranging Baby Ella on her lap. "He's not an animal, honey. He didn't do anything like that the last time."

That's because last time I wasn't messing stuff up around the house, trying to get him mad, I think. *Last time, I wasn't trying to get you guys to fight all the time, until it got so bad that Slade snapped. Last time . . .*

I stop, forgetting about the notebooks for a moment, as I realize again that it is my fault that Slade hit Mom. It is my fault that Slade's annoyance grew into a frightening, tangible rage, so much so that he himself admitted that things would only get worse. Now we're on our way to a battered women's shelter. All because of me and my stupid plan.

I'll make it up to you, I think. *I don't know how yet, but I swear on everything I know and everything I am, Mom, that I will make it better.* I press my face back up against the window. The darkness flies past me like a sheet of ink.

And as soon as I figure out how, I'm going back to the house to get my notebooks.

FIVE

I've never been to this part of Sommersville, but the view from the cab doesn't look too bad. The wide streets are clean, shaded by heavy elm trees, and the houses are neat, with small well-kept yards. When we drive by the Wal-Mart, a feeling of reassurance washes over me. The familiar white and blue letters glow warmly in the dark. Even better, I know they sell bags of Cheetos.

McLean Street, where the shelter is located, looks like any old regular street. In fact, when we first pull up to the shelter, I wonder if the cabdriver has made a mistake. Mom does too, apparently, because she doesn't move until the driver looks at her in the mirror and says, "This here's your stop, lady." Mom glances out the window next to me.

"That one?" She points to the white two-story house sitting in front of us. It's the very last house on the block. There are green shutters on the outside and a brick chimney sticking out of the roof. Even in the dark, I can see curtains on the windows and a heavy silver knocker on the front door. "That's the . . . ?"

The cabdriver nods. His oily little ponytail slithers up and down his neck. "That's it."

Mom squints, then shades her eyes with her hand. "I don't see any kind of sign," she says. "There's no—"

"It doesn't *have* any signs," the driver says, cocking his head and looking at Mom as if she is retarded. "It's a shelter, lady. People in there are hiding from someone."

Mom gives the driver a sidelong glance. "Oh," she says. "Of course."

"It looks like someone's house," I say. "I mean, it's . . . kinda nice."

"What'd you expect, a dump?" The cabdriver sounds indignant. "It *is* someone's house." I glare at him as he holds out his hand for the fare. Mom blushes and presses a sweaty twenty-dollar bill into it. We get out of the cab, dragging our clothing-stuffed garbage bags along a stone path. Mom gives me a quick glance before she reaches out and grabs the knocker. Baby Ella is still asleep on her shoulder. After a moment's hesitation, she raps the knocker once.

"Who's there?" A low voice comes out from behind the door.

Mom leans in. "Brer Rabbit," she says. The door opens immediately. A woman with glasses and short black hair smiles at us and opens the door wider. A plastic card pinned to her shirt says: KATE BORIS, WOMEN'S COUNSELOR.

"Daisy?" she asks. Mom nods. Kate glances out toward the street. "Is there any chance he may have followed you?" Mom and I turn our heads simultaneously, looking for Slade's car, but no one is there.

"No," Mom replies. "He's not here." Kate seems satisfied.

"Follow me," she says, grabbing two of our garbage bags, one in each hand, and turning back around.

"*Brer Rabbit?*" I whisper, as we follow Kate down a hallway.

"Shhh," Mom whispers back, not turning around. "It's just a password. Kate gave it to me earlier on the phone so I could identify myself." I don't know what to think of that, so I keep quiet. We traipse behind Kate as she leads us through an enormous kitchen covered with white and yellow wallpaper, a living room with old blue couches, and down a set of stairs.

"I know it's late," Kate says apologetically. "But you have to talk to Naomi before you can go to bed. She has papers and things for you to sign." She drops our bags to the ground and gives Mom a quick squeeze on the shoulder. "It won't take long."

Naomi Shonko's office is in the basement of the women's shelter. It's a dim room with orange walls and frayed furniture. A cloud of cigarette smoke hovers above a desk cluttered with piles of paper and empty styrofoam cups. Wedged alongside a dead plant there is a narrow gold plaque in the middle of the desk that reads: NAOMI SHONKO, DIRECTOR. Naomi herself is sitting behind the desk, talking urgently on the phone. Mom, Baby Ella, and I sit down in the yellow chairs across from her and wait.

"I know, I know," Naomi says. "You're going to tell *me* what these guys are like?" She has circles under her eyes, and blond curly hair. Her head is resting against the back of her chair and she is rubbing her eyes with her free hand. A Mickey Mouse clock hanging on the wall above her head indicates that it is eleven thirty at night. I don't feel tired at all.

"Do whatever you can," Naomi says again into the receiver. "Bribe her. Lie to her. Whatever you think might get her in here. Tonight." I pretend not to listen. Baby Ella begins to whimper.

"Here," I whisper, holding out my arms. "Let me have her." Mom hands her over and gives me a grateful smile. I put the green binky back into Baby Ella's mouth and push her head gently against my chest. I can feel her tiny body sagging into mine as I start to hum "The Muffin Man." It's her favorite song in the world. Mom is perched on the edge of her seat, looking around the room. I sit back and follow her gaze.

There are pictures on every wall. Some are thumbtacked carelessly to bulletin boards; others are hung neatly on the wall in small plastic frames. Hundreds of pictures of babies clutter the bulletin board, some professionally taken, with ribbons in their hair, wearing starched pink Easter dresses and little patent leather shoes, surrounded by plastic ABC blocks or teddy bears. But most of the pictures seem to have been taken at random, snapshots of kids swinging high on swings, or hanging loosely from jungle gyms, laughing with delight. There are a few birthday parties, the children's mouths each in the shape of an O, awestruck at the flaming cakes in front of them. One little boy, standing waist-high in a pool of water that shimmers like glass around him, has his arms thrown toward the sky, a gigantic smile on his face.

But it is the pictures of all the women, assembled on the wall facing Naomi's desk, that Mom is staring at. I look too, wondering what she is thinking. Some of the women are sitting on couches, holding cigarettes in their hands, their heads bowed low, looking shy and afraid. A young girl in a black graduation cap and gown, her head tilted at a sharp, unnatural angle, beams with joy. There are pictures of women standing next to other women in the kitchen we just walked through, holding each other tightly, as if they might never let go. Up in the far left-hand corner is a picture of a tall, thin woman standing on a highway with a little kid in red overalls next to her. The woman is holding a cardboard sign that says SAN FRANCISCO OR BUST, and the sky overhead is blue and gold as the road before them stretches on endlessly.

The phone plunks down in the cradle with a click. Mom and I look over at the same time.

"There's quite a lot of them, aren't there?" Naomi asks, referring to the pictures. Mom nods mutely. "They've all stayed here at one time or another." I look over at Mom. Her face is getting red. I rub her hand. Naomi stands up.

"I'm Naomi Shonko," she says, extending her arm. "You must be Daisy. Welcome to Sunrises Women's Shelter." Mom gives Naomi a small smile and shakes her hand. I struggle to free my other hand out from under Baby Ella, but Naomi stops me.

"It's fine, sweetheart. I was just going to ask your name."

"Hershey," I say, squeezing Baby Ella. "And this is Baby Ella."

"You're both beautiful," Naomi says. "I love your glasses, Hershey. And I bet you're a huge help to your mom."

"She is," Mom offers, glancing over at me. "I don't know what I'd do without Hershey."

"I bet." Naomi nods and then looks at Mom carefully, as if seeing her for the first time. "Did you get that cut on your lip tonight, Daisy?" Mom nods and stares at the floor. A muscle in her cheek moves. Naomi turns back to me and gives me a wide smile. Her teeth are brown and old-looking. "Listen, sweetheart, would you like to go upstairs with Ella and lie down while I talk—"

"No," I interrupt, looking over at Mom. "Um, I mean, I already know what happened, okay? You don't have to hide it from me."

Naomi tilts her head. "I'm not trying to hide anything from you, Hershey." She's using that voice that means she's probably had this exact conversation before with some other kid—and won. "It's just that your mother and I have to go over some details that she might want to keep private." I stare at Mom, willing her with a steady gaze to disagree with Naomi, to say instead, *Hershey's been through this before. She doesn't need to leave.*

Instead, Mom squeezes my hand and gives me a sad look. "Actually, honey, I think that's a good idea."

"But . . ." Just then, Baby Ella grunts. Her eyelashes flit open like two worn-out hummingbirds and close lightly again.

"Just for a few minutes, Hershey," Mom says. She's pleading with me, her voice on the edge of breaking. I gather Baby Ella into a little bundle and stand up.

"We'll be in the hall," I say, looking at Mom. "In case you need me or anything." Naomi smiles and walks out from behind her desk. She's shorter than she looks, and she walks with a limp.

"I appreciate it, Hershey," she says, opening the door.

I slit my eyes at her when her back is turned. "We won't be long." Little silver earrings sway next to her face while she talks.

I walk down to the end of the hallway and sit on one of the three steps. There is a grimy cigarette odor in the air. Baby Ella's body feels like dead weight in my arms. Her lips fall slack around the binky and it slides out of her mouth. In another minute, she is asleep. I rest my head against the wall and close my own eyes. If I weren't holding Baby Ella, I'd scream. Or, better yet, eat. There's gotta be a vending machine around here somewhere. I stand up slowly and press my ear against Naomi's door. I can hear Mom crying softly.

"It'll be okay," I whisper. "Everything's going to work out, Mom. I promise." I lean my forehead against the dark wood and shut my eyes. I'd kill for a bag of Cheetos. But then another sound, coming from the end of the hall, makes me lift my head. I take a few steps toward it. It sounds like a piano. At least I *think* it's a piano. It's definitely music of some sort. I move my ear closer to the doorjamb and lean in as tightly as I can. It's a lovely melody, slow and sad. I listen more closely. Goose bumps rise on my arms. If the music was a person talking, she would be crying.

I'm leaning in so hard that I accidentally bump Baby Ella. She lifts her head before I can hush her, and lets out a wild, high-pitched scream. Pressing my hand gently over her mouth, I step back away from the door. But Baby Ella writhes and wiggles in my arms, bellowing as if I have just stuck a safety pin into her arm. I hang on as tightly as I can, so that she won't fall to the floor, and try to quiet her down.

"Shhh, baby. Shhhh, it's okay." But Baby Ella doesn't think it's okay at all. She pummels me with her tiny fists, her face getting as red as a tomato. The screams coming out of her are as loud as I've ever heard.

Suddenly the door flings open.

"Que es ese *ruido*?" Baby Ella stops crying instantly. We both stare at the tiny woman standing before us. She looks old, like someone's grandmother, and she's at least half my size. Her skin is the color of butterscotch candy, and her eyes, which are as black as eight balls, are surrounded by dark bruises. A large, flat Band-Aid covers the bridge of her nose, and a heavy necklace made of twisted rope and carved blue beads hangs around her neck. A flat silver medallion, like a sea dollar, hangs down in the middle of it. The woman steps forward. A sheet of long black hair sways behind her as she peers down the hallway.

"Que es mamá?" she asks harshly. I don't have the faintest idea what language she is talking in, but I think she just asked me something about Mom.

"My mother's, um, down the hall. Talking to Naomi." The woman's dark eyes flash. I wonder if the bruises hurt when she blinks, the way mine did after my surgery.

"You have just arrived?" I nod slowly, relieved that she is speaking English. The woman rolls her eyes and then stamps her foot. She is wearing brown sandals and no socks. Her toes are unpolished and ragged-looking.

"Ay, dios mío," she says. "Another pack of rats."

I shift Baby Ella in my arms and glare at the woman. "We're not *rats*." The woman snorts and begins to close the door. But I step forward. "Were you playing the piano in there?" She looks curiously at me.

"You could hear?" she asks. I nod.

She looks down and touches the silver medallion on her chest. It has a hole in the middle and little squiggly lines all around the outside. "I was playing a little."

"It sounded amazing," I offer.

The woman makes another snorting noise and steps back into the room. "You have never heard the piano played correctly, then!" She slams the door with a sudden bang. I jump. Baby Ella turns and, burying her face into my neck, begins to wail again.

"It's okay," I soothe, staring at the closed door. "I won't let her hurt you, baby. I promise." Before I let myself stop to think what I am doing, I rap hard on the door, once, twice, three times. Inside, the piano playing stops. I hold my breath as footsteps move toward us.

"*Sí?*"

"I . . . I . . . was just wondering . . ." I swallow hard. "I mean, I have to just sit out here in the hall and wait while my mother . . ." My voice trails off as I gesture toward Naomi's door with my arm. "Would you mind if maybe we just came in and—"

"No," the woman says abruptly, disappearing behind the door once more. I stare, dumbfounded, and then look at Baby Ella. She has stuck her thumb into her mouth and is watching me with sleepy interest. I can feel the blood rushing to my ears and a pounding behind my eyes. I lean in and bang hard on the door with the side of my fist.

"Que *tienes*?" the woman barks, flinging the door wide once more. The Band-Aid on her nose wrinkles as she speaks. Baby Ella hides her face in my neck, but does not take her thumb out of her mouth.

"Um," I say, holding Baby Ella a little more tightly, "I don't mean to upset you or anything. It's just . . ."

Just then Naomi's head pops out from her office. She looks one way down the hall and then the other. A flutter of concern crosses her face when she sees the woman and me standing face-to-face

"Lupe?" she calls out. (She pronounces it *"Loo-pay."*) "Is everything okay?" The woman stares at me for a moment, and then at Ella. A look of disgust passes over her face.

"Sí," she calls out to Naomi. "It is okay."

Naomi holds up an outstretched palm. "Five more

minutes, Hershey. I promise. We're almost finished." She steps back into her office and shuts the door.

Lupe is scowling at Baby Ella. "The baby will fuss. I cannot play if there is noise."

I put my hand over the top of Baby Ella's head. "The music will help her go back to sleep. I promise you she won't make a sound." Lupe's eyes continue to dart back and forth between me and Baby Ella. Finally she takes a step back and walks over to the piano. She leaves the door open.

The room looks like some sort of broom closet. Mops and buckets, brooms and dustpans, are leaning against every available wall. Bottles of Lysol, coated with thin films of dust, have been scattered carelessly on the floor. The piano, which looks more or less like a narrow cardboard box, has been shoved into a corner on the other side. I settle myself into a corner, next to four mops and a broom, and arrange Baby Ella in my lap. She leans heavily against my chest and closes her eyes. The piano is only about three feet away from me, but I sit up straight as Lupe begins to play again. I watch her fingers as they move slowly over the keys. She plays the same piece of music I heard earlier. It is mournfully slow, each individual note as delicate as a strand from a spider's web. Lupe stares at the sheet music resting on the piano ledge, even as her fingers move nimbly over the keys. *How does someone do that?*

I wonder. *How can a person learn to play something so well without looking?* My breathing slows as I listen. It is as if the music is a living, breathing thing, separate even from Lupe herself. And although I have never heard anything so sad, I have also never heard anything more beautiful. *How can that be?* I wonder. How can something be sad and beautiful at the same time?

Lupe's fingers move more quickly across the keys as the melody gains momentum. She must know this part by heart, because her eyes are closed and she does not even look at the sheet music.

But she stops all at once as the door opens. Mom and Naomi are standing there, staring at us with stupid grins on their faces.

"It looks like you found a friend," Naomi says, glancing at Lupe and then over at me.

"Bah!" Lupe says, not turning around.

"This is Lupe," Naomi says, talking to Mom. "Lupe, I want you to meet Daisy. She'll be staying here for a while with her girls, whom . . . I guess you've already met." Lupe doesn't budge. Mom glances at Lupe and then holds out her hand toward me.

"I'm sorry you had to wait so long, honey," she says. "Let's get to bed."

I struggle to my feet, careful not to jostle Baby Ella.

"It was nice to meet you," I say, staring at Lupe's back.

"Maybe I can come down again sometime and listen to you play?" In response, Lupe stands up, shuts the piano top with a loud bang, and walks out of the room. Naomi comes over and squeezes my shoulder.

"That's just the way Lupe is, Hershey. Try not to take it personally. She's been through a lot. She doesn't talk to anyone here. In fact, you're the first person I've ever seen her talk to besides me."

"Really?"

Naomi nods. She gives me a little wink. "Don't let her rudeness scare you off," she says. "Lupe could use a friend."

SIX

The room Naomi shows us to is upstairs on the first floor, directly across from the kitchen. It's nice enough, with a bunk bed, clean green carpeting, and two dressers. There is a tiny lamp on one of the dressers, and a crib has been set up in the corner for Baby Ella. The slats are old and worn-looking, but it has a clean yellow sheet on it. A soft bumper pad dotted with panda bears surrounds the mattress. Kate has put our black garbage bags on the bottom bunk. There is a large window at the end of the room, but it is locked shut with two iron bars that crisscross in an ominous X on the outside of the glass.

"I know it's been a long night," Naomi says as we look around the room. "Do either of you have any questions before I leave?" Mom shakes her head, but I gesture toward the window.

"Are the bars on the window so we can't get out?" I ask.

Naomi smiles grimly at Mom and then looks back over at me. "Unfortunately," she says, "the bars on the window are there so that certain people can't get *in*, Hershey."

I can feel my face flush hot, first with embarrassment, and then with fear. "You mean . . . there have been guys . . . who have tried to get in here?"

Naomi nods once. "Yes. But not for a long time."

"Like how long?"

"A pretty long time ago," Naomi says. "Actually, there haven't been any incidents since we had them installed several years ago." I can tell by the calm expression on Mom's face that she has already been told all of this, but I feel panicky inside. Naomi puts her hands into her pockets. "You remember the lady who let you in? Kate?" I nod. "She's on duty in the room right next door to this one." Naomi taps the wall. "She'll be up all night, so if you need anything, or if there is any kind of emergency, you just let her know, okay? Don't worry, sweetheart. I promise you're safe here." I swallow hard, wanting desperately to believe her. "I won't keep you any longer," Naomi says, closing her hand around the doorknob. "Try to get some sleep now." Mom smiles her thanks as Naomi shuts the door softly behind her.

"Well," she says, putting Baby Ella down in the crib and rubbing her eyes. "Naomi's right. It's almost twelve thirty in the morning. Should we try to get some sleep?"

"Did everything go all right downstairs?" I ask, side-stepping the question.

"Yes," Mom says uncertainly. "I think so. Naomi is a very nice lady." She brings her hands down on either side of her cheeks. "Oh, that reminds me, Hershey. She gave me something for you. I put it on the dresser over there."

"Oh, brother." I walk over to the dresser slowly. It's probably some dorky pamphlet for kids about how to recover from domestic violence. Just what I need. Instead, on the dresser is a wide-lined two-hundred-fifty-page wire-bound notebook. I crack it open. It's brand-new, with a purple cover. Not a mark on it. I turn and look at Mom.

She gives me a small smile. "Just until we can go back and get your other ones, Hershey."

I hug the slim notebook to my chest. I am already thinking of a list. "Thanks, Mom." I slide the notebook under the pillow on the top bunk. "Do you mind if I sleep up top?"

Mom shakes her head. "Be my guest." She sits down on the lower bunk and starts to untie her dirty white Keds.

"Do you know how long we'll have to stay here?" I ask.

Mom grunts, struggling with a knot in her laces. "Naomi seems to think we could be here for a month at least."

"A *month*?"

"Shhh!" Mom says. "You'll wake Ella!"

How am I going to practice with Phoebe for the talent show? Will I even be allowed to visit with her while I'm living here? And what about school? We have two weeks left, not to mention final exams. I'm no honor roll student, but I don't want to fall behind. Especially since I'll be starting high school next year.

"Am I going be able to finish out the school year?"

Mom nods and pulls off her socks. "Of course, honey. Naomi says that the bus comes right to the corner of McLean Street. You'll have to get up a little earlier too, since the drive will be farther now." She pauses a moment, as if to catch her breath. "I'm going to have to file for custody of Ella right away too. In court."

"And that's going to take a whole month?" I ask. Mom's shoulders sag. She leans over, resting her elbows on her knees, and lets her head sink against her hands.

I bite my tongue and run over to her. "I'm sorry. I won't ask any more questions, Mom. Let's just get some sleep." She nods and falls back against the mattress like a sack of flour. I cover her up with a thin yellow blanket and give her a kiss on the forehead. Within two minutes she is snoring.

I get into the top bunk, wincing as the mattress creaks and groans under my weight. The airlessness of the room combined with my close proximity to the ceiling makes me feel as if I am in a coffin. Too spooky. Climbing back out of bed, I take the tiny lamp off the dresser and plug it into the wall across the room. Even under the tiny circle of light, my brand-new notebook looks and smells wonderful. I inhale deeply, relishing the scent of pink bubble gum rubbed around on the bottom of an old, soft shoe. I write and write and write until my hand gets a cramp in it that takes hours to go away.

THE SHELTER:
1. Bars on windows, thanks to past psychos.
2. Looks like a regular house.
3. Smells like cigarettes.
4. Okay bedroom. Bunk beds.
5. Already met a lady. Plays piano. Kind of freaky.

HOW TO KEEP THINGS STRESS-FREE FOR MOM:
1. Take care of Baby Ella as much as possible.
2. Don't mention Slade (like I would anyway).
3. Don't say anything else about my notebooks.
4. Think of funny jokes to make her laugh.
5. Don't complain.

WHAT TO TELL PHOEBE ON MONDAY ABOUT A.G.:
1. He only eats tuna-flavored cat food.
2. His favorite thing to do is play with yarn.
3. He cries when he's lonely.
4. He doesn't like it when people yell.
5. He sleeps a whole lot.

NOTEBOOK RETRIEVAL PLAN (IF SLADE IS THERE):
1. Crawl in through window. (Get trash can to stand on.)
2. Have a garbage bag stuffed in pants.
3. Put notebooks in garbage bag and throw out window.

4. Go back down through window, get bag, and run.

NOTEBOOK RETRIEVAL PLAN (IF SLADE IS GONE BUT HOUSE IS LOCKED):

1. Crawl in through window.
2. Get notebooks.
3. Go out through front door.
4. Leave door unlocked.

THINGS I'D GIVE MY LEFT ARM FOR RIGHT NOW:

1. A supersize bag of Cheetos.
2. A kiss from Mom.
3. Having Augustus Gloop next to me.
4. Being able to wake up and find out that this is all a bad dream.

I look over at Mom when I'm done writing. The light illuminates the soft planes of her face. Except for the cuts on her lip and forehead, her skin looks as soft as a peach. The furrow in her brow has disappeared and her hair hangs as limp as silk around her shoulders.

"Oh, Mom," I whisper. "I'm so sorry."

Minutes tick by as she snores. On the opposite side of the room, Baby Ella inhales in and out, her breath coming in deep and hoarse sweeps. Taking my glasses off, I put my head down against the cool notebook sheet and close my eyes.

"Mom." My voice floats through the dark room. "I'm scared."

SEVEN

A loud clanging sound, followed by the trampling of what sounds like hundreds of feet, wakes me from a sound sleep the next morning. I am still on the floor, my face drool-glued to the front of my notebook. Mom bolts upright and bangs her head on the top bunk.

"OUCH!" she says, falling back into her pillow. I sit up, rubbing the sleep from my eyes. It takes me a minute to remember where we are. Then I see Baby Ella's panda bear crib and the metal bars across our window. Baby Ella stands up in her crib and stretches out her arms. "Mama, Mama, I want out!"

"Are you all right, Mom?" I ask, feeling around for my glasses. I put them on.

Mom sighs heavily. "I will be." She swings her legs out of bed. I scramble to my feet, over to Baby Ella, and lift her out of the crib. She smells like baby shampoo and lemon yogurt, which, aside from hot dogs, is pretty much all she eats.

"How are you, baby girl?" I ask softly, pressing my nose against the top of her head. But she pulls away from me, reaching for Mom.

"Mama!" she cries. "Mama!" I hand her over, but my disappointment must show in my face because Mom says, "Oh, Hershey, don't take it personally. She's confused is all." She turns to Baby Ella, talking in her little-kid voice. "We're in a new place, aren't we? Yes, Ella, new. Very different. But Mama's here, baby. And Hershey, too." Baby Ella puts her chubby arms around Mom's neck and holds on for dear life. I wish I didn't want to do the same.

The noise outside our room gets louder and louder until it sounds like a stampede of cattle is right outside our door. A clattering of strange voices—women's and children's—begins to seep under the door. For some reason, I had forgotten about the fact that there would be other women here. Or kids. We didn't see anyone last night, except Lupe. Everyone must have been asleep. It sounds as if there are a hundred of them out there.

"Don't you even *think* of sitting down at that table without washing your hands! You get yourself right over to that sink and *use* that soap!"

"Radiance! Where is that girl? I told her six times it was time for breakfast! Come on now!" Chairs scrape against the floor and a child starts crying. It's a small sound that rises above the din like a puppy whining. Then a banging sound punctures the crying, eight or nine harsh sounds that end abruptly.

"Reggie *Marks*! What did I tell you about banging that truck? You better watch it, 'fore I bang your head off this table, you got that?"

"Who going to call the new girls?" someone asks. It's another, older child's voice. Mom and I stare at each other as footsteps move toward our door. There is a knock, timid as a mouse. "Yes?" Mom says. A little girl in white shorts and a yellow T-shirt opens the door slowly. Her greasy hair has been pulled off her face with a yellow giraffe-shaped barrette, and her nose is running. She peers into our room.

"You coming out to eat?" she asks, looking first at Mom and Baby Ella, and then over at me. Her voice, soft and sweet as a flower, hangs in the air between us. Through the crack in the door, I can see the rest of the women in the kitchen. They are craning their necks behind the girl, waiting for Mom's response.

"We'll be out later, sweetie," Mom says. "Thank you."

"You can't eat later!" one of the women calls out. "No eating allowed here in this kitchen after hours. We got rules. You gotta eat when we eat." Mom looks over at me. I shrug. "All right," she says through gritted teeth. "Come on."

With the lights on, the kitchen looks a lot bigger than it

did last night. It's divided into two parts by an open door-way. The first part, which is closest to our room, consists of a rectangular table and seven or eight folding chairs. Three narrow windows across the room are draped with nice-looking curtains, but the windows have metal bars across the outside, just like the one in our bedroom. The green linoleum floor is filthy. Ten steps away from the table is the actual kitchen, where it looks like Big Bird exploded. Everything, including the stove, the sink, the countertops, and the floor, is bright yellow. Boxes of Rice Crisps and Oatie-O cereal sit next to a pile of spoons on a counter. Next to the cereal is a microwave oven and a toaster that has six slots in the top. A skinny woman with long braids and a leather bracelet around her wrist is watching the toast. Next to her, a large pot of coffee is gurgling its own good morning.

I sit down, trying hard to ignore the stares and side-long glances from the strangers across the table, but when you're new, there's no getting around it: People want to look. I bring my fingers up to my bad eye and rub the lid, which I always do whenever I think someone's going to say something about it. Mom is busy at the other end of the table, trying to wedge Baby Ella into a high chair. The scrawny-looking woman from the kitchen comes into the room carrying a plate of toast. Up close, I can see a blue dragon tattoo on her arm. Her braids hang down under a beat-up baseball cap, and her T-shirt says, JESUS LOVES YOU. EVERYONE ELSE THINKS YOU'RE A DORK in big pink bubble letters. She pops a corner of toast into her mouth and looks directly at me. There is a pale green bruise under her left eye.

"I'm Josie." She pats the head of a little boy sitting next to her. "This here's my boy, Galvin, and over there"—she jerks her head toward the little girl who knocked on our door—"is my daughter, Macy." She points at the others with her fork. "That's Deletha over there, and those two, Reggie and Radiance, are hers."

I stare at Deletha, who is sitting at the opposite end of the table. She has dark black skin and is dressed in a fuzzy green bathrobe. Hundreds of long, thin braids hang from her head, each one secured with a heavy gold bead. She is shoveling scrambled eggs into her mouth and does not look up when Josie says her name. Her little boy, Reggie, who's maybe four years old and also has a head full of braids, is sitting next to her. He's picking his nose. Radiance is nowhere to be seen. I look away uncomfortably.

Josie twirls her fork and with a movement that is sort of like the flourish I've been practicing for the juggling show, says, "And this is Gracie." She points to another black woman who, as if on cue, walks out of the back of the kitchen. She is dressed in a long white tunic and soft black pants. Her lips are red and the palms of her hands are pink. She nods at me and takes a sip from a blue coffee mug. "There's a few more ladies upstairs," Josie says, pouring milk into Galvin's cereal bowl, "but they don't like eating breakfast with all the kids. Except Gracie here. She don't mind the yelling." Gracie makes a *harumpf* sound with her lips and takes another gulp of coffee. When she opens her mouth, I glimpse a dark, cavernous space where her two front teeth should be.

"Speak for yourself," she says, lisping her *S.* "Anyone know if the newspaper got here yet?"

I look around one more time quickly, just in case I have missed her, but I don't see Lupe.

"What about Lupe?" I ask quietly. No one says anything. Then Josie bursts out laughing.

"Lupe?" she repeats. "What, did you meet her last night? In her little broom closet?" I nod, embarrassed.

Josie laughs again. "Did she curse at you?"

"She wasn't very nice at first," I admit. "But she was playing the piano and I accidentally interrupted her."

"That's Lupe," Gracie says. "She's crazier than a loon. Stay away from her. She spends all her time in that closet downstairs, playin' the piano. She's been here about a month. She doesn't eat with us or talk to anyone."

I'm intrigued. "Why's she crazy?"

"Why's anyone crazy?" Gracie says, peeling red nail polish off her nails. "You can only take so much, I guess."

Josie laughs again. "I actually had the nerve to go down there and ask her if she would play some of my songs for me." She tosses her hair. "I'm a singer, you know. I have to practice constantly, to keep my voice in shape for auditions. You have to be serious about that stuff if you want to make it big someday." I notice Deletha rolling her eyes as Josie keeps talking. "I went down there one night and asked Lupe if she would play for me so I could practice my singing." Josie shudders at the memory. "You woulda thought I asked her for a pint of blood or something. Started cursing at me in Spanish, acting all wacky and stuff."

Gracie turns her attention back to me. "So you all got here last night?" I look around; Mom has disappeared into the kitchen, preparing breakfast, I guess, for Baby Ella. She doesn't like talking to strangers; she says it makes her nervous. The table is quiet; it seems even the children are waiting for me to answer. I nod.

Gracie pushes a paper plate toward me and motions toward a blue platter of scrambled eggs and bacon. I hate eggs. "Come on, eat something," she says. Josie hands the egg platter to Gracie, who places it in front of me.

I shake my head. "I don't really eat breakfast."

"What about something to drink?" Gracie asks. Without waiting for an answer, she walks back into the kitchen, opens the refrigerator, and takes out a plastic pitcher. After pouring a purple liquid into a tall glass, she sets it down before me.

"Kool-Aid. All we got, but it's cold."

I take a small sip. It tastes like cough syrup, but I drain it anyway.

"Thank you," I say quietly.

"So, you from Sommersville?" Josie asks. I nod and look down at the bottom of my empty cup.

"Which part?" she asks.

"By the Coca-Cola factory. Over on Lilac Lane." Josie nods in recognition.

"Funny," she says, scratching her stomach. "We just live a few blocks away from you, but I can't say I've ever seen you in the neighborhood before." I stare down at the table-cloth. What should I say?

Suddenly, Reggie and Radiance, who have reappeared from underneath the table, start to bicker alongside their mother.

"Gimme back my fork!" Radiance screams, slapping her little brother on the back of the head. Reggie bellows with pain and turns, burying his face into the middle of Radiance's stomach. A piercing scream comes out of the girl's mouth.

"He *bit* me!" Radiance wails. "Mama, Reggie bit me again!" But Deletha, whose long braids are dangling in her food, is still cramming pieces of toast and egg into her mouth. She doesn't even look up. I start to relax a little as heads turn toward the crying children, shifting the atten-tion away from me.

"Shhh . . . ," Josie tries, tapping the table in Radiance's direction with her fingers. "It's okay, sweetheart. Don't cry." She holds out her arms. "You want to come sit in my lap, baby?" Radiance shakes her head and screams even louder, clutching her mother's shirt. Deletha takes a long swallow of her orange juice, and pushes the little girl off of her. Gracie sits up straighter in her seat. Setting her fork down, she points in Deletha's direction.

"Deletha, how many meals you expect us to sit through, listening to those children holler and yell like stuck pigs, while you stuff your face?" Gracie's words stop Deletha mid-chew. She swallows slowly and then looks up. Her dark eyes gleam as she swats at the braids swinging around her face. She shoves her plate toward the middle of the table.

"I got enough to deal with in this place, Gracie, without you bossing me around." Deletha's voice is deep and gravelly. Three front teeth jut out painfully from her mouth, as if someone has yanked them forward with a pair of pliers. "Why don't you mind your own business for once?" Out of the corner of my eye, I can see Mom over Gracie's left shoulder. She is stirring Baby Ella's cereal slowly, watching the scene with frightened eyes. Josie's eyes dart back and forth between Gracie and Deletha.

"You're not *dealing* with anything," Gracie says, and glowers. "You sit there like you got earplugs in your head, while your kids run wild." Now Deletha gets up on her feet. Her height shocks me. Even in her green bathrobe, she could pass for a basketball player with her skinny, towering frame and yard-long arms. Already just a few inches away from Gracie's face, she leans in even closer.

"Hey, hey, hey!" a voice barks, charging into the kitchen suddenly. It's Kate, waving her arms over her head. Her plastic name card bobs up and down on her T-shirt. "What's going on here?"

Deletha, who is breathing hard through her nose, ignores Kate. She leers a moment more at Gracie, and then yanks Reggie's arm.

"Let's go," she says fiercely. "Radiance!" The tiny girl stops crying and trots after her mother. Kate watches them leave. No one says a word. And then, as if nothing has even happened, Kate turns toward me and puts her arm around my shoulders.

"Everyone meet Hershey?" she asks. Josie and Gracie nod. Kate twists around and catches Mom's eye. "And Daisy, too? And the baby, Ella?" Mom gives a weak half-hearted wave from the kitchen. Josie gives me a little grin.

"Is that really your name?" she asks. "Like the Hershey bar?"

It drives me crazy when people say that. Just for once, I wish someone would come up with something a little more original. "Yeah," I say politely. "That's really my name."

"It's cool," Josie says. "Different." She leans back so she can see Mom. "You eat a lot of chocolate or something when you were pregnant, Daisy?" Mom shakes her head and touches the back of her neck self-consciously.

"The doctor had to use forceps on me when I was born," I explain, coming to Mom's rescue. It's the least I can do. "They made my head pointy, and when I finally came out, the doctor said I looked just like a little Hershey's Kiss." The women break into wide grins.

"I *love* that!" Gracie says, smacking the side of the table with her hand.

"Hoi-shey baw!" Galvin says, grinning. His mouth is full of tiny silver teeth. I smile back at him, despite myself.

"Hoi-shey baw!" he says again, delighted.

EIGHT

After breakfast I go back into our room and unpack my bag of clothes. Mom is busy stacking Baby Ella's diapers in a neat pile against the wall. It feels weird putting my stuff in a strange drawer, weirder still to think about having to open it every morning from now on when I need to get dressed. But I do it anyway. I even fold all my T-shirts, so that Mom won't have to call me back later to redo it.

"Can I take a bus over to Phoebe's?" I ask Mom. She turns around on her heels.

"*Phoebe's?* Hershey, you can't go anywhere around our neighborhood now. At least not until I get a protection order against Slade. He doesn't know where we are, and I need it to stay that way."

"But I just—"

Mom cuts me off roughly. "But nothing, Hershey. Do you not understand the magnitude of our situation? We're in *hiding*, honey, because Slade threatened our safety. We cannot be seen. Period." Guilt surges over me again. We're in hiding. Mom has to get a protection order. All because of me. I stare at the floor.

"Why don't you call Phoebe when you're done with your clothes?" Mom tosses me a quarter. "See how Augustus Gloop is doing."

I catch the coin with two hands. "Where's the phone?"

"The pay phone is at the end of the hall," Mom says. "Didn't you see it?"

"Why do we have to use a pay phone?"

Mom bites her lower lip. "Well, Naomi said something to me last night about people outside not being able to trace the pay phone number to the shelter."

"People outside?" I ask, as another shot of fear courses through the middle of my chest. "You mean those psycho guys who try to climb through the windows?" I think about the bruise on Josie's face, Gracie's missing teeth.

"Yes," Mom says firmly. "I think that's exactly what she meant."

"Okay," I say, taking a deep breath. "No big deal."

But it is a big deal. It's the *real* deal. An unidentified building, passwords, bars on the windows, pay phones, and who knows what else just to keep these nuts out. I wonder what kind of guys Josie and Gracie have left behind. And what about Deletha? I've seen *COPS* on TV. I know the kinds of crazies that are out there.

Kate knocks on our open door and then sticks her head

into our room. "Group meeting at ten o'clock, girls," she says. "I'd appreciate it if you'd both come."

Mom nods. "We'll be there." It's nine thirty. I head down the hallway and insert the quarter Mom gave me into the pay phone.

Phoebe answers the phone on the first ring. I wonder if she's been waiting for me to call.

"Hey," I say. "How's it going?"

"Hershey! How are *you*? How's your mom? What's it like there?"

"We're okay. It's . . . different. Kinda weird. There's bars on the windows."

Reggie and Radiance come tearing down the steps, hollering and screaming.

"Bars?" Phoebe repeats. "Like jail?"

"Yeah," I say. "Sorta."

"Are there tons of women there?"

"Not *tons*. Like eight, I think. I've only met four so far, though."

"Oh." Phoebe sounds disappointed. "I thought it would be packed, for some reason. It sounds packed."

"It's not Walt Disney World, Phoebe. It's a shelter. There's a bunch of little kids here too. They're running around and stuff."

"Oh." She pauses. "Okay."

"How's Augustus Gloop?"

"Well . . ." Phoebe hesitates.

"What? Is he okay?"

"Yeah," Phoebe says uncertainly. "I think so. It's just that he won't come out of his cage. He's been in there ever since last night when you dropped him off. I think he's kind of scared."

"Oh, that's just because he's never been inside your house before," I say. "If you take him outside, he'll be fine. He knows the area, remember? And he loves that little space on your front porch."

"Do I have to touch him?" Phoebe asks.

"What do you mean, do you have to *touch* him? He's not a mountain lion, Phoebe!"

"I know. But I'm not good with animals like you are."

"Just carry the cage outside with him in it. And then open the door and let him come out by himself. You'll see. It'll work."

"Okay," Phoebe says. "I'll give it a try."

"I never thought I'd look forward to going to school so much," I say. "Especially on a Monday."

"It's that bad, huh?"

I step on my toe. "No, it's not that bad. I'm just looking forward to doing something normal again."

The ten o'clock meeting, which Kate directs, is held at the kitchen table. Mom and I sit next to each other in the same chairs we sat in for breakfast. Baby Ella sits on Mom's lap. Everyone who was at breakfast this morning is there, as well as another woman I haven't seen before.

"This is just a quickie," Kate says. "Nothing serious, girls. I just want to formally welcome the newest members of the house and introduce them to everyone. Then we can give them a quick overview of how we all do things." The unfamiliar woman introduces herself as Rose Pewter. She's young, maybe twenty, with bright green eyes, bud-shaped lips, and a silver stud in her nose. Both of her arms, from finger to elbow, are wrapped in white gauze. She lets Macy, Josie's little girl, sit on her lap.

"Now tell 'em what they gotta do." Deletha smirks as the introductions come to a close. She is sitting across from us, still in her bathrobe, leaning heavily on both elbows. Mom and I look expectantly at Kate. But before Kate can speak, Josie jumps in.

"Oh, it's no big deal," she says. "It's just like living at home. Everyone's gotta pitch in and do their chores."

Deletha snorts. "Right. *And* look for a new place to live. *And* find a job. *And* go to all your court dates." She puts her head down on the table. "It's too much, man. It's just too much."

Ignoring Deletha, Kate nods encouragingly at us. "We actually have a chart that has everyone's chores marked on it." She points to the kitchen behind her. "We keep it on the refrigerator so that everyone can see it easily." Mom and I exchange glances.

"Like a Job List?" I hear myself asking.

Kate nods. "Yes, exactly, Hershey. It's a list of jobs like cooking, doing the dishes, vacuuming, helping out with the children, taking out the garbage, and other things. Everyone living here gets assigned one job a week so that the place keeps running smoothly. Daisy, I was thinking we would start you out with something simple, being it's your first week and all. How about the vacuuming?" Mom smiles and nods, ducking her head behind Baby Ella's. "Great," Kate says, writing something down on a piece of paper. "Thanks, Daisy." She puts her pen down.

"Um . . ." I raise my hand tentatively.

Kate raises her eyebrows. "Yes, Hershey?"

"You didn't give me a job," I say. "For the Job List, I mean."

Kate grins. "That's because you don't get one."

"Why not?"

"Because you're a kid."

"She's no kid!" Deletha asserts, sitting up straight again. "Look at the size of her!" I blush angrily.

Kate looks at Deletha, steeling herself. "This will be the last time, Deletha, that I will ask you not to yell out during meetings." I hold my breath, waiting for another scene like the one this morning with Gracie, but Deletha just sighs heavily and drops her head down again onto her folded arms.

"Now," Kate says. "As I was saying, Hershey, you are exempt from the chore chart, as is everyone under the age of sixteen. You've got enough on your plate right now with school and everything else." She gives me a wink. "Of course, if you find yourself absolutely *yearning* one night to busy yourself, just let me know. I'll find something for you to do. But for now, just relax, okay? Just be a kid."

"I can't believe it," I say to Mom later when we are back in our room. "I just can't be*lieve* it."

"Believe what?" She is changing Ella's diaper. It always amazes me how such little people can make such large, disgusting smells.

"I can't believe you have to do chores here, too! You shouldn't have to do them, Mom. Didn't you tell Naomi about Slade's Job List at home? That it was the whole reason why he—"

Mom holds up her hand, waving it in front of me. "I need another wipe," she says. "Over there, in the black bag." I grab the box of wipes and shove them at her.

"Are you even listening to me, Mom?"

"Of course I am," she says, grimacing as she wipes Baby Ella's behind. "And it's no reason to get all upset. It's not the same thing as Slade's Job List at all."

"How can you say that? It's got your names, the check marks. It's even on the re*frig*erator!" I went into the kitchen after the meeting disbanded, to study the loathsome thing myself. It was set up almost exactly like Slade's, with the list of names and corresponding jobs. I noticed Lupe's name was on it, at the very bottom. She has bathrooms this week.

Mom seals Baby Ella's diaper shut and pulls up Ella's baby bloomers. Baby Ella claps her hands. "All done!" she says. "All clean!"

Mom tweaks her on the nose and hands her a blue sippy cup. "Hershey, it's not the same thing, and I'm telling you, it's not worth getting all worked up about. This shelter is harboring six women. They're feeding us, helping us find new houses, new jobs, all of it. The least we can do, honey, is pick up after ourselves and keep the place neat."

I sniff. When she puts it that way, I don't feel quite so outraged anymore. "Well," I say. "I still think it's kind of weird."

"Weird or not," Mom says, "that's the way the world works in most circles, sweetheart. You're just going to have to get used to it."

NINE

WHAT I WOULD DO IF I WEREN'T HERE:

   1. Play with Augustus Gloop.

   2. Write in my notebook (which I'm doing anyway).

   3. Walk to Phoebe's place.

   4. Rent *Willy Wonka + the Chocolate Factory*.

   (that would make it 108 times)

   5. Go buy a supersize bag of Cheetos.

THINGS I CAN DO WHILE I AM HERE:

   1. Take care of Mom/Baby Ella.

   2. Keep room neat.

   3. Homework (bleech).

   4. Make friends. (?????)

THE WOMEN I'VE MET SO FAR:

   Deletha-bully, terrible mom, TALL!!!

   Gracie-pushy, nice, no front teeth

   Josie-loud, obnoxious, good mom, kind of rude

   Rose-nose stud, arms wrapped???

   Kate-tiny, strong, counselor

   Naomi-in charge, secretive, annoying

Lupe-piano player, Spanish (I think), mean!!
THINGS THAT ARE SAD AND BEAUTIFUL AT THE
SAME TIME:
  1. Twilight.
  2. The last snowfall of winter.
  3. Rain.
  4. Baby Ella crying.
  5. The look on Augustus Gloop's face when he knows
  I have to leave for school in the morning.
  6. The music Lupe plays.
WHO I CAN SEE MYSELF HANGING OUT WITH HERE:
  Gracie-because she looks like she could have fun
  Josie-because she reminds me a little bit of Phoebe
  Lupe-because I want to learn how to play the piano

I put my pen down. I didn't know I wanted to learn how to play the piano until I wrote that last sentence. I know it's crazy, but before I can talk myself out of it, I scramble out of bed and creep downstairs. Mom and Baby Ella are napping in the bottom bunk, which means I have at least an hour to myself. At the very least, I can sit outside Lupe's door again and listen to her play. I walk softly, holding on to the side of the wall as I go, grateful for the bustle and clamor of the kids upstairs, who will muffle any sounds I might make. But I forget about the last three steps outside of Naomi's office, and when I fall, it sounds as if a bulldozer has just dropped on the building. I freeze, holding my breath, expecting a stampede of women to come rushing out. No one comes. Carefully, I pick myself back up and creep closer to the broom closet. Thinking about what Gracie said at breakfast about Lupe being crazy sends a little shiver of fear down my spine. Pressing my ear against the door, I listen closely. Nothing. I knock. Once. Twice. Three times. Nothing. I turn the knob, blinking several times until my eyes adjust to the dark. No Lupe.

Shutting the door tightly behind me, I turn on the light, and sit down at the piano bench. The room is stifling hot, but I don't care. I've never sat in front of a piano before. It feels exciting. I lift up the lid and rest my fingers on the glossy black and white keys. They are cool and smooth to the touch. I can hardly breathe, I'm so worked up. And I don't even know why. It's not like I can *play* or anything. The music book is open, perched on a thin ledge above the keys. The words "Moonlight Sonata" are displayed at the top of the page. If only I could read music. What would it be like to read music and then play? Really *play*? What if I could play the way Phoebe can juggle? What would it feel like to glide my hands over the keys and have a real song emerge from them?

I press down on a few of the keys. They ring out in the tiny room, small and alone. I push my glasses up along the bridge of my nose and press a few more. And then . . . *wait a minute*! Weren't those the same notes that Lupe played in the beginning of that song I heard last night? The one I've been humming in the back of my head for the last twelve hours? I press the same keys down again. Yes! I think that's right! At least, it sounds familiar. I hum the tune out loud and poke around for the next note. Dum, dum, dum. No. Dum, dum, dum. DUM! Yes, dum! That's the one! I play all three of the familiar notes together, pausing at the end of the fourth one to lift my hand in a melodramatic flourish.

Now wait, I know I can find the next three notes. It can't be that hard. But it takes me a while. I poke around, giggling as I stumble on notes that are obviously wrong. Soon I find the first one in the next set, and then the second, and finally the third. Now I can play all six notes, one after the other, just as Lupe did. I close my eyes, feeling the slender keys under my fingertips as I begin. I play the two sets of three notes at least twenty times before I hear the creak of the door opening behind me.

"What are you *doing*?" The harshness of Lupe's voice frightens me so much that I nearly fall off the bench. I collapse forward, my arms landing heavily on the keys. Lupe winces at the ugly sound.

"Oh!" I say, struggling to get up from the bench. "Oh, Lupe! I'm sorry! You weren't here . . . and I thought . . .

I thought . . . I would just . . ." Lupe strides forward, her dark hair swinging from side to side.

"You thought you would just *what*?" she snarls. "Do you have permission to be down here?" I shake my head, mute with fear. "Get out!" She points to the door with a rigid finger. "Get out before I . . ." Her voice trails off, but I don't wait for her to finish. Scurrying backward, I slam into the wall behind me. Brooms and mops rain down in a torrent of wooden handles and damp foul-smelling sponges, and I sit down hard. My hand comes down on something metal and sharp. "Ouch!" I yelp. A scurrying sound, followed by a series of high-pitched squeaking noises, makes me yell again. "Oh!" I look around frantically. The sound of scraping claws continues. "Oh, jeez, where is it?" I yell. "Where is it?" Lupe is standing a foot away from me, her hands on her hips, eyes glowering like marbles above the Band-Aid on her nose. The frantic squeaks get louder and more desperate-sounding. Suddenly, Lupe pushes past me, shoving the mops and brooms aside. I watch with my mouth open as she pulls a metal cage out of a tiny spot, holds it up, and starts clucking to the small animal inside.

"Shhh, Chili," she says. "Shhh. Mamacita is here."

I lean as far away from the cage as possible, scrambling backward on my arms and feet. "You have a pet rat?" I shriek.

Putting the cage back down on the floor, Lupe pushes the flat of her hand so quickly against my mouth that I gasp. "Quiet!" she says hoarsely. "Do you want me to get thrown out of here?" I shake my head from side to side. The weird-looking medallion on her chest is swinging at my eye level. Up close, I can see that the little squiggly lines are in fact letters, spelling out many different words. It looks like some sort of saying or quote. But I can't read it. The words are not English. After a few seconds Lupe lets her hand drop and redirects her attention to the brown animal in the cage. I stare at it for a few minutes, realizing to my great relief that it is not a rat. It's not even a mouse. I don't know *what* it is, but it's actually kind of cute. It has big black eyes, wide ears, and a small, bushy tail. The floor of its cage is covered with a layer of chunky sawdust, and there is a yellow plastic wheel, three red hollow balls, an upside-down water bottle, and a tiny food dish.

"Did you catch that thing in here?" I ask breathlessly. "I mean, was it living here in the closet?"

Lupe gives me a strange look. "Of course not. Chinchillas don't live in this country. They live in South America."

"Chin what?" I ask.

"Chinchillas," she repeats, sticking her finger into the cage and shaking it back and forth. "This is my pet chinchilla. Her name is Chili." She pronounces it "Chee-lee." The tiny animal moves forward timidly, its nose wiggling and trembling inside a set of nearly transparent whiskers.

"But I thought pets weren't allowed."

Lupe gives me a dark look. "They're not."

"So then why—"

Lupe cuts me off roughly. "Because I had to. I do not know anyone here and I could not leave my Chili behind." She tilts her head and pushes her lower lip out. "Ricardo knows how much I love her. I don't know what he would . . ." Her unfinished thought makes me remember how unsafe I felt leaving Augustus Gloop alone with Slade.

"Is Ricardo your husband?" I ask.

Lupe nods.

"I have a cat," I say slowly. "I didn't want to leave him home either."

Lupe's eyes squint. "Where is he?"

"With my best friend," I say. "She hates cats."

Lupe grunts. Then she turns her head suddenly and slits her eyes at me. "If anyone finds out that Chili is here, I will be forced to leave. It is against the rules, and breaking the rules means you must go."

"I . . . I wouldn't do that," I say, getting slowly to my feet. "Don't worry. You can trust me." Lupe turns back to Chili, clucking her tongue again and making shushing noises with her mouth.

"Bah," she says. "We'll see."

I don't know what to say to that, so I just look down and rub the spot on my hand where I jammed it into the cage. "Well, I guess I'll go," I say, taking a few steps toward the door. "I'm sorry I came in here without asking. And I'm sorry I touched your piano."

"It is not my piano," Lupe says, not turning around. "It belongs to the shelter. But I have permission to use it because I can play. You do not. You . . . you . . . were just . . . banging away . . . like it is some kind of toy. And the piano is not a toy!"

"I wasn't banging," I protest. "I was just trying to play that song that I heard you play last night." There is a pause.

"'Moonlight Sonata.' By Beethoven. It is my favorite."

"Beethoven?" I repeat. "The Furdelis guy?"

Lupe turns around. "Do you mean 'Für Elise'?" she says. I nod. "You have heard of Beethoven, then?"

"Sorta. I mean, we learned about him in school. Third grade, I think. Him and Mozart and another one whose name I can't pronounce. And one time I heard my mom play the piano and she told me it was that Furdelis song of his."

"Für. Elise," Lupe repeats, enunciating the words slowly. "It is pronounced 'Für Elise.'"

"Yeah," I say, scratching my leg. "Okay." There is a pause. "So you were playing Beethoven too, then?" I ask.

"Last night, when you let me and my little sister listen?" Lupe nods. "It sounded so good. Really. It was amazing."

Lupe snorts. "I was just practicing."

"Oh, no! You can really play."

"I used to be able to really play," she says, her voice quiet. "I cannot play well anymore."

"Well, I think you can." She doesn't respond. "Did you hear *me* playing?" I ask softly. "I found the first six notes all by myself just now, before you came in. Just from memory. Do you want to hear?" Lupe gives me a disgusted look.

"Playing by memory is nothing. Have you ever had a piano lesson from a real teacher?" I shake my head. "And you do not know how to read music?" I shake my head again. "Bah!" she says.

"Are *you* a teacher?" I ask.

She nods and touches the Band-Aid on her nose gently. "I was. But not anymore."

"Why not anymore?"

"You ask too many questions," Lupe says. "I don't like people like you. You should go. I'm tired."

My shoulders droop. I don't want to go. "Yeah. Okay, then. I'll see you around, I guess."

"What is your name again?" she asks.

I freeze. "Hershey. Hershey Hollenback."

"Hershey?" Lupe turns her head slowly. "I have never heard of a girl with that name before."

I shrug. "It's actually the name of a candy bar." Lupe smiles in recognition. Her teeth look like little pieces of Chiclets gum.

"Ah . . . sí." She turns back to Chili's cage. "Good-bye, then, Hershey."

TEN

On my way back upstairs, I notice that the back door is open, leading to a tiny yard behind the shelter. Tufts of pale grass, like blotchy chunks of hair, dot the otherwise dirt ground, and the entire yard is enclosed by a wooden fence. Deletha is sitting on the lone swing on a rusty swing set planted right in the middle of the yard. She is smoking a cigarette, swinging slowly, back and forth. In the opposite corner is a green plastic sandbox shaped like a turtle. Macy is sitting in the middle of it, filling a bright pink bucket with scoops of sand. I push open the door and step outside. The light makes me squint, but the warm air feels good on my face. Overhead, the sky is a brilliant blue.

I sit down against the part of the fence that is closest to the door and watch Macy for a while. She's lost in her own little world, babbling something about sea lions and a person named Princess Minook. I sneak a glance over at Deletha. She's changed out of her bathrobe and is wearing a purple sweat suit with silver stripes running down the sides. The shiny material glimmers in the sun. I stare at her nails when she brings her cigarette to her lips. They are so long that the ends actually curl over. Each one is painted a blinding neon green with a diagonal gold stripe across the middle. They look like alligator claws. I can't believe I didn't notice them this morning.

"Whatchou lookin' at?" Deletha asks suddenly, making me jump.

"Um . . . your nails," I say. "They're so long." Deletha stretches her hand out and flutters her fingers proudly.

"Took me almost a year to get them like this. They're four and a half inches now. I'm trying to get them up to twelve."

"Won't they break?"

"Nah. I got this strengthening stuff I put on 'em at night." She taps the side of her plastic swing with the nail on her index finger. It makes a dull sound, like a heavy shoe. "These babies are so thick right now I could chop wood with 'em." I shudder inwardly, careful not to let my disgust show. Why in the world would someone want twelve-inch long nails?

"Don't they make it hard to do stuff?" I ask.

Deletha shrugs. "You get used to it." I can't see any outward or visible marks on Deletha, and I wonder what kind of man she left behind. He must be enormous.

"Where's Reggie?" I ask. "And Radiance?"

Deletha shrugs. "Watchin' cartoons, I think."

"You don't have to stay with them?"

Deletha's eyebrows narrow as she takes another drag from her cigarette. "You're new, right?" I nod. "Then why you axing me twenty questions and all?" I shake my head and look down at my legs. I wish they weren't so wide. "How old are you, anyway?"

"Thirteen."

She snorts. "You big for thirteen."

"You mentioned that," I say, wishing I had the nerve to tell her to shut up.

She puffs again on her cigarette. "You in school?" I look over as Macy gets up out of the sandbox, brushes herself off, and walks back inside. She doesn't say a word to either of us.

"Eighth grade."

"Almost done, huh?"

I smile a little. "Two more weeks."

Deletha makes a *pphhhfff* sound with her lips and crushes her cigarette out with the toe of her purple sneaker. "That's nice—you spend the last two weeks of school in this dump."

"I don't think it's a *dump*."

Deletha jerks her head toward a spot over the fence. "Half the place still ain't even built." I look over across the fence. Metal scaffolding bars are attached to the back of the house where the kitchen is, and part of a wooden frame leans heavily against the opposite side. The beams are long and narrow, a pale, syrupy color under the sun. "That was s'posed to be some sort of playroom for the kids and a den or something for us girls. But Naomi said the guys working on it just up and left a few weeks ago." She snorts. "I guess they can't find no one else to finish the job."

I look away from the partially constructed room. "Well, anything's better than being at home with my mom's boyfriend." Deletha raises her eyebrows. She grabs hold of the chains on the swing and leans backward in her seat. Her arms are so long that they almost touch the top of the swing set.

"We going home in a few days," she says, looking straight at me.

I don't know if this means she's going back to the place she left, or if she and her kids found somewhere new to live, but I decide not to ask. "That's great." I wonder if Gracie knows.

Deletha's head is bobbing up and down like it has a spring in it. "Yeah. We been here two weeks. That's long enough. He learned his lesson."

"Who learned his lesson?"

"Douglas." Deletha pumps her legs so that the swing carries her up. "My boyfriend." She looks like a gigantic bird silhouetted against the sky, the braids flying back from her head like gold-tipped feathers.

"Oh." I don't say anything for a minute. But I have to know.

"Is he the reason you came here in the first place?" Deletha stops pumping. She brakes herself with her foot on the ground, so that she is barely moving at all anymore. Her sweat suit makes a crinkly sound.

"Yup," she says slowly. "He is."

"Then, why are you going back to him?" Deletha stares at me with an intensity I've never seen before. I can't hold her gaze, so I drop my eyes. She stands up, brushing off invisible crumbs from her legs, and shakes her head. The beads on the ends of her braids make a light, tinkling sound.

"I just came here to scare him," she says finally. "We ain't never been gone more than a week. Now he knows I mean business." She gathers her hair up into a sloppy ponytail and secures it with a rubber band from around her wrist. "You shoulda heard him last night on the phone when I called, cryin' and blubberin' like a fool. He was begging for us to come home." She waves her hand. "Douglas be fine. And we over it. We'll all be fine now." I try to picture Douglas crying and begging Deletha to come back home to him. I wonder if he misses his kids.

"Do your kids want to go back?" Deletha looks up from studying her nails and shoots me a scornful look.

"Well, *yeah*, they wanna go back. What d'ya think? He's their daddy."

"Oh. Yeah, I didn't know." Deletha gestures toward me with her chin.

"Don't you miss your daddy?"

I study the creases in my blue jeans. No one's ever asked me that question before. "I've never met my dad. He took off right after I was born. The guy we left last night is just my mom's boyfriend." Deletha seems to consider this for a minute, nodding her head in silence. Then she bends over, tucking a green package of cigarettes inside one of her socks. "Well," I say, "good luck."

Deletha gives me a fake smile. "Thanks," she says. "But you the one gonna need luck, living in this place." She heads for the door. "You'll see."

WEIRD THINGS ABOUT LIFE:
1. That adults can act like kids.
2. That adults get to break the rules they tell us to keep.
3. That some people go back to people who hurt them.
4. That dads can leave their kids behind.

IF I HAD A HUNDRED DOLLARS, I WOULD BUY:
1. Ten new notebooks.
2. Forty-seven supersize bags of puffy Cheetos.

3. Three new binkies for Ella.
4. New Keds for Mom.
5. A glow-in-the-dark collar for Augustus Gloop.
6. A new cardigan sweater for Phoebe.

ELEVEN

S tanding on the corner of McLean Street the next
morning waiting for the bus is an exercise in self-
restraint. By that, I mean I have to restrain myself
from telling Kate, who has informed me that she "has"
to come along with me, to beat it. Another shelter rule,
apparently. All kids living here have to be chaperoned
outside if a parent can't be around. And Mom is feeding
Ella, so Kate's got the honors this morning. I don't know
if I'm more embarrassed by the fact that at thirteen I
am still considered kid enough to be chaperoned, or that
Kate is wearing blue camouflage pants and white high-
top sneakers. Either way, as the minutes tick by, I keep
taking baby steps in the opposite direction, trying to put
as much physical distance between us as possible.

"Don't worry," Kate says, pulling the string off the end
of a package of Wrigley's gum. "I'll stand way over here,
okay? Pretend I don't even know you." She holds the gum
out in my direction. "Want a piece?"

I grin, despite myself. "Offering someone a piece of

gum is a great way to pretend you don't know someone."

Kate shrugs and stuffs the package back into her pants pocket. "So how are you doing, Hershey? I mean here, at the shelter. You all right?"

I scuff the sidewalk with the toe of my sneaker. "Yeah, you know, it's fine."

"Yeah?" Kate encases both of her arms inside the sleeves of her shirt. "Is there anything I can do for you? Anything you need to help make things a little easier? I know it's a lot right now."

You can promise me that no one's crazy husband or boy-friend is going to throw a rock through our window at night, I want to say. *Or that Slade isn't driving around town right now, looking for us.*

"Oh, no," I say instead. "I'm okay. Thanks." I look at the sky, and then at my shoes, exhale loudly, and drum my fingers off my arms. The truth is, though, I am kind of glad Kate's here. I don't *really* think Slade is driving around Sommersville at this hour looking for Mom and me, but, well, you never know. And what *would* I do if I ran into him all of a sudden? What if he tried to grab me or follow me back to the shelter? I feel inside my front pants pocket for the letter Mom gave me this morning. I have to give it to the guidance counselor when I get to school. I haven't read it (since Naomi wrote it and then put it inside a sealed envelope), but Mom told me that it's informing the school of our situation. Also, until the protection order is filed, the school is supposed to report any Slade sightings around the school to the police. Mom hugged me hard after she gave me the letter, but I'm not too worried about it. Slade's never been to my school. I don't even think he knows what school I go to.

My thoughts are interrupted by the familiar rumble of the school bus coming down the street. I look over nervously at Kate.

"Don't worry," she says, as if reading my mind. "I'm not gonna stand here and wave to you. You're not in kindergarten." The bus gets closer and closer. I can feel panic in the back of my throat, a small butterfly thrashing. What if someone is looking out the window? Does anyone at school know that the shelter is on this street? Does anyone know Kate? "I'm gonna start walking back real slow," Kate says. "I won't turn around or anything. Okay?"

"Yeah," I say, not moving my lips.

"See you, Hershey," she says, ambling down the sidewalk just as the bus pulls up in front of me. I get on and, staring ahead at the black rubber tracking on the floor, make my way to the very back of the bus. Until a patent leather ballerina flat blocks my progress.

"What are *you* doing on this bus?" Andrea Wicker glares at me with a pair of eyes lined heavily with electric blue mascara. Her hair has been scraped back with a pink and green plaid headband, and diamond studs glint on either side of her face. Can things possibly get any worse? Of all the buses in Sommersville, why does this one have to be Andrea Wicker's? I try to force my way past her, but she stands up, straightening her pink button-down cardigan and swinging her long blond hair over one shoulder. She smells good, like toothpaste and pineapples. "I asked you a question," she says. "Don't ignore me."

I take a deep breath. "What do you care what bus I take?"

Andrea's blue eyes narrow. "I *care* because this is my bus, and you're smelling it up." Rhonda Livingston, who worships the ground Andrea walks on, titters next to her. Rhonda thinks she's a prep because she wears clothes from the J.Crew catalog and hangs out with Andrea, but she's not really. She was actually a skater-girl last year and wore things like shrunken T-shirts and superskinny jeans. She never came to school without her skateboard, which she kept in her locker and then rode home every day with the rest of her crew. Then, inexplicably, she became friends with Andrea, and in a week's time, she had ditched her skateboard completely. Now she walks around with a fake leather purse and wears things like Izod shirts and madras shorts. People who are that easily influenced don't scare me.

"Could you just let me through?" I ask, shifting my weight onto one hip.

"Not until you answer my question," Andrea says, moving her face closer to mine.

I think fast. "We're visiting one of my mom's friends. And we're staying at her house for a while, okay?" Andrea moves her head back an inch. I can see Rhonda's greasy black hair—the only reminder of her previous skater-girl image—dangling behind her like seaweed.

"Why are you staying at her house?" Andrea asks.

"None of your business," I answer. "It's personal, all right?"

Andrea sticks a finger into the soft part of my chest. "You watch the way you talk to me." Her lips, smeared with a thick peach gloss, curl up into a sneer. "I mean it. You don't want to tick me off. Especially on a Monday." I don't say anything as Andrea sits back down next to Rhonda. But as I take my seat in the back, underneath the red EXIT sign, and stare out the window, my mind starts to wander. What if I started a rumor that Andrea has lice? No, no one would believe that one. Andrea takes great pains to make sure that her long hair looks and smells as clean as possible. She brushes it so hard in between classes that it actually crackles when someone walks by. Static electricity or something, I guess. Maybe I could bump into her in the lunchroom and then "accidentally" sneeze all over her lunch tray. Boy, would that throw her for a loop. She'd probably faint before she got the chance to do anything back to me. Sitting down deeper into the seat, I pull my legs up against my chest and bury my face into my knees. No one needs to see the grin on my face.

Seeing Phoebe at her desk in homeroom makes me so happy that I want to grab her and hug her tight. Instead I meander over to her desk and tug gently on the velvet crescent moon pinned to her hair.

"Hey!" she says, whirling around. The moon flops over the top of her ear. "How're things going? You're never here this early!"

"I know." I lower my voice. "The new bus I have to take gets us here at seven forty-five."

"Cool!"

"Yeah, cool," I repeat. "Except that Andrea Wicker takes that bus."

Phoebe looks at me with wide eyes. *"No!"* I nod. She rubs my hand. "You let me know if she starts anything with you, Hershey. I'll talk to her."

"I don't want you talking to her. You're not my body-guard." Phoebe withdraws her hand, hurt. "I'm sorry," I say hurriedly. "I didn't mean it like that. It's just that . . . I mean, I can fight my own battles." Phoebe's face relaxes.

I don't know how to explain it, but in the past month or so, Andrea has completely stopped bugging Phoebe. About everything. No more taunts about her hair ornaments, no more dirty looks, no comments about her smelly sweater or red boots, nothing. Nada. At first I thought I was just imagining it, because Andrea hasn't eased up on me at all. Last week, in fact, as I was standing in front of my locker, she came up behind me, stuck her finger into my back, and then said, "Ewww, look! My whole finger, like, disappears when I do that!" But when Phoebe appeared, her face flushed pink and her fists clenched, Andrea just walked away without another word. It's so weird. I just don't know what to make of it.

"Well, we have, like, ten minutes before announcements." Phoebe tucks her skirt under her legs and pats the empty desk in front of her. "Sit down and tell me everything else that's been going on." This is what I love most about Phoebe. Even though I talked to her again after dinner last night, she still always assumes that I have more to say. Which I usually do. I start to tell her about Lupe and Chili and the piano, when the bell rings. "Oh, shoot," Phoebe says. "Well, write me a note about the rest if you can. And if you can't, I'll see you at lunch."

Although I'm glad for the familiar monotony of school, it's a peculiar feeling going about my day, knowing that when it's over, I am going to have to take the bus back to the shelter. I feel displaced and out of sorts, as if I am walking around inside a bubble. The never-ending jostling and shoving between classes doesn't feel real, as if I am watching it in a movie instead of walking through the middle of it. Even the random screams of students, something that usually aggravates me no end, sound muted, as if someone has turned the volume way down. It's a curious feeling, walking from class to class knowing that at the end of the day I am going to take a bus back to a place that is hiding us from the rest of the world. It's an odd, unsettling kind of secret.

During biology I catch myself playing invisible piano keys on the top of my desk, humming along to the "Moonlight Sonata" melody.

"Miss Hollenback!" Mr. Diggs, my biology teacher, doesn't tolerate any kind of goofing off. He considers it a personal insult if you're not staring at him the entire class. Which is kind of hard to do, since he has hairs growing out of his nose like weeds. "Are you with me?" I stop moving my fingers and nod.

"Sorry," I mumble.

It's a relief when the lunch bell finally rings, even though I'm not aware of being hungry. Phoebe's already at our table, ripping open a bag of peanut M&M's, and sorting them into piles by color. I head over to the lunch line and just order fries. Mrs. Levandowski, who is the nicest of all the lunch ladies despite the weird little mustache on her upper lip, hands me the red and white paper boat piled with french fries and raises her eyebrows.

"That's all, honey?" I nod and smile. "You come back if you want more," she says. "We have a lot today."

"Thanks," I say. Mrs. Levandowski always gives me extras of everything.

"So where were we?" Phoebe asks, studying the green pile of her peanut M&M's as if they are about to break into song. For all the time I've known Phoebe, I've never seen her eat anything else at lunch besides peanut M&M's and chocolate milk. The girl is addicted to sugar. I am about to resume my Lupe story when Andrea Wicker walks by. Staring at me as I chew, she crosses her eyes and makes a grunting sound like a pig.

"Seconds, Hershey?" she asks, glancing at my fries. "Or is that thirds?" The other preps, sitting at a table nearby, erupt into peals of laughter. Rhonda pushes her finger against her nose and oinks.

Phoebe whirls around as Andrea passes us. "Shut up, Andrea!"

Andrea laughs loudly and keeps going. She doesn't say a word to Phoebe.

"I told you, you don't have to do that," I say, chewing harder.

Phoebe pops an orange M&M into her mouth. "I know. I can't help it. It just makes me so mad when she does that stuff."

I reach over and sneak one of Phoebe's blue M&M's.

They're the only ones she doesn't eat. "It's so weird that she never bothers you anymore," I say. "Remember in the beginning when she just wouldn't leave you alone?" Phoebe rolls her eyes and takes a sip of her chocolate milk. "Did something happen?" I press. "Did you and she have a fight or something that you haven't told me about?"

"If Andrea Wicker and I got into a fight, don't you think I'd tell you?" Phoebe asks.

"Well, how come she doesn't say things to you anymore?" I take another M&M. "She obviously still hates *me* enough."

"Who knows?" Phoebe shrugs. She looks uncomfortable. "She's weird, Hershey. You know that. She'll probably start picking on me again when she gets bored enough."

"Still. Remember a few weeks ago in the hallway when she was following me around, calling me Cyclops? As soon as she saw you, she just stopped and walked off in the opposite direction." I pause and look up at Phoebe. "How come?" Phoebe looks down quickly at her candy.

"No clue," she says. "No clue." She changes the subject quickly. "So listen, I've been meaning to ask you about our practice schedule. We're still going to be able to get together and practice for the talent show, right?"

"Um, yeah." I am still distracted by the whole Andrea-Phoebe thing. Something tells me there's more to this than meets the eye. "Probably just on weekends, though, Phoeb. And I think you're gonna have to take the bus to the Wal-Mart. I can meet you there. I'm not allowed to walk around here anymore. Mom thinks Slade might see me." Phoebe stops chewing.

"But it's almost time, Hershey! The show is in the beginning of June, which means we only have two more weeks to practice. And if you can only do weekends, that means . . ." She stops and counts on her fingers. "That means we'll only have *four* more practices? Hershey!" Her eyes are enormous, her brows arched so high they look as though they might take flight off her forehead. I shove three fries at once into my mouth.

"Phoebe, look. It's not like I *planned* it to happen this way or anything. Jeez, I mean, you think you'd try to be a little more understanding, considering the circumstances." Phoebe's fingers disappear behind the velvet moon in her hair as she scratches her neck.

"I am trying to be understanding, Hersh. Believe me, I am." She moves her hand over to her forehead. "It's just that, man, I don't know if we'll be *ready* with only four more practices. I just don't know."

"Sure we will," I say. "We'll just have to make each practice count. No fooling around or talking or anything." I place my palms flat out on the table. "We just *practice*. That's it." But I can tell by the way Phoebe is looking at me that she's not buying it.

My mind drifts all afternoon. We prep for final exams

in every class, but I don't hear anything. All of it—biology, Andrea Wicker, the prep table, even practicing for the talent show with Phoebe—seems so inconsequential all of a sudden. In an odd sort of way, I feel older than everyone around me. And none of it, for some reason, seems to matter half as much as it did before.

TWELVE

Andrea's not on the bus after school. I breathe a sigh of relief. She's probably at the coffee-house downtown with the other preps, where she drinks coffee and sneaks cigarettes. On the corner of McLean Street, where the bus lets me out, is a Rite Aid. I walk in immediately. The chip rack is all the way to the right, behind the magazines. I can't decide between the puffed Cheetos and the crunchy ones. I wish I had enough money for a supersize bag, but I've only got a dollar fifty left over from the lunch money Mom gave me this morning. It's enough for two small ones. Supersize bags are $3.49. Maybe next time. I settle on one of each kind, pay at the front counter, and walk toward the shelter.

It's incredibly warm for May. The air feels heavy, like I'm walking through a thick fog, and new leaves droop heavily from the elm branches. I keep the Cheetos inside my backpack and eat them quickly, before anyone can see me. For some reason, they don't taste as good as they usually do. And while I finish both bags, I'm still hungry afterward, which is really odd. I catch sight of Kate suddenly, who is running toward me, waving her arm. My throat tightens for a moment. Is Mom hurt? Did something happen?

"Hershey," she says, finally catching up to me. "Honey, I'm sorry. I should've been at the corner when the bus came. I lost track of time. Is everything okay? You didn't see Slade, did you?"

"No. He's not around. Don't worry about it." I had forgotten that she was supposed to be there. "It's fine."

"Your mom took Ella over to the Wal-Mart," Kate says, shoving her hands down into her pants pockets. "They'll be back in a little while. Your mom seems to think that some new binkies might help Ella settle down a little." She laughs and gives me a pat on the back. "Wouldn't it be nice if that worked for all of us?"

I lie down on the bottom bunk when I get back to our room. Rolling over, I push my face down into Mom's pillow, trying to inhale the scent of her. When I was little, way before Slade came around, she used to let me crawl into bed with her every night. I couldn't fall asleep unless I rested my face against the curve of her neck and curled my legs around her stomach. Her skin smelled like the Jean Nate bubble bath she poured into her tubs at night, and her hair was as soft as a rose petal. I breathe in hard, but I can't smell her scent now. Eventually I get up and wander around the room. My eye falls on a loose piece of paper on top of the dresser. I pick it up and slowly read Mom's handwriting. It says:

> My goals while living here include the following: 1) File for custody of Ella. 2) Get a restraining order against Slade. 3) Look for new housing. 4) Apply for financial assistance, food stamps, and medical coverage. 5) Move out of the old house. 6) Find a new job.

Holy cow. I read the list over again, more slowly this time. Is Mom going to be able to *do* all of this? Plus the chores she has to do for the shelter? It just sounds like so . . . much. I should try to help her. At least offer to do the vacuuming—

"Hershey?"

I whirl around. "Hi!" I say. "How was your day?"

"Fine, honey." Mom walks slowly into our room, looking at the piece of paper still in my hand. "You found my goal sheet?"

I nod silently, placing the paper back down on the dresser. "It looks good, Mom." I hope I sound encouraging. "You know, I was thinking . . . why don't you let me do the vacuuming for you this week?" I nod toward the goal sheet. "You've got enough on your plate right now without having to . . ." But she is shaking her head.

"Thanks, sweetie," she says, shifting Ella on her hip. "But it's okay. I just want you to focus on your schoolwork right now. Don't worry about me." She gives me a tired smile. "I'm going to lie down for a little while with Ella." We lock eyes for a minute and do this thing where we communicate without saying anything. *Go ahead,* I tell her. *It's okay. Everything's fine.* I grab my book bag and shut the door as I go out. The kitchen table is empty. Thank goodness. I take out my history book from inside my book bag. If I don't pass my history final next week, I'll flunk the class for the year.

I'm trying to memorize the list of things the Inca tribe contributed to our culture when Josie appears with a small gray radio under her arm. She gives me a nod and plugs the radio into the wall, tuning it to a country station called Froggy 101. Then she starts taking things out of the refrigerator. Pretty soon, there is a haphazard line of different barbeque sauces, tomatoes, a carton of eggs, an orange block of cheese, and a quart of milk arrayed on the counter. I pretend to keep studying.

"You like beef macaroni?" Josie calls out, her head partially obscured inside the refrigerator. She straightens up and looks at me expectantly. I hate casseroles. With a passion.

"Um, yeah," I say. "Sure." Josie rolls up her sleeves and plops an enormous hunk of ground beef into a bowl. She's wearing old jeans and has her long black hair pulled up into a ponytail at the top of her head. Her legs are so thin, they look like matchsticks.

"It's my week to cook," she says, mashing the meat between her fingers. "My kids love this dish. I put a can of tomato soup in it and they think they're eating a T-bone steak."

"You really have to cook all the meals this week?" I ask. "For *everyone*?"

"Yup," Josie says. "But it's not as bad as it sounds. Breakfast and lunch are no-brainers. I mean, I just set out boxes of cereal in the morning and throw some cold cuts on a plate in the afternoon. Everyone pretty much just helps themselves. The only meal I really have to worry about is dinner. And Kate buys us all the stuff after we tell her what kinds of things we know how to cook." She shrugs. "I don't mind it, really. It sure beats scrubbing out the toilets." Lupe's job. I wonder if she minds it.

Suddenly she drops the meat and leans over, turning the radio way up. "God, I love this song," she says, and starts singing at the top of her lungs.

Josie has a great voice. I'm not kidding. I don't know very many country songs, but listening to Josie sing along with some guy about a little girl hiding behind a chair while her mom and dad fight makes me sit up straight. The way she closes her eyes and whispers some of the words, it's as if Josie is the little girl herself, lost, scared, alone, praying to a picture of Jesus on the wall above her to make the fighting stop. I sit there with my hands resting on top of my book, watching her.

Josie closes her eyes as the song ends and folds her hands, as if in prayer.

"Man," she says, shaking her head. "That song just about kills me every time." Then another, faster song comes on, and she lifts her head again.

"Yeah!" Josie yells, slapping the counter with both hands. "Jo Dee Messina! Sing it, girl!" She tosses her ponytail from side to side, wailing about a girl who's just ditched her boyfriend and is driving away in her car, feeling free and happy. It's a fun song, and before I know it, I'm tapping my foot along to the music. Josie gets back to work on the meat mixture, still singing as egg and bread crumbs and ground meat start to drip down her arms.

Deletha might roll her eyes when Josie sings, but I like her voice. For some reason, it makes me feel a little hopeful. The way I see it, if someone can sing in a battered women's shelter, maybe, just maybe, things will work out after all.

Dinner is complete chaos. Josie has overcooked the beef macaroni, and none of the kids will eat it. "It tastes like burned stuff!" Macy cries, pushing her plate away from her. Galvin throws his spoon across the table and screams, "Yucky!"

"Stop it!" Josie barks. "Both of you! It's fine!" She yanks the plates back under her children's chins. "Now eat!" The kids throw their heads back and wail simultaneously. Reggie and Radiance don't even bother complaining. They just get down from their seats and run around the perimeter of the table, screaming and yelling at each other. Once again Deletha sits at the other end, cramming pieces of bread into her mouth, ignoring them. Rose, who is sitting cross-legged in her chair, stares out the window and lights a cigarette, holding it between her cocooned fingers. A single tear, perched on the edge of her lower eyelid, rolls like a tiny pearl down the front of her face. Baby Ella won't touch the macaroni, but Mom spoons some of the lemon yogurt she picked up earlier at Wal-Mart into Ella's open mouth. Gracie comes in, takes one look at the situation, and heads back upstairs, shaking her head and muttering under her breath.

I get up too.

"Where are you going, Hershey?" Mom asks, handing Baby Ella the empty yogurt carton to play with.

I point to the bedroom. "In there. To study for finals."

"You're not going to eat dinner?" Mom asks. I shake my head, pretending not to notice the dirty look Josie shoots me across the table.

THIRTEEN

As the night wears on, the house bustles with bedtime preparations. Tubs are drawn, and the sound of crying and hair dryers blowing fills the upstairs. Padded pajama feet race up and down the hallways, and then, after what feels like forever, a miraculous sort of quiet begins to descend again. Mom brings Baby Ella down from her bath, dressed in a Tinker Bell nightgown and little yellow slipper socks. She lowers her into her crib and then rubs a towel back and forth over Baby Ella's wet head.

"Would you finish this for me, Hershey?" she asks. "I have to go back out to the kitchen for some kind of women's meeting."

"Women's meeting?" I take the towel from Mom. "What kind of women's meeting?"

Mom runs a comb through her hair. "Oh, Kate said some therapist comes here on Monday nights to talk to us about things. No big deal."

"What kind of things?"

Mom shakes her head and gives me one of those fake smiles. "Just stuff," she says. "You know, about our situations." She leans over and kisses Baby Ella on the cheek. "You be a good girl for your big sister now, okay, Ella? Mama will be right out here if you need me." Ella whimpers and then puts her arms around Mom's neck. "She's tired," Mom whispers, sliding out the door. "She should go right down after *Goodnight Moon*." She squeezes my arm. "Thanks, Hershey."

I rub Baby Ella's hair as dry as I can. Then I spray it with that no-tangle stuff that Mom uses and comb it out with her little plastic Ernie comb. Baby Ella sits as still as a statue, yawning every few minutes. When I'm finished, I tuck the loose strands behind her ears and run my finger over her cheek. It's smooth and pink and perfect. She's asleep before I get to the fourth page of *Goodnight Moon*, about the old lady who says hush. Just as I bring her blanket up around her shoulders and turn off the light, I hear someone crying in the kitchen. Opening the door a crack, I peek out, turning my head so that I can see with my good eye.

Josie, Mom, Gracie, Rose, and a woman I have never seen before are sitting at the end of the kitchen table closest to me. From where I am standing, I can see all of them except Josie, who is hidden by the wall. But there is no mistaking her voice. It's Josie who is crying.

"He just pushed all three of us out and locked the door," she weeps. "I sat down on the front steps and had a few cigarettes and told the kids some stories, thinking he'd let us back in when he simmered down. But when he opened the door a few hours later and we were still there . . ." Her voice trails off. "He just went off on me." Her voice is very quiet. "Galvin's so little. I don't think he really understands yet. But Macy . . ." Josie stops for a moment. "Macy understands." She takes a deep breath. "So, anyway, I had to come *here* because it's like the seventh or eighth time I've left him. And my parents don't want to hear it anymore, I guess. When I called them the other night, after he went crazy on me again, my mom just hung up the phone." Josie's voice breaks on the word "phone." Across from her, Gracie's eyes squint.

"Why you keep going back?" she asks. Josie cries harder, but she doesn't answer. I watch Mom carefully. She is staring at something on the tablecloth in front of her, not making eye contact with anyone. The tips of her ears are bright red.

"Let's talk about this for a minute," the strange lady sitting at the end of the table says. Her straight red hair is parted in the middle, and she is wearing gray silk pants, a white short-sleeve blouse, and black patent leather flats. "Women who return over and over again to men who abuse them are not uncommon. In fact, most women leave and return at least once before they find the courage to leave for good." Mom's eyes scoot across the tablecloth.

"Who says?" Josie demands, blowing her nose behind the wall.

The red-haired lady smiles. "*I* say," she says, not unkindly. "I've been working with women for over twenty years now. I'm telling you what I see and observe every single day."

"So why you keep going back?" Gracie asks, turning to Josie again. "I mean, you know he just gonna hurt you again, right? So why you keep giving him chances?"

Josie sniffs. "It's just . . ." Her balled-up tissue flies across the table. "It's just that when he apologizes, he's so sin*cere*. I mean, you should hear him. He cries. No, he doesn't cry. He *sobs*. He holds me so tight and he swears up and down it's never going to happen again." She pauses, taking a shuddering breath. "And I want so bad to believe him."

"Why?" the red-haired lady asks. "Why do you want so badly to believe him?"

"'Cause he's all I got!" Josie sputters, choking on tears again. "I mean, if we split up, where does that leave me? I'll be all alone!"

"What about your kids?" Rose asks. She's sitting cross-legged on her chair, her bandaged arms in her lap. "You're not alone if you have your kids, right?"

"That's not the same," Josie says. "Kids you have to . . .

take care of." She sighs deeply. "I need someone to take care of me, too." Rose nods slowly. So does Gracie. And then, to my horror, I see Mom's head bob up and down, ever so slightly.

"You agree with that, Daisy?" the red-haired lady asks. Mom's head shoots up. She swallows, shrugs, traces an imaginary line on the tablecloth. I have to strain forward to hear what she says.

"You know . . . we all want to be taken care of." Her face flushes as she talks. "It's . . . something . . . I guess that . . . never really goes away." My legs give way beneath me when I hear Mom say that. I mean, I literally sink to the floor. It's the saddest thing I've ever heard her say. It also frightens me. If Mom feels that way about needing someone to take care of her, who's going to take care of me and Ella?

"But you don't need a *man* to do that for you." Gracie's voice makes me raise my head again. "Yeah, we all need to be taken care of. That's human nature. But you can get love and support from lots of people, not just some dolt." Mom blushes deeply.

"No, I'm serious," Gracie says. "You too, Josie. And I don't mean to lecture here, 'cause Lord knows I got my own set of problems, but I've been doing a lot of thinking these past days upstairs in my room. I'm here at this shelter 'cause . . ." She pauses for a moment, examining the red polish on her fingernails again. "Well, 'cause I'm afraid *not* to be. My husband's a scary man when he gets angry." She turns her hand over, stares at the center of her palm. "Last week, I spent all day cooking his favorite foods— chicken-fried steak, mashed potatoes, corn bread, mustard greens . . ." Her face darkens. "He said it wasn't to his *liking*. The potatoes were runny, the greens were wilted. He chucked the frying pan at the wall and then threw my food all over the house. Made a mess of my kitchen curtains, let me tell you. Then he left again. I spent all night cleaning and crying, trying to get things back the way they were." Gracie stares at something behind Mom's head. "I've never left Bernie before. No matter how bad things got, I always told myself I would make it work. But for some reason, that night, leaving him seemed like the only sensible thing left to do." She shakes her head. "I'll never go back. It takes too much outta me, trying to love someone who can't love me back. It's like trying to fit my foot into the wrong-size shoe. It don't feel good."

The only sound in the kitchen is the ticktock of the clock on the wall. Mom is biting her lower lip. Gracie is studying her fingernails. Rose is staring out the window.

"I have to go back," Rose says slowly.

"You don't *have*—," the red-haired lady starts.

But Rose lifts her head, cuts her off. "No, I do," she says. "It's my grandfather who does this kind of stuff to me." She lifts her bandaged arms. Gracie and Mom get strange looks on their faces.

"Whatchou talking about?" Gracie asks.

"My parents ran off when I was little," Rose says, a far-away look coming into her eyes. "He's the one that raised me. He was good to me too, gave me everything I needed, everything I wanted. Then, when I left for college, he got sick. He doesn't have anybody but me, so I came home to take care of him." She pauses, running the tip of her finger along the edge of her lip. "I think it was the sickness that made him mean," she says.

"And you saying you *have* to go back?" Gracie challenges. "Why? You think you owe him or something for taking care of you all those years?"

Rose lifts her face. Her pretty eyes are wide. "Well, yeah," she says. "Of course. If he hadn't taken care of me, I would've been an orphan."

"Sick or not, he hurtin' you, baby. Bad." She shakes her head, points to Rose's arms. "You cut your losses, girl, and get on with your own life. You given him enough already."

"What if he was your grandfather?" Rose asks. "Would you let your grandfather die alone?"

Gracie winces and then reaches up and yanks her earlobe. No one, not even the red-haired lady, says a word.

I shut the door and sink down to the floor.

I don't ever want to be an adult.

FOURTEEN

The broom closet door is partially ajar when I creep downstairs the next night. It's nearly midnight. Gracie and Rose stayed up talking in the kitchen until ten thirty, and there was no way I was going to have them asking me any questions about going downstairs. I pause just outside Lupe's door, pondering the possible reasons why it is open. Could she be expecting me? No. I haven't set foot near Lupe's room for two days now. After the whole piano-Chili fiasco, I was afraid she would bite my head off if I did. Maybe she just went out for a minute to use the restroom and forgot to shut the door? Maybe she fell asleep inside and doesn't know that the door isn't shut. . . .

A mutter drifts out from inside, making the little hairs on the back of my neck stand up straight.

"Lupe?" I whisper. "Is that you?" There is no answer. I push against the door slightly. "Lupe? Did you say something?" She whirls at the sound of my voice, nearly falling from her crouched-over position in the corner. When she sees me, her face softens.

"Hershey."

I push open the door a little wider. "Is it okay? Can I come in?"

"Sí." She beckons me forward with her hand. "I am just feeding Chili. She has been such a good girl. I am giving her treats." I sit down and watch as Lupe pushes a raisin through the little slats of Chili's cage. To my amazement, the little animal picks up the raisin with both hands and chews it, just like a baby squirrel gnawing on a nut. Within ten seconds, the raisin is gone.

"She's cute." I twirl my finger around my shoelace, staring at Chili's still-moving jaws. "I miss my cat."

Lupe stops pushing raisins through the cage. "I know," she says slowly. "I'm sorry. He is okay, though, no? He is with someone who is kind?"

"Oh, yeah. Phoebe's my best friend. She'll take good care of him. I trust her."

Lupe smiles and nods. "I have a question for you," she says, standing up and draping a cloth over Chili's cage. "The other day, when you were playing some of the notes . . ." She pulls on one of her earlobes. "That was just from memory? From hearing me play?"

I nod so hard that I pull a muscle in my neck. "And you know, I haven't been able to forget the song since I heard you play it that first night." I try not to stumble over my words in my excitement. "I have it memorized, I think. At least that first part of it. And I just sort of poked around until I found the notes that matched what I heard." Lupe is looking at me differently now, as if she is interested in something.

"That is very good," she says, raising her eyebrows. Some of the bruises around her eyes have started to fade to a pale violet. Her long hair has been braided into a thick rope. Now she brings it around the top of her shoulder and threads the ends of it between her fingers. "Did you like it? Playing, I mean?"

"I loved it!" I burst out.

A tiny smile crooks the edges of Lupe's mouth. Then she shrugs. "Sit down for a moment." She points to the bench. "Let me hear you again." I gulp nervously and make my way over to the bench. I was just fooling around before, but now suddenly it feels like the pressure is on. What were those notes again? I scan the keys quickly and find the first one. Lupe is standing to my right, watching intently as I use my index finger to push down on the keys.

"Ay!" she says, tapping me on the shoulder. "Move over."

"But I haven't even . . ." Lupe glares at me. I scoot over.

She reaches over and grabs my hands. "The first thing you must learn if you want to play the piano is how to hold your hands." She takes my wrists between her first two fingers and shakes them hard. "Relax the bones in your wrists."

"What do you mean, my bones?" I ask, perplexed. "How do you relax bones?" Lupe grunts.

"Let your fingers hang down," she says. "Loose. Free. As if they are weightless." I let my hands drop forward. "Ah!" Lupe says. "That's it! Now this is the way they must be positioned when you begin to play. You cannot have them rigid and tight, or your music will sound the same way." *She is talking about my music, about me playing*. I try to keep my breathing steady, but I feel as though I might start to hyperventilate. Lupe places my hands down on the keys.

"Do you see your longest finger?" she asks. "The middle one?" I nod. "That one will go over the C note. The C note is the center of everything, like the heart." She taps her chest and then points to a note on her book. "That is a C note," she says. Pushing down the key under my middle finger, she says, "And that is what a C note sounds like." I push it down again, just for the heck of it. "Good," Lupe says. "Notes are arranged alphabetically, and I don't think they will be very difficult for you to learn. "She points to the thumb on my right hand. "This is your A note. B comes next. We've already talked about C. After C, of course, is D, and then E, F, and finally, G."

"That's it?" I ask. "It's just A, B, C, D, E, F, G?" Lupe shakes her head.

"Sí. But they're not all played the same when you read

a piece of music. There are treble clef notes and bass clef notes. There are half notes and full notes, quarter notes and eighth notes, sharps and flats, all of which you must know before you understand how music should sound." My head is swimming. She is going too fast, but I don't want to tell her that.

Lupe points out a note on her book and then plays it on the keyboard. Then she has me do the same thing.

"You will learn the notes," she says to me, "but your real goal is to learn the music. They are two different things." I nod, not really understanding, but thrilled that she thinks I can learn. Then she closes the music book. "'Moonlight Sonata' is tricky," she says. "Not one for a beginner student." She reaches into a brown leather satchel next to the piano bench and pulls out another, much thinner book. "This," she says, holding it up in front of me, "is much simpler." The cover reads "Für Elise." I smile broadly, making room for Lupe as she sits down next to me again. Arranging her fingers carefully over the keys, she closes her eyes, pauses for a moment, and begins to play. Within the span of ten seconds, I am back at Sally's Thrift Store, standing at Mom's elbow, watching her fingers fly back and forth across the keys. I hold my breath as Lupe gets to the part where Mom stopped—and exhale as she continues, playing the rest of the piece all the way to the end. When she finishes, Lupe turns to look at me.

"You are crying," she says softly. I shake my head, then reach up and rub my tears away. I had not known they were there.

The next two hours fly by as Lupe goes over and over the notes of the first four bars of "Für Elise." Again and again and again. She shows me how to use my left hand and then my right. Then we practice using them both together. I play the treble notes with my left hand, the bass notes with my right. When I get through the fourth bar without faltering, Lupe squeezes my arm and then claps her hands together once, as if she has just caught a fly.

"You are very quick," she says. Her black eyes are shining and her dark skin has a sheen to it, as if she has been perspiring. "Maybe the fastest-learning student I have ever had."

I blush. "Really?"

Lupe nods. "And you have the passion," she says, fingering the medallion on her chest. "Who knows? Maybe you have a gift." We look at each other for the merest second, contemplating this possibility. Then Lupe glances at the clock on the wall.

"Ay dios mío!" she says, clapping her hands to her head. "It is almost three o'clock! You must get to bed, Hershey. You have school in a few hours, si?"

I get up slowly. "Yes, but I'm not tired. I feel like I could play all night." I mean it.

Lupe snorts. "Let's not get carried away. Come downstairs again tomorrow night. We will have another lesson."

I float back to bed. Inside, it feels as if something has shifted, like one of those tectonic plates deep in the earth that move just before an earthquake.

"Maybe you have a gift!" She said those exact words! *"A gift!"*

FIFTEEN

Andrea looks as though she's been waiting for me as I climb up the stairs to the bus the next morning. For a split second I look past her, out the window. Kate is hurrying back to the shelter, her hands shoved deep into her pockets. *Turn around,* I think. *Just once, just for a second.* But she hurries on, vanishing from sight as the bus turns the corner. Andrea's squinted eyes relax and she sits back a little in her seat as I head down the aisle. Something that looks like a boy's tie is around her neck. Rhonda is sitting next to her. She clutches Andrea's arm as I pass. I hear the word "Now" a second too late. The shock of coldness against my skin is nothing compared to the sudden realization that Andrea has lifted my shirt, displaying my waistline for the entire bus to see. I drop my arms quickly enough so that my bra stays hidden, but still, having my belly rolls exposed feels worse. The bus rocks with laughter. A kid I've never even seen before points at me and covers his mouth with his other hand, his eyes wide with shock and disgust. I clutch at my shirt, holding it tight against my waist as I make a beeline for the back of the bus.

I am almost at my seat when I turn around again, rage coursing through my arms like electricity. I don't even know what I am going to do. But I've got to do something. And then, two steps away, just as my hand reaches out for Andrea's hair, another thought stops me. If Andrea and I get into a fight, the bus driver will call the school and the school will call Mom, and then everyone will find out where we are living. Everyone will know that we lived with a psycho named Slade West. I freeze as Andrea turns around again, her eyes wide with surprise.

"What do *you* want?" I watch my hand lower itself, trembling, against the green leather seat. I hug my book bag tightly against my chest. Try to take deep breaths. But nothing blocks out the sound of the terrible laughter. There is no way to ignore the eyes that glance at me over and over again, full of glee.

I used to think there was no one in the world as awful as Slade.

Now I know I was wrong.

The first thing I do when I get to school is sneak down to the cafeteria. Pulling out the four singles that Mom gave me for lunch, I insert each of them into the vending machine and start pressing random buttons. C-1, which is the slot that holds the Cheetos, is empty. Figures. Still, in less than thirty seconds, I have a bag of Mini Oreo cookies, a sleeve of salted peanuts, a bag of Cheese Nips, a bag of buttered popcorn, and a package of wheat crackers spread with cream cheese. I huddle in tightly against the wall, crammed in between two of the vending machines in case anybody walks by, and stuff my face.

The cafeteria looks enormous with no one in it. The long brown lunch tables are lined up in neat rows, and the kitchen, which I have never seen without food or trays, looks like one big empty silver table. I stare at the ugly mural painted on the wall across the room depicting kids our age of every race and size and color, holding hands, smiling gaily. The words "Together, We Can Do Anything," painted in black, arch over the tops of the kids' heads like a rainbow. Tearing open the salted peanuts, I shove a handful into my mouth. Then, one by one, I throw the rest as hard as I can at the mural.

In biology I make a list. We are supposed to be taking notes for our final exam, so Mr. Diggs doesn't think there's anything unusual about me writing in my notebook while he is talking.

WAYS I COULD LOSE WEIGHT:
  1. Don't eat so much. (Duh.)
  2. Give up Cheetos.

3. Walk more.

4. Have only one bag of Cheetos a day and nothing else.

WAYS I COULD MAKE MYSELF LOOK BETTER:

1. Lose weight.

2. Cut my hair. (Too many layers.)

3. Get my ear cartilage pierced.

4. Buy cooler clothes.

5. Wear sunglasses.

6. Get a padded bra.

WHAT I WANT TO DO WHEN I GROW UP:

1. Be able to play the piano as well as Lupe.

2. Go to college.

3. Travel with Phoebe.

4. Come back to our ten-year high school reunion and rub it in Andrea Wicker's face that I just won a ten-million dollar lottery.

5. Be pretty. Just for once.

SIXTEEN

By the end of the day, I am dreading getting back on the bus so much that when the final bell rings, I seriously contemplate walking back to the shelter. But it's at least eight miles. The farthest I've ever walked in my life is to Phoebe's, which is a little less than eight blocks. And I'm always exhausted by the time I get there. But by some miracle of fate, the afternoon bus is nearly empty. There is no sign of Andrea or Rhonda. I breathe a deep sigh of relief and plop down in my seat in the back.

The first thing I see when I walk into our room is Mom sitting with her back against the bunk beds, twirling a piece of her hair around one of her fingers. I can tell by the vacant look on her face that she can't see or hear Baby Ella, who is running up and down the length of the room, screaming like an overjoyed lunatic.

"Hey, pudge!" I say, scooping her up as she flies past me. "What's all the yelling about?"

Baby Ella squirms in my arms. "Let go! Down, Shee!"

I put her back down gently and watch her race across the room again.

"Mom?" I ask, sitting across from her on the floor with my legs crossed. Our knees barely touch. "How'd it go? Did you get over to the courthouse today and file the papers?"

"Slade was there," Mom says, taking her eyes off Baby Ella and looking directly at me.

"He was at the *court*house?" I ask.

Mom nods grimly. "Apparently, he had the same idea I did. He wants custody of Ella too."

"That's the dumbest thing I ever heard," I say. "Slade doesn't even know how to take care of her!" It's true. Slade has never done a thing when it comes to Baby Ella. He insisted it had nothing to do with the fact that she was born a girl, telling Mom instead that he just didn't "do" babies. That meant he never changed a diaper, fed her a meal, or gave her a bath. It kills me that Baby Ella loves him anyway. Babies are cute and all, but they are so stupid. Now I catch Baby Ella around the waist again as she flies past me. She shrieks and kicks.

"Let her go," Mom says tiredly. "She's probably overtired. She stayed with Josie this afternoon while I went to the courthouse, and I don't think she got a nap." She looks back up at me.

"Did Slade say anything to you?" I ask.

Mom drops her eyes. "Not really."

Baby Ella bumps into me on what must be her forty-third trip across the room.

"Bam!" she says. "Gotcha!"

"Yeah, gotcha," I say, not turning around.

"Did you talk to *him*?" I press.

Mom shrugs. "Yeah. You know, just a few words. Nothing to worry about or anything." She gives me a weak smile.

"Well, I hope not. I mean, there's really nothing to say, is there?"

Mom bites her lip. She's getting that weird look in her eyes the way she did the night I found her with the cut lip. "No," she says.

I push my knees against Mom's. Her kneecap feels flat and hard against mine. "You know, because nothing he could ever say to you, Mom, can excuse what happened."

Mom swallows and wrinkles her nose. "I know that, Hershey."

Baby Ella hollers from across the room. "Mama, look!" She is bent over at the waist, looking at us through her fat, dimply knees. "I see you, Mama!"

"I see *you*!" Mom says, talking in her baby voice. Baby Ella plops down on her stomach and stares at something under the bed.

Mom turns back to me. "You know, the one thing he did say was that he just wanted to find out how Ella was doing."

"Oh, please," I say, rolling my eyes again. "Give me a break."

"Don't say that," Mom snaps. "You've never had a baby taken away from you. You don't know what it's like." I look at her, too surprised to answer, and then drop my eyes. There is a blue stain on the rug next to my leg.

"I just . . ." I stop, unsure of what to say next. I just what? Don't want to hear her excuses? Don't know what I really think of her at all anymore? Mom stares past me at a point on the wall. Then suddenly she begins to cry.

"What?" I ask. "What is it, Mom? What's wrong? Did he say something else? Did something happen?" She shakes her head and then raises her hands helplessly.

"I . . . I . . . just don't know how all of this is going to work! We're going to have to find a new apartment, and I don't even have a lousy nickel to my name. Anything extra I ever had I always gave to Slade for the rent." She cries harder. "You and me and the baby are going to have to go on welfare, and what kind of life is *that* going to be? Everything's just gotten so out of con*trol*. I mean, first the shelter and now custody and protection orders." She stares at me with leaky eyes. "I mean, Slade could get arrested now if he even tries to call me on the *phone*."

"But that's a *good* thing, Mom. We don't want him bothering us."

Mom wipes her eyes. "But Ella is his baby too. What

right do I have to take her away from him? He'll want to—"

I snatch Mom's hands out of her face and hold them tight. Her wrists are so thin that I am afraid for a second that I might snap them.

"Weren't you listening?" I hiss. "Didn't you hear anything Gracie said the other night during that therapy thing?"

Mom's eyes get big. "You were listening? *Eaves*dropping? Hershey!"

I don't blink. "You're wearing the wrong shoe, Mom. Just like Gracie said. It's the wrong shoe. It's never gonna fit."

She stares frantically at me, as if I am speaking another language. I try hard to read what is going on behind those eyes, but for some reason I don't recognize them. At all. There's something in there that I've never seen before. I wonder, if she had let me see her all those years ago when we sat at Aunt Kemi's kitchen table, would I have seen the same thing then that I do now?

My heart starts doing that downward plummet thing, exactly the way it did at Aunt Kemi's when I knew we were returning to Slade. I was ten then. I couldn't do anything except go with Mom when she decided to go back. But I'm thirteen now. Next year I'll be in ninth grade. I love Mom more than anything, but at this moment, sitting on the rug across from her, staring into her wistful eyes, I can feel myself becoming separate from her. Like a snake wriggling out of its skin, I am starting to detach from what it is she thinks she wants out of life. For the first time, I understand that I want something else, something better.

"You go back, then," I say, dropping Mom's wrists slowly. "But you're not going to take me with you this time. I'll stay here, Mom, or do whatever I have to do. But I'm not going back to live with Slade. Not ever." Mom catches her breath and presses her fingers against her lips. Her eyes are pale blue, but when she cries, they look almost purple. After a few more seconds she blinks and the wet amethyst color disappears. She stands up and holds out her hand to Baby Ella, who has now settled herself into the corner behind the door and is trying to pull her diaper off.

"Come on, baby," she says.

Baby Ella trots over and grips Mom's hand with one of her own pudgy ones.

"Juice?" she asks, tilting her head back to look up at Mom.

"Yes," Mom answers tenderly. "Let's go get you some juice."

"Mom?" My voice is breaking. *Please turn around. Look at me. Tell me you understand. Tell me that I mean more to you than Slade West does.*

But she walks out of the room swiftly, holding Baby Ella's hand.

Behind her the door closes with a thud.

SEVENTEEN

Mom and I don't talk—or even look at each other—for the rest of the night. I lie on the top bunk as she busies herself beneath me with Baby Ella's needs, drying her hair and getting her into her red Elmo pajamas. But when the two of them snuggle up on the floor together to read *Olivia*, Baby Ella's favorite book, something cracks inside of me. It hurts worse than anything I've ever felt before, and for a minute I don't know if I am going to be able to keep breathing. I climb down from the top bunk, grab my biology book, and leave the room.

I have an hour until I can sneak downstairs and practice with Lupe. Heading back out to the kitchen table, I flip the pages of my biology book listlessly, trying to remember what sections of the text Mr. Diggs told us to go over for the test. But nothing registers. Plus, it's *hot*. There must be something weird going on with the weather; I can't remember any weekend at the end of May ever being this warm. It's almost eight at night and it must be 85 degrees outside. My forearms are sticking to the tablecloth, and my forehead is damp with sweat. I read the same line about amoebas three times. It's impossible to concentrate. All I can think about is how much I hate Slade. How much I miss Mom.

Suddenly Josie appears with a Scrabble game tucked under arm. She places the box on the other end of the table and uncovers it, while glancing at my biology book.

"You studying?" she asks.

I nod and smile wearily. "Trying to, anyway. I have finals next week."

Josie nods. "Gracie and Rose and I got a Scrabble competition going on here. They'll be down in a few minutes. Can you study while we play?" I nod eagerly, hungry for any kind of excuse not to stare at the swarm of incomprehensible information in front of me.

Josie sits down in one of the chairs, her dragon tattoo glaring out at me from her bare arm. Gracie arrives a few minutes later, rubbing her hands together, as if she is trying to warm them up.

"Let's go, girl," Gracie says. "I'm out for *blood* tonight."

Josie grabs her pack of Marlboro Reds and a pear-shaped ashtray. She lights a cigarette with one hand as she arranges herself in a chair, and grabs the bag of letters with her other hand. "Dream on, Chiquita. I'm already fifty-six points ahead of you."

Gracie waves her hand at the offending smoke. "Fifty-*five*," she says. "And that's just because you got lucky on that last triple score last night. You just wait. I'ma be all over you tonight." Rose appears a few minutes later. She has a bag of tortilla chips under her left arm and is balancing a bottle of orange soda in the other. Gracie jumps to her feet.

"You shouldn't be using those arms," she says, taking the soda.

Rose smiles softly at her. "Thanks."

"What are you doing, homework?" Gracie asks, as if she has just noticed that I am sitting here. I nod silently. "Can you study while we're here? Won't that bother you?"

I shrug, shake my head a little. "Not really."

Josie laughs. "Yeah, right," she says, and gives me a wink. "That's what I used to tell my mom when I studied with the TV on." I sit back in my seat and relax a little. Rose opens the bag of tortilla chips and dumps them into a plastic bowl. A salty smell fills the air as she pops one into her mouth.

"Help yourself," she says to me. "Soda, too, if you want. There's plenty." I smile my thanks but don't take any.

"Well, thank God Deletha's finally gone," Josie says, arranging her tiles in a neat row along the tiny ledge in front of her. "I don't think I could have gotten through another day with all that hollering." I had forgotten that

Deletha left. She must have gone this morning, while I was at school. I wonder if anyone said good-bye to her. I wonder if Douglas will kiss her on the lips when she gets home, tell her, *Baby, I missed you so much.* I wonder what Reggie and Radiance will think.

Gracie shakes her head, examining her letters with a serious expression. "You know, I woulda knocked those buck teeth right down that woman's throat if she got in my face one more time." I sidle a glance over at Gracie's hands. Her fingernails have been filed smooth and repainted a bright red, but her fingers are thick and meaty. She probably could've given Deletha a serious run for her money. I wish I could take her on the bus with me tomorrow. I'd give a million bucks to see the look on Andrea Wicker's face if Gracie was standing behind me.

The Scrabble game is fierce, right from the get-go. From what I can tell, it has been going on for more than a week now, and the stakes are high. The woman that reaches five thousand points first will win—and be relieved of any and all chores for the upcoming week. A paperback dictionary lies close to the board; if the word is not in the dictionary, it cannot go on the board. Rose is a slow, steady player, but Josie is an amazing speller. Her first word is "visceral," which I have never even heard of. Apparently, neither has Gracie, because she challenges her, clucking her tongue and demanding proof. Josie slashes open the dictionary and points out the word impatiently, much to Gracie's dismay.

"Well, *I* never heard of it," she says.

"And that's why I'm going to leave you in the dust," Josie says, lighting what must be her fourteenth cigarette of the night. I stifle a laugh from my end of the table.

But the conversation takes a more somber turn after Gracie asks Josie about the apartment she went to see today. Josie licks her lips and pretends to study her tiles.

"Hey," Gracie says. "Did you hear me? I asked you what the place looked like that you went to see today."

"I didn't go," Josie says finally.

"Why not?" Gracie asks.

Josie looks sideways at her ashtray. "I had an audition," she says. Her voice is so low that I have to lean forward so that I can hear her.

"An *audition*?" Gracie repeats. "You went to a *singing* audition instead of going to see a new apartment?" Rose leans in, pretending to be absorbed with her tiles. Josie fingers another cigarette out of the red and white box. She lifts it to her lips and lights it with her powder blue Bic lighter. Her face is defiant behind the flickering flame.

"Yeah. I did. So what? I can schedule another appointment to go find an apartment."

But Gracie is shaking her head. "Girl, you got your priorities all mixed up."

Josie inhales fiercely, her upper lip twitching. "Don't start on me, Gracie, okay? I got a mother and an ex-husband who criticize me every chance they get. I don't need anyone else jumping on the bandwagon."

Gracie picks up one of her tiles and rolls it back and forth between her thumb and index finger. "Josie, you got to get custody of your kids, find a place to live, and get a job. Those things come first, girl, before any pipe dream that you think you need to be running after. That's the way life is." Gracie's voice is hard, unforgiving. "You can't be wasting your time right now running around to auditions. Your kids *need* you." Josie's posture slumps, listening to Gracie talk. She stubs her cigarette out listlessly in the ashtray and stares at it with blank eyes.

"I know," she whispers. "But I've got to hold on to this part of me, Gracie. It's all I've got left." The silence in the room is deafening. Josie gets up. "I'm going to bed," she says. She walks out of the room, leaving the Scrabble game unfinished, broken and silent.

EIGHTEEN

It's only eight forty-five, but when Gracie and Rose finally leave the kitchen and head upstairs after Josie, I can't wait another minute. I walk down to the broom closet and knock gently on the door.

"Hershey?"

"Yeah! It's me! I know I'm early, but I can't wait around anymore. It's killing me."

"Come in," Lupe says. "You're just in time. I need help."

"With what?"

Lupe lifts the top of Chili's cage and sets it down on the floor. Then she scoops Chili up in her palm and walks over to me. "I have to clean her cage. Will you hold her for me while I work?" I nod eagerly as Lupe slips Chili into my outstretched hands. "Keep your other hand over the top of her," Lupe instructs. "That way she won't startle. In a few minutes we'll let her run around. She's ready for a little exercise about now." I do what she says, cupping my hands around the tiny animal as she begins sniffing my skin. She is as light as a thimble. Her tiny nose looks like a pink pencil eraser.

"You let her run around in here?" I ask. "Don't you worry about losing her?"

Lupe shakes her head. "Chinchillas sleep all day, so she gets restless at night. I always let her out for an hour when it gets dark. And Chili is very well trained. She comes when I tell her to."

"She's so adorable." I run the tip of my finger over the edge of her wide ears as Lupe empties the soiled sawdust into a plastic bag. "How long have you had her?"

"My sister gave her to me when Ricardo and I left Colombia," Lupe says, straightening up. "Which makes her almost twenty years old."

"Holy cow!" I say. "That's old!"

Lupe smiles. "She is very healthy. And strong."

I stroke Chili's back with the back of my index finger. I can feel her spine just under her fur, like a tiny chicken bone.

"Where is Colombia?" I ask.

Lupe stops swabbing the cage with her rag. "They do not teach you geography in school?"

I blush. "Yeah, they do. I just don't pay attention."

"It is in South America," Lupe says, turning her attention back to the cage. "At the very top. Near Venezuela." She stops. "You have heard of Venezuela?"

"Yes," I say uncertainly, watching her dip her rag into a bucket of water. She squeezes, wringing it dry, and then starts cleaning again. "Why did you leave your country?" I ask.

"Colombia is a dangerous place to live." Lupe makes little grunting noises as she rubs the rag along the bars of the cage. "There has been a guerilla war going on there for years. Ricardo and I wanted to get away and start a new life."

"And so you came here?"

"No, we have only been in Sommersville for six months," Lupe says. "We moved to Texas first and lived there for a long time."

"Why'd you come to Sommersville?" I ask. "It's so . . . boring here."

Lupe smiles. "I don't think it is boring. I like the mountains. I think it is pretty." A thoughtful expression comes over her face. "We came here . . . for another fresh start. Things had gotten very difficult in Texas. We thought . . . maybe a new place . . . another chance . . ." Her voice drifts off as she stops cleaning. She sits back on her heels and tosses the damp rag back into the bucket. I stare at the bruises around her eyes, the bandage on her nose. Did Ricardo do that to her? Did he do it in Texas, too? "Bah! Enough talk." She gets up and scoops Chili out of my hands. Then she walks over to the piano and slides a deck of cards off the top.

"What are these?" I ask as she hands them to me.

"Look." I glance down at them. They are not playing cards. Instead, drawn on the front of each card is a picture of a blank staff with a single musical note drawn on it. I flip one over. On the back is the letter that corresponds with the note on the front. "Flash cards," Lupe says. "And your assignment tonight is to memorize them. Not just the letters, Hershey. The kinds of notes." She taps the side of her head with a finger. "I want you to be able to see them in your head. Each one. Tomorrow night we will see how well you do. Good night."

"Wh—"

Lupe holds up her hand. "A student does not argue with her teacher."

"But I *know* my notes!" I protest. "I played almost all of them last night!" Lupe reaches out and, holding my gaze, draws a random card out of the deck. She holds it up in front of me. I don't know what it is. An F, maybe? An A-flat? I grimace. Lupe slides the card back into the deck and turns around.

"Good night, Hershey," she says. "Let's hope you do better than that tomorrow night."

"What about Chili?"

"What about her?" Lupe asks.

"I . . . I . . . wanted to see her run around," I say lamely. "I wanted to . . . play with her."

"There will be time for that later," Lupe says. "Good night, pepita."

I plod upstairs and crawl into bed. I look at Lupe's flash cards for a while, but the sound of Mom snoring underneath is too distracting. The conversation we had this afternoon is still banging around in my head. I can't forget the way Mom's eyes looked when I told her I'd never go back with her. My heart feels like it's beating more slowly, as if it has gotten too heavy to beat any faster. When I take a breath, it hurts. Darkness has never frightened me before, but the room seems to be turning a deeper black with every second that passes. I shut my eyes, reach under the pillow, and plug my ears, as if to block out the sound of Mom's voice all those years ago.

"It'll be different this time, honey," she said, glancing at me in the rearview mirror as we drove back down along Route 80, getting farther and farther away from Aunt Kemi. "He won't pick on you anymore. I promise." I was packed in again under the peach blanket in the backseat, but this time I could not get warm. The white sky above us looked ominous, as if a snowstorm was coming. I pretended not to see Mom's anxious eyes or the way her chin trembled as she waited for me to respond. "Look at me, Hershey." She wasn't watching the road. It was making me nervous, so I looked up for just a second. A red highway sign on the side of the road flashed past.

WRONG WAY, it read in huge letters.

"Mom!" I yelled.

She shrieked as a car came barreling toward us, and swerved off the road. I slid off the seat and landed in a heap on the floor. The car came to a shuddering stop as Mom slammed on the brake. Clutching at the front of her shirt, she leaned over the seat to look down at me. Her face was as white as milk.

"Oh my God. Are you okay, Hershey?" she asked. "Did you bump your eye?" I shook my head. Mom reached down and helped me back up. She tried to smile, but it just came out as a quiver. "You're sure you're okay?" she asked. "You're positive?"

"Mom," I said, grabbing her hand as she pulled the peach blanket back over my legs. "Please, let's turn around. Let's go back to Aunt Kemi's. Please. I don't want to go back, Mom. Please. Don't make me go back." Mom's hand froze under mine. I could see the hesitation in her face, the mistrust of her decision in her eyes. I held my tongue between my teeth—hard. But she blinked, and the doubt was gone. She began to tuck the blanket around my legs with quick, tight movements.

"I told you, Hershey, it's going to be different now. Slade swears it was an accident, and I have to believe him. We've got nowhere else to go, baby. I have no money. It's going to be fine. I won't let anything happen to you, okay? I promise."

I kept my eyes closed the whole way back, pretending to sleep, so that Mom wouldn't keep talking, and so she wouldn't be able to see the tears behind my eyelids. Whenever one slid out, sneaking its way down my cheek like a little raindrop, I brushed it away angrily. I knew nothing she said from that moment on would make any difference anymore.

Remembering now is painful. I cry into my pillow and wipe my eyes and wait, but the hurt doesn't go away. Not even a little bit. My heart feels like a stone in the center of my chest. And so I get up and head out into the kitchen. The first cupboard is filled with little red spice tins: allspice, cloves, basil, oregano, garlic powder, all arranged in a neat little row. Above the spices is a gigantic box of raisins. I hate raisins, but I grab the box and dump a handful into my palm. They taste like hamster pellets. No wonder Chili likes them. I shove a handful into my pants pocket for her and poke around a little more. The only things I see are three boxes of artificial sweetener, coffee creamer, and orange-spice tea bags. Ugh.

The next cupboard is stuffed with snacks. Blue bags of Doritos, yellow bags of crinkle-cut potato chips, pretzel rods, and corn chips. My breath catches in the back of my throat as I see the familiar orange of the Cheetos bag. I stand on my tiptoes. Yes! They're the puffy kind—my favorite. Now, this is real food. Nothing like that junk in the cafeteria vending machine.

There is only one problem. Across the front of each bag is a strip of masking tape bearing a name written in black. The Doritos and pretzels belong to Josie. The potato chips are owned by Rose. Kate's name is slashed across the front of the corn chips. And Gracie owns the puffed Cheetos.

I hesitate only for a moment, knowing that what I am about to do is wrong. It would definitely even be considered stealing in some circles. But after the moment passes, I sit down in the middle of the kitchen floor. I spread all of the bags around me, like a little fence. And then in the dark, with only the moon outside watching me like a white eye, I eat the contents of each and every bag.

NINETEEN

Andrea is missing from the morning bus too, but Rhonda leers at me as I climb on. She looks ridiculous in her black-and-white-striped polo T-shirt with the collar flipped up, and spiderlike eyelashes. How can Andrea not see what a fake she is? Rhonda lowers her head, squeezing her nostrils hard with her thumb and forefinger as I move past her.

"Get lost, you wannabe," I mutter under my breath.

"*What* did you say?" Rhonda asks, swiveling around hard.

I keep moving. "You heard me."

Rhonda stares hatefully at me as I settle into my seat and look out the window. What a moron. Without Andrea next to her, she can't do anything.

I make my decision as the bus scuttles on toward school. I'm going to skip the afternoon bus back to the shelter and walk back to our apartment instead. I know it's forbidden for me to walk around my neighborhood, not to mention going back to my house, and Kate is probably going to have a heart attack when the bus comes and I'm not on it, but I want my notebooks. Not having them with me is starting to give me the heebie-jeebies. I know they are well hidden, stuck on the shelf all the way in the back of my closet, but I'm getting more and more worried about Slade. He'll be served with the protection order that Mom filed any day now, and who knows what he'll do once that happens. I know he blames me. He blames me for everything. I just want my notebooks safe. They belong with me.

That settled, I pull Lupe's flash cards out of my backpack and start studying them for real. The notes between the lines spell F-A-C-E. Not so bad. The notes in the middle of the lines spell E-G-B-D-F. I try to remember the hint Lupe gave me about remembering these. "*Every Good Boy Does Fine.*" Yes, I think that was it. It's basic memorization. I go through them once, twice, twelve times before the bus pulls up alongside Sommersville Middle School.

Phoebe has a different flower in her hair today. It's just as big as the red one, but the petals are snow white. Tucked in the center, like large blackberries, are three blue stones.

"Are those real?" I ask, peering inside the flower.

Phoebe laughs. "Yeah. They're genuine sapphires. I bought it for ninety-nine cents at the Dollar Store. They were having a special." I smile and sit down.

"I think Jack is starting to bond with Augustus Gloop,"

Phoebe says. I rest my head on my arms, struggling to keep my eyes open. It was a long night. And although I demolished six bags of junk food, I crept back to bed feeling even emptier than before. I don't understand it.

"Why do you say that?" I ask, pushing down a twinge of envy.

Phoebe laughs. "I came home from school yesterday and he was sleeping on Jack's bed, right next to him. It was so cute."

"Really? That's weird. He's never slept with anyone but me."

"Why's that weird?" Phoebe asks. "I thought you'd be glad."

I chew on my thumbnail. "Well, of course I'm *glad*. I guess I'm just surprised a little too, that's all. Is he eating that tuna stuff?"

"Yeah," Phoebe says. "And last night he enjoyed a fat little mouse he found in the field." She shudders, and I laugh.

"Are you going to be able to meet me this weekend?" I ask. "So we can practice?"

"Maybe," Phoebe says. "I still have to ask Jack. I don't know how he's going to feel about me going to a shelter, though."

"Oh, you can't come to the shelter. We'll have to meet at the Wal-Mart and then go somewhere else."

"Oh." Phoebe looks distracted. "Well, I don't really know that part of town very well. How would I find you?"

I look hard at her. "Do you still want to do the talent show together, Phoebe, or not?"

"Well, *yeah*," she says. "Of course." There is a long pause between us.

"I'm going back to the apartment after school today," I say.

Phoebe looks at me like I'm crazy. "What are you talking about? Why would you do that?"

"I have to get my notebooks. I forgot to pack them the night we left. They're in a bag in the back of my closet."

"Why don't you just get them later?" Phoebe asks. "After everything gets worked out in the courts between your mom and Slade?"

"Because that might take a while, and he'll prob'ly destroy them if he finds them."

"Oh, Hershey, come on. Slade's not going to go looking through your things. . . ."

"Why not? I'm the reason he hit Mom to begin with—"

Phoebe cuts me off, dropping her voice to a harsh whisper. "No, *Slade's* the reason he hit your mom to begin with. I don't care how messy you left things that night, Hershey, or how far along we got with our plan. Neither of us thought he was going to *hit* her. It's not your fault."

My skin feels prickly hearing Phoebe say the words "mom" and "hit" out loud. "Whatever. I just want my notebooks back. They're really important to me."

"What if Slade's there?" Phoebe asks.

"Well, obviously I won't go in if *Slade's* there. But he should be at work. He doesn't get home until six thirty."

"Do you want me to come with you?" Phoebe asks.

I look up in surprise. "You mean it? You would do that?"

"Well, yeah," Phoebe says. "I don't think it's a good idea for you to go alone."

"What about Jack?" I ask. "Won't he get mad?"

"Jack doesn't have to know," Phoebe says. "Not that he would, anyway."

I must look over my shoulder a hundred times as Phoebe and I walk down Lilac Lane. The sun is behind us, slanting through a curtain of lush green trees. Across the street a woman in a yellow sundress is pushing a little girl in a stroller, and two boys roll by on skateboards with red and blue Dairy Queen cups in their hands. They are yelling to each other and laughing. One of them has his T-shirt off. It's tucked in at his waist and blows behind him like a kite. It feels weird to see people going about their dumb everyday activities, taking a walk, going for ice cream, while Phoebe and I are headed for . . . what? Are we in danger?

I stop when we reach the house. Someone has kicked the potted geranium off to the side of the road. It's still a mess, half out of the pot, its green leaves turning brown at the tips. I pick it up and put it back in the pot, even though it's broken. Tamping down the rest of the dirt, I carry it over and place it back on the first step, where Mom used to keep it. Then I look in the driveway for Slade's car. It's gone.

"Okay, he's still at work," I say, grabbing Phoebe's hand. "Come on, let's go. I want to get in and out of there as fast as we can."

"What if the door's locked?" Phoebe asks.

"Let's check. If it is, then we're going to have to figure out a way to bust in through the upstairs window." I'm running full speed up the front steps, dragging Phoebe behind me. If I don't run, I will stop to think about it, the way Phoebe is doing, and I will lose the little courage I have now.

"*Bust in?*" Phoebe says, "What're you, crazy? I'm not getting arrested here, Hershey!" We're standing directly outside the front the door. The numbers 113 hang small and neat on the wall, next to the little wicker basket Mom keeps out for the mail.

"Would you be quiet?" I say. "Just relax. Let's just see." My heart is pounding like a drum. I turn the doorknob and push on the door.

It's open.

"Oh, man," Phoebe whispers, holding her nose. The inside is filled with a terrible odor, as if something is rotting inside. There are newspapers thrown on the living room floor, and dirty clothes scattered across the couches. Crushed cigarette butts litter the carpeted hallway like bugs, and in the kitchen the entire silverware drawer has been torn out from the counter. Now it is sitting upside down in the trash. Forks, spoons, and knives are strewn all over the place, as if Slade picked up a handful of them and threw them across the room.

"Man," Phoebe says. "It looks like ol' Slade's gone off the deep end."

I glance toward my bedroom. "I'll be right back. You stay here and keep watch."

"Hurry up," Phoebe says. "This place is creeping me out." I feel like I might throw up as I head toward my bedroom. With the rest of the house in the state it's in, what in the world will my room look like? But it's exactly the way it was the night we left: my unmade bed with the purple comforter thrown aside as I looked frantically for my biology book, my dresser drawers still hanging open, emptied of their contents. Even my old tennis shoes, which I decided to leave behind at the last minute, are in the same pile where I threw them, alongside my desk. I walk over to my closet and turn on the light. Standing on my tiptoes, I reach all the way up until my fingers close around the paper bag.

A scream in the next room makes my blood rush hot in my head. It's Phoebe. Pulling the bag down from the shelf, I clutch it to my chest and run toward the door. Before I have a chance to open it, it flings wide, nearly knocking me down.

There in the hallway, waiting for me, is Slade.

TWENTY

Slade's got Phoebe around the wrist. Hard. She's wincing and struggling, but he doesn't seem to notice. His eyes are glazed and heavy, but they shoot through me like laser beams. I can smell the beer on his breath. Before I can say a word, he leans forward and with his free hand snatches the bag from my arms. I hang on with all my might as he pulls me into the hallway, but Slade is stronger and when the bag comes loose, I fall down backward, banging my head on the wall. Slade pushes Phoebe down in a heap next to me. She whimpers a little and clings to my shoulder.

Sliding back into the corner, I keep my knees up against my chest and my eyes on Slade as he glares at me with puffy, wild-looking eyes. Dark whiskers pepper the line between his chin and neck. His mustache hangs ragged and uneven above his upper lip. I stare at the spaghetti sauce splattered across the front of his T-shirt and wonder how long it's been since he showered.

"You touch either of us and you're gonna be sorry," I

say. "Mom just filed a protection order against you." Slade laughs and digs into his front pocket. Without taking his eyes off me, he pulls out a wrinkled piece of paper and throws it in my direction. It hits my leg and slides to the floor.

"You mean that?" he asks. I unfold the paper with shaking hands.

It reads:

Now, on this 28TH day of May, in the year 2004, it is hereby ordered and decreed that Slade West, Defendant in the above captioned complaint, shall have no personal, physical, or telephone contact with Daisy Hollenback, Plaintiff in the above captioned complaint, for a period of sixty (60) days. Failure to comply with these terms and regulations may result in the arrest and subsequent jail sentence of no more than thirty (30) days.

I look back up at Slade. He grins, exposing a row of dirty, slimy teeth.

"Don't say anything about you, now, does it?" he sneers. "Just Daisy." His face darkens at the sound of her name. "It's Daisy who don't want to see me. Just Daisy." He starts to pace up and down the length of the hallway, stepping on chunks of balled-up newspaper, kicking empty beer cans out of his way. "Daisy," he keeps saying. "It's *Daisy* on the order." I place the protection order down on the floor because I don't know what else to do with it. The only thing I can think about is what Slade said to Mom the night she left: *"If you or anyone else is here when I get back, I'm not going to be responsible for what happens next."* I'm not stupid. I know who "anyone else" refers to. I've got to get us out of here. Suddenly, Slade stops pacing.

"Where have you been all this time?" he asks. "Where you staying?"

"I'm not allowed to tell you." I clear my throat so that my voice doesn't come out in a whisper.

"You got a message for me? Did Daisy send you here to tell me something?" I shake my head and stand up slowly, balancing myself against the wall behind me. Phoebe stands up too. I can feel her fingers sliding around one of my belt loops on the back of my pants.

"I just want my notebooks, Slade," I say, pointing to the paper bag that's still in his hand. He looks at the bag with confusion, as if he has forgotten he is holding it.

"What are you talking about, notebooks?" he says. "What notebooks?"

"They're just notebooks," Phoebe says. She tries to shrug nonchalantly, but her voice comes out all nervous. "You know, for school. We have finals next week." Slade peers at us for a minute. It takes all of my strength not to look away.

"You're a liar," he says finally. "You all would never come back here for a schoolbook." I bite the inside of my cheek as he opens the paper bag and pulls a notebook out. He turns it right side up and studies the green cover. "Notebook number seven," he reads aloud. I lurch forward, begging. Phoebe moves with me, her finger still entangled in my belt loop.

"Slade, please. Just give them to me."

But he holds out his hand and points his finger. His eyes stop me cold. "You take one more step and I'll wring your neck."

"You can't threaten her!" Phoebe says, finally finding her voice. "We'll call the police!" Slade gives Phoebe a withering look.

"You *call* the police," he says. "I'll sit them right down on the couch and tell them about a piece of white trash I know who's milking the workers' comp situation for all it's worth." I can feel Phoebe's finger loosen and then fall from my belt loop. Slade stares at her for another few seconds and then drops his eyes. He begins flipping through my notebook, blinking stupidly as he reads a page and then another and then another. On the fourth page a slow grin spreads across his face. He starts nodding his head up and down.

"Well, well, *well*. What have we here?"

I close my eyes as he begins to read aloud.

"Slade Plan. Week One. Don't line up shoes in the hallway. Leave one of Ella's dirty diapers in his closet. Don't sweep under the bed. Mess up the soup cans in the pantry. Only clean litter box once a day—instead of three." Slade pauses between each sentence, as if pondering their significance. My heart is pounding so hard that I can hear it in my ears. He goes on. "Slade Plan. Week Two." He is getting animated now, reading the sentences in a dumb, falsely comical way. "Don't put sofa pillows back in order. Sit on his bed after he makes it." He pauses after that one and flicks his eyes over at me. "You been sittin' on my BED?"

"Slade," I try again. "Please. Please just give it—" He cuts me off, starting up again with a roar.

"LEAVE out the butter after making grilled cheese! Leave one saucepan in the sink—still dirty! Leave TOENAIL clippings on the bathroom rug!" He slams the notebook shut. It makes a loud smacking sound in the air between us, and Phoebe and I both jump. Slade laughs a horrible laugh and clenches his teeth. "I knew it was you," he says. "I *knew* it!" He moves closer to us as he speaks, his fists clenched, spit gathering in a corner of his mouth. The front door is right behind him. I know he is off balance from the booze. I am going to have to make a run for it and drag Phoebe along behind me. "You've been plotting all along," Slade says. "I *told* Daisy you were doing stuff to make me crazy, but she wouldn't believe me. But now I have proof. You've been trying to get your mother away from me ever since that accident with your eye, and now I can prove it."

"It wasn't an accident!" I scream. "You threw that glass on purpose! You were trying to hurt me!"

A vein in Slade's forehead bulges like a serpent under his skin. "Because you wouldn't *shut* up! Always whining and complaining about the Job List and how much you had to do! Wah, wah, wah! Do you have any idea how much *I* had to do? How hard I was working back then to find another *job*? Putting up with your mother needling me, day in and day out, to find work? Huh? Do you have any *idea*? And then *you* start in, complaining about having to stack the cans in the pantry! I was just trying to scare you! It wasn't supposed to hit you! You were in the way! And your mother will never forgive me because of that!"

"Why should she?" I scream back. "You never even said you were sorry! Not once! You almost blinded me, Slade, and you never even apologized!" Slade straightens up. His breathing slows down a little. He cocks his head and squints at me, as if he hasn't quite heard me correctly.

"Is *that* what this is all about?" he asks in a guttural voice. He taps the front of my notebook. "You been doing all this just because I never *apol*ogized?"

I stand there, trembling. I'm not sure anymore why I've done any of it. Has it really been all about me? Have I let things get this bad just because Slade never came to me and said he was sorry? Suddenly I wish Phoebe wasn't here. I don't want her to hear any more.

A sneer slides across Slade's lips. "Well, I'm *sorry*," he says. "I'm sorry you got in the way the night Mommy and I were arguing." He takes another unsteady step toward me. "*Okay?* All better now?" It feels as though I am choking on my hate for him, as if an arm is reaching up inside my throat and squeezing the breath out of me. Slade takes another step and then another until he is inches away from my face. His body odor, a combination of old sweat and beer, makes me gag. "Now you listen to me for once." His voice is deadly calm. "You got what you wanted. Now it's time to give me something." I don't move. Phoebe clutches the back of my shirt.

"I don't have to give you anything," I say. Slade blinks three times, quickly, as if the movement will prevent his rage from spewing out. He gives me that terrible smile again.

"You do if you want to see your mother again."

I shake my head. "You don't know what you're talking . . ." But he is nodding his head rapidly. His eyes are big circles. His nostrils flare open like potholes.

"Oh, yes I *do*, Hershey. And I think you do too." I bite my tongue until I taste the salty tang of blood. I don't feel any pain. Slade holds the notebook out in front of me.

"See, you've made things easy for me. All I have to do is show this to your mother when I see her in court in two weeks and you're done."

"She won't care," I say. It comes out in a whimper.

"Oh, she'll care," Slade says slowly, tapping the front of the notebook with the back of his palm. "She'll care. See, if there's one thing I know about Daisy Hollenback, it's that right about now, she's just looking for an excuse to come back." He smacks the book once, hard. "And this is it." There is a long, dead pause.

"I hate you!" I scream. "I wish my mother had never met you!"

"The feeling's mutual," Slade says, throwing my notebook back into the paper bag with the rest of them. "Now the two of you get out of here before I call the police. You're trespassing, in case you weren't aware of it. You don't live here anymore."

"Can I have the rest of my—"

"*Get out!*" Slade screams. "Now!"

Phoebe and I run to the door as one body. We don't stop running until we are a full three blocks away from my house. Finally, at the corner of Vanguard and Franklin Street, Phoebe slumps against a sidewalk bench and sits, gasping for breath. I stop too, and lean over, holding my kneecaps with my palms. After a minute Phoebe points to a pay phone across the street.

"Call the police," she gasps.

I stare at her. "For what?"

"To press charges," Phoebe pants. "He threatened you, Hershey. I heard him. He said he was going to wring your neck if you took one more step. I'm your witness. I can come—"

"I don't want to press charges."

"*Why?*" Phoebe is aghast. "This is your chance to get him, Hershey! He *threat*ened you! I heard him with my own ears! You can have him put in jail!"

I shake my head. "If we go down to the police station, they're gonna call my mom. She's gonna find out everything about these notebooks and it'll just make things even worse than they already are."

"How can it possibly get any worse?" Phoebe asks.

"I can't explain it right now." My voice trails off. "Believe me, it's better if we just don't say anything about any of this. I've got enough to worry about, figuring out what I'm gonna tell Mom before Slade sees her in court."

"So you're just gonna let him get away with what he did to you?" Phoebe asks. Her hands fall helplessly to her sides. "God, I never thought I'd say this, Hershey, but you're as bad as your mother. You'll let anyone walk all over you, even—"

I shove her so hard that she goes flying off the side of the bench, landing in a heap on the sidewalk. Sometimes even I forget how big I am. She stays on the ground for a second, just staring at me. I stare back, unmoving. *Oh my God*, I think. *That was meant for Andrea Wicker.*

"I can't be*lieve* you just did that," Phoebe says in a hollow voice.

I move toward her quickly. "I'm sorry!" My words flow out in a torrent. "Oh, Phoebe, I'm so sorry. I'm so sorry. Please. I'm all screwed up inside right now. . . ."

"It's okay," Phoebe says, but she takes a step backward. "I shouldn't have said what I said." She rubs her arm where I shoved her. "Man, you're stronger than you look."

I drop my eyes. "I'm so sorry," I whisper. "I didn't mean to hurt you."

Phoebe shakes her head. "Yeah," she says. There is a long, painful silence. Across the street is the Dairy Queen. I think stupidly how great it would be if we could walk across the street and get in line and order an extra large peanut-butter-crunch Blizzard to share. "Well, I gotta get home. Jack's gonna be wondering what happened to me." She looks down the street, still holding her arm. "The bus stop is on the next corner. I'm pretty sure there's a four thirty one that goes across town." I follow her slowly, staring at the black rubber soles of her shoes as she walks in front of me. My legs feel incredibly heavy.

The sun is glaringly bright on the horizon, nearly white with heat. I shield my bad eye with my arm. The street is empty, the air is warm, and a soft breeze blows through my hair. I pick up my pace a little so that I am walking alongside Phoebe. She is running her fingers along her bottom lip.

"Are you okay?" I ask softly.

She nods distractedly. "Yeah." She's biting the edge of her pinky. Suddenly she stops walking and turns to face me. "How did Slade know about the situation with Jack's workers' comp?"

"What do you mean?"

"I mean, where did he get that whole thing about ratting him out? Where did that even come from?"

"That's how Slade is," I say. "He's always saying horrible things about people."

"But how did he *know* that one thing?" Phoebe pushes. She's spinning her rubber bracelets around her wrists furiously. "He's never even *met* Jack."

"Phoebe, *I* don't know. What, do you think *I* told him?" She raises her eyebrows. "I didn't, Phoebe! I don't even know what the heck workers' comp is, if you want to know the truth. And if you think I sit around at night chatting things up with Slade, you're crazy. Anyway, who cares what Slade thinks about Jack? It's no big deal."

Phoebe drops her eyes. "It is a big deal, Hershey.

Workers' compensation is money the government gives you when you get hurt on the job and can't work. Slade was right. Jack's cheating the system."

"What do you mean?"

Phoebe swallows. "His back is fine. It's been fine for weeks. But something else is wrong and I don't know what it is. He won't go look for a job; he won't even get out of bed. All he does is drink that stupid beer and sleep. And when the papers come about his workers' comp checks, he lies and says that he's still injured. So they keep sending him money." I don't know what to say to that. Sometimes I wish I was older and had more answers. But then again, who says when you're older you have answers? It seems some things in life are impossible no matter what your age.

"Phoebe . . ." We stand there for a minute and I hope, although I don't have the slightest idea what to tell her to do about Jack, that she knows I am here for her. And I hope she knows that, despite what just happened between us, I will always be here for her.

"I lie in bed at night, and I pray that someone will just call him and offer him a job." Phoebe shrugs. Her eyes are getting glossy with tears. "I just can't think of any other way he would get out of bed. It's like he's turned into a little baby. Someone's gotta spoon-feed him to get him to do anything."

Another adult acting like a kid, I think. *What is it with these people?*

"Well, maybe somebody will call him," I say.

"Oh, yeah? You on a first-name basis with Santa Claus?" Phoebe's voice is bitter. She wipes her eyes roughly. The sun feels hot on my neck. I'm sweating all over, but I feel cold. I want to reach out and hug Phoebe. I would give anything to hear her say, *Don't worry. Everything will work out. You'll always be my friend, Hershey. No matter what.* Or something like that.

After a bit Phoebe looks up.

"Here comes the bus." We watch the lumbering vehicle in silence as it creaks up next to us and opens its enormous doors. I climb two of the steps and then turn around.

"Phoebe," I say. But nothing else comes out. Maybe it's because I know the bus driver is watching me, or maybe it's because Phoebe's sad eyes are saying enough for both of us. Maybe it's just because I don't know what else to say to make anything better anymore. Maybe sometimes there isn't anything left to say at all.

"See you in school," Phoebe says flatly as the doors close. I walk all the way to the back and sit behind a sleepy-looking man with dreadlocks. He's eating french fries out of a paper napkin. I wonder briefly what he'd do if I grabbed them and shoved them into my mouth.

As the bus rumbles to life again, I watch Phoebe out

the window as she walks down the street. I stare at that dumb flower in her hair as long as I can, until the bus turns the corner and she disappears from sight.

"Tell Augustus Gloop I said hi," I whisper.

TWENTY-ONE

Mom and Kate are standing in the kitchen, talking in low voices, when I finally walk into the shelter at five thirty. Baby Ella is in a high chair, chasing several green peas around the plastic tray with her fingers. Rose is sitting at the opposite end of the table, flipping through a magazine. Mom jerks her head up when she sees me, eyes flashing. I'm startled by how much older she looks lately. Her forehead is mapped with creases and she has gray bags under her eyes.

"Where were you?" she demands. They are the first words she's said to me since our conversation yesterday. Kate doesn't give me a chance to answer.

"I waited on that corner for you, Hershey, for over an hour," she says. "Not coming back here on the bus like we talked about is unacceptable. We were really, really worried."

"Where *were* you?" Mom says again.

I glance over at Rose, embarrassed, but she doesn't lift her head. "I stayed after school to practice for the talent show with Phoebe. I'm sorry I didn't call, but I didn't know the number."

Mom rests her forehead in the heel of her hand. "Well, you're going to have to *learn* the number, Hershey. And you're going to have to call if you need to stay late again. I can't go through another afternoon like . . ." Her voice breaks and she covers her face with both hands. I don't move, although part of me wants to run over and hug her.

"We understand that things can come up," Kate says, putting an arm around me. "Especially at the end of the year. But it's never a problem for one of us to come pick you up at school, Hershey, if you need to stay late. You just need to call and tell us, okay?" I nod. Kate squeezes my shoulder.

"Mama?" Baby Ella says uncertainly. She is holding a pea in her hand. It's squished flat. She looks at me. "Shee?"

"Okay," I say. "I'll memorize the number, Mom. It won't happen again. I promise." She nods behind her hands. I walk into our bedroom, shut the door, and climb up to the top bunk. I stare at the ceiling for a long time before I reach over, grab the notebook Naomi gave me, and open it up to a clean sheet.

WHAT WOULD HAPPEN IF I PRESSED CHARGES:
 1. Slade might go to jail. (!!!!)
 2. Mom will find out about the notebooks and figure out that all this is my fault.

3. She will never forgive me.

4. Baby Ella won't have her daddy around.

WHAT I CAN TELL MOM BEFORE SLADE DOES:

1. Nothing.

2. I'm sorry.

3. I didn't know things would get this bad.

4. I was only trying to get you to leave.

5. I wanted you to see how mean Slade can get.

WHY I SHOVED PHOEBE:

1. Because what she said was true.

2. Because what she said hurt.

3. Because I'm a jerk.

HOW I CAN PAY PHOEBE BACK:

1. Be the best friend I can be.

2. Save up to buy her a really cool present.

3. Help her figure out what to do with her dad.

I sit up quickly after I write the last sentence.

I have an idea.

It might work and it might not, but it sure as heck is worth a try. I have to wait until I see Naomi again, and then I will give it a shot.

Lupe is impressed by how well I know the flash cards. I don't miss a single one, not even when she shuffles them and holds them up randomly.

"Excellent, Hershey. You have done your homework." I don't tell her that it is rage that has sharpened my concentration, or that everything right now is being propelled forward by a new, blinding fury. I notice that she has changed the Band-Aid across her nose; it is much smaller now, with two little pinchers at either end. The black circles under her eyes are fading to purple and yellow shadows.

But when I start to play, Lupe grabs my wrists and shakes them. "You are still not holding your hands correctly! The first knuckle of the finger must be round. Your arch must be high. Like this. Like I told you." I rearrange my fingers once more over the keys, rounding the tips of them and keeping my wrists loose, as Lupe has instructed.

Once I get my fingers in order, Lupe has me play whatever notes of the first section of "Für Elise" that I can. It is basically the same six notes, played over and over again in a different order. She sits next to me on the bench, holding Chili in her hands, eyes closed. I ease through the first four lines and then stumble through the fifth. I hit many of the remaining notes on the next two pages, but my playing is stilted and hesitant, and sounds nothing like any music I've ever heard. A few times Lupe winces, or she makes a strange sucking sound with her front teeth. When I reach the end of the page, she shakes her head.

"Again," Lupe says. I sigh and begin again from the top. Once more when I get to the fifth line, I start to stumble, looking frantically from my hands to the keys and then back up again at the music. Lupe stays silent, stroking Chili's fur with the back of her knuckle. Chili does not move. Her tiny tail is wrapped around her hind legs and her eyes are closed.

"Again," Lupe says. I go through it one more time. The first page does not seem as difficult this time, but I hesitate terribly on the last two lines and even hit three wrong notes toward the end.

"Again." I look at her in disbelief. *"What?"* Lupe says. "I thought you said you could play all night! You want to play, you practice. This is practice, Hershey. Even if some of it comes easily, you must practice and practice and practice if you want to get better." I know she is right. I shake my hands out and place them down again on the keys.

By the ninth time through, I play the first two pages of "Für Elise" without an error. The fourteenth time, I play the entire three pages all the way through without stopping or making a mistake. By then my bad eye is throbbing, but I am so excited that I can barely feel it.

"Did you hear that, Lupe? I played every note without stopping! The whole first movement!"

"You did play every note," Lupe says, placing Chili, who is sound asleep, back into her cage. "But your music is dead." I rub my bad eye behind my glasses and blink a few times.

"Dead?" I repeat.

Lupe nods. "There is no feeling, Hershey. You have not gotten behind the music yet, because you do not know what it is about." She pokes me in the arm. "You do not know what *you* are about. And because of that, you cannot bring anything to the piece. It is dead." Lupe pulls her braid over her shoulder and strokes the tip of it against her cheek.

"One of the reasons Beethoven was considered a master of music was because of the emotion he brought to the piano." She speaks slowly, concentrating on her English. "People had never heard anything like it before." She stops and looks at me. "Some people say that he wrote that piece for a woman he loved, named Elise. If you listen closely to the piece, you can feel the love he had for her."

"Well, if he loved her, why is it so sad?" I ask.

Lupe shrugs. "Maybe she didn't love him back," she says. "That kind of love can be the saddest of all."

"Has that ever happened to you?" I ask, thinking about Ricardo. "I mean, being in love with someone who didn't love you back?" Lupe looks away. "I'm sorry," I say. "I don't mean to pry."

She lifts her hand, waving away my apology. "It is why I am here," she says softly. "Sometimes, the only thing left to do is leave." I think about what Gracie said the other night about leaving. How is it that these women are so different and at the same time so alike? "But I am not the only one, pepita. Did you know Beethoven had a terrible relationship with his father? It started when he was very young. Mr. Beethoven drank too much and he used little Ludwig to fulfill his own desire to be famous. The man used to wake his son up in the middle of the night when he was only four years old and force him to practice."

"Ugh. How awful."

Lupe nods. "He lost his mother when he was only eighteen, as well as his baby sister. And for all the success Beethoven enjoyed as a musician, he was never able to find a wife." Lupe shakes her head. "He had terrible problems with women."

"Why?"

"He was a crab! Ornery, rude, arrogant. Although . . ." Here Lupe pauses for a moment, resting her hand on her chest. "Although I am sure he was that way because of a deep, deep sadness that was born out of having such a cruel father. One time he wrote his younger brother a letter and said that he was not really grouchy at all, that he ignored people simply because he could not hear them."

"He really couldn't hear them?" I ask.

"No," Lupe says sadly. "Can you imagine? He couldn't hear his own piano when he played, he couldn't hear the orchestra when he conducted, he couldn't even hear what people were saying across the room. He actually thought of taking his own life when he began to go deaf, because he did not know how he was going to be able to go on."

She closes her eyes. "But then he decided that, deaf or not, he had too much inside of him that still needed to come out." She smiles hugely and raises her hands up toward the ceiling. "Ay dios mío! And look what he gave us!"

"Well, I'm still confused about something," I say. "What am *I* supposed to feel in order to play the piano the way you want me to?"

"Music," Lupe says, "is like a baby, Hershey. It is a living, breathing thing." She nods toward the sheet music resting on the piano. "Right now, it is asleep on the page. When you play, you wake it up, warming it under your fingers, until it begins to breathe again. But you must *love* it, Hershey—the way a mother loves her baby—for it to come to life under your touch. If you do not, it will stay asleep." Lupe draws her eyebrows together. "And if it stays asleep, it can never touch anyone else." I think about Mom, how silent she has been toward me for the past two days, how angry she is with me now, and how much it hurts.

"Do you love music?" I ask. Lupe reaches out and strokes one of the ivory keys with her finger.

"I try to love it like he did," she says. "But I am not perfect."

"I think you must love it," I say. "Because when I heard you play, I couldn't stop listening."

Lupe smiles gently at me. "Gracias."

My bad eye twitches once, and then again. I take my glasses off and rub it.

"Your eye is tired?" Lupe asks.

I nod. "It's hard for me to read across the page like that." I tell her about my lists, how I have found that reading only halfway across a page is much easier on my eye than having to read all the way across.

Lupe nods somberly. "It was hurt in an accident?"

"My mom's boyfriend threw a glass at the wall," I reply. "A long time ago. It smashed and one of the pieces got stuck in my eye. I had to have an operation on it."

Lupe reaches out and touches the side of my face. "It is still a beautiful color," she says. "Like sea glass." I drop my eyes and look at my hands.

"I think it makes me look like a freak. The big white scar and everything running right down the middle . . ." I can feel something tight and sour rise in the back of my throat, and I swallow hard.

"Tsss . . . ," Lupe says, turning away. "You are just feeling sorry for yourself."

I stand up, furious. "I'm not feeling sorry for myself! *You* try being fat, and having a messed-up eye, and living with a mother who would rather be with her wacko boyfriend than her own daughter!" I'm not sure where that last part comes from, but suddenly there it is, out on the floor of the broom closet, as angry and alive as a scorpion lashing its venomous tail. Lupe turns back around slowly, just as I cover my face with my hands, overwhelmed by the painfulness of my admission. I stamp my foot, willing my tears back, and shake my head angrily. "I just want her to love me!" I cry. "Why can't she love me enough to put me first? Just for *once!*" Lupe's arms around my shoulders only make me cry harder.

"Shhhh . . . ," she murmurs. "Shhhh, pepita." I let her hold me, which surprises me, but I don't think I could pull away even if I wanted to. Her arms are like a fence around my shoulders, holding me up, keeping me in. My cheek presses against the rope part of her necklace. It's surprisingly silky against my skin. After a few minutes Lupe stops rocking.

"I do not know the whole situation, Hershey. It is difficult for me to say what is right and what is wrong." She reaches out and pinches my cheek. Hard. "But I think you must find a way to use this sadness when you play your music. You will be surprised what it can do. Sadness can sometimes be made into something very beautiful." I sit down and rub my nose. "Listen to 'Für Elise' when you play, Hershey. Really, really listen to it. And you will understand what I am telling you." I think about the things on my list—sunsets, the last snow of winter, the look on Augustus Gloop's face when he knows I am leaving for school—and I think I do understand.

"You know, the ladies upstairs think you're crazy. They all told me to stay away from you."

Lupe laughs. It's a high-pitched tinkling sound. "That is fine with me what they think. And you, what do you think?"

I shake my head. "I don't think you're crazy. Maybe just sad."

Lupe holds me close again. "Sí, pepita. Your eye may be damaged, but you see plenty."

It feels so good to be held. Lupe's small body is warm and she smells like sawdust and grass. For the first time in three years, I realize slowly, sitting down here in this tiny broom closet with Lupe, I feel safe.

I stare down at the silver medallion dangling at the end of the rope cord and try to read the strange lettering again. But it's no use.

"What does your necklace say?" I ask finally. Lupe slides her fingers under the medallion until it rests heavily in the center of her hand.

"My mother gave this to me when I left my country to come live here in America. It says, 'La memoria del corazon elimina los malos recuerdos y magnifica los buenos.'" The words spill off her tongue like butterflies racing toward the sun.

"What does that mean?"

"It means: 'It is the memory of the heart that eliminates

the bad and magnifies the good,'" Lupe recites, looking down at the medallion with a tender expression.

"It is the memory of the heart that eliminates the bad and magnifies the good," I repeat. "Who wrote that?"

"A great writer named Gabriel García Márquez." Lupe says the long name slowly and with great reverence. "He is from Colombia, like me. He is as good with words as Beethoven was with music. He won the Nobel Prize for his writing."

"Will you ever go back to Colombia?" I ask.

"Sí."

"When?"

Lupe looks at me with sad eyes. "I don't know. I am waiting here for my transportation papers because it is not safe for me to be in my house anymore. Naomi says the papers may come anyday, or it may take months."

"Why isn't it safe to be in your house?" I ask.

"For the same reason it is not safe for you to be in yours," Lupe answers. I stare at the ivory keys on the piano. Some of them are worn yellow with age. Pockets of dust have collected along the corners, and the wood along the edges is marked and stained. "I know it sounds selfish, but I hope you stay for a little while," I say. "I would really like you to keep teaching me." Lupe smiles and puts her arm around me again.

"Sí, pepita," she says. "I would like that too."

TWENTY-TWO

A ndrea is in the middle of the aisle the next morning when I get on the bus. A tiny plaid flower is tucked behind one of her ears. Rhonda is standing an inch behind her, her hand on a skinny hip.

"Listen, fatty," Andrea says. "Rhonda told me you called her some kind of name the other day when I wasn't here. Is that true?"

I stare at the floor. "Maybe."

"Maybe?" Andrea repeats.

"You know you did," Rhonda pipes in. "Don't lie."

Andrea reaches out and sticks a finger on my shoulder. "Don't start with us, blimp-ball, or you're going to regret it." The bus lurches forward, nearly throwing me and Andrea off balance. She grabs the seat next to her, which is where my hand is resting. "Ugh!" she says, snatching her hand back as if she has been burned. "God, you're, like, all soft and clammy."

"Like a whale," Rhonda sneers.

"Sit down!" the bus driver roars from the front. "The bus is moving!" Rhonda and Andrea sit back in their seat and watch me with cold eyes as I move toward the back.

From my window I can see the streets of Sommersville getting ready for the eagerly awaited one-hundred-year celebration. With a little more than a week to go, it is as if the town itself has come alive with excitement. Red, white, and blue streamers have been hung from all the streetlights and on the town green, where the mayor will make a speech and Hillside Farms will be giving away free ice-cream cones. New shrubs and flowers have been planted. Even the metal garbage cans have been painted a new coat of green. A brand-new banner, hanging like a flag between two of the biggest buildings on Main Street, spells out in bright red words:

SOMMERSVILLE'S FIRST
ANNUAL TALENT SHOW!
COME ONE! COME ALL!
$1000.00 GRAND PRIZE!!!

I look away, feeling a twinge against the swell of happiness inside my chest. I haven't had a chance to practice with Phoebe once since we left for the shelter. And now, after yesterday's run-in with Slade, I don't know if she'll want me to practice with her at all. Maybe she'll want to ditch the whole thing. I lean my head against the window of the bus and close my eyes. I try to erase the way her face looked when I pushed her yesterday out of my head. But instead of going away, the picture gets bigger. Her pretty eyes, so wide and round, were full of something I did not recognize. Was it fear? Could I really have made my best friend afraid of me? Was it possible that Phoebe felt about me now the way I felt about Slade?

My eyes fill with tears as the middle school comes into view. The sun glints off the brick siding and the grass on the front lawn has just been mowed. The American flag waves and snaps in the morning breeze. I wipe my face hurriedly as the bus pulls up alongside the front door. I still can't believe that this is our last week of school.

What a way to kick off summer vacation.

At lunch I take a bite of my mashed potatoes, savoring the salty yellow gravy. They taste good today. Not like soap. Mrs. Levandowski has given me an extra ladleful of the gravy, and two scoops of mashed potatoes.

"Come back for more," she said, giving me a wink. "I made extra."

I hold my breath as Phoebe approaches our table. She seems to hesitate for a split second and then, thinking better of it, sets her tray down. This is the first time I have seen her since yesterday.

"Hey." I chew rapidly, hoping I don't sound as nervous as I feel.

Phoebe takes her carton of milk off the tray. "Hey." Our eyes meet for a split second, but she looks away so quickly that I can't tell what she's feeling.

"How come you weren't in homeroom?"

"I got a pass," she says. "I had to go talk to someone."

"Oh." I let it drop.

Suddenly, she leans forward.

"Did you press charges against Slade?" she whispers.

"No." I shovel a forkful of Salisbury steak into my mouth. "And I don't mean to be rude, but I'd rather not talk about it anymore."

"Fine." Phoebe eyes my food as she pulls a banana out of her backpack. "How can you eat that stuff? There's like deer guts and eyeballs in it, you know."

I keep chewing, trying not to smile.

She's back.

Which means we're still friends.

I think.

"Thanks," I say. "I'll try not to throw up now. When did you start eating bananas?"

Phoebe shrugs. "Jack says I'm going to stunt my growth if I keep eating M&M's all the time. Bananas are the only other food I like."

"Oh." I stir my potatoes with my fork. It occurs to me

that, with everything else going on, I still have not had a chance to tell Phoebe about Lupe and the piano. "Listen, I want to tell you something."

"What?" Phoebe asks.

I put my fork down slowly and wipe my mouth with my napkin. "I think I have a gift. A real one, just like your juggling." Phoebe takes another bite of her banana. She smacks her lips together when she chews. It's kind of disgusting.

"Oh, yeah? What, can you stand on your head or something?"

"I'm serious, Phoebe. Don't make fun of this. Something really amazing happened to me at the shelter. I've been trying to tell you about it for the last four days, but everything's been so nuts."

"So go ahead, then. Tell me about it now."

I tell her the whole thing, starting at the very beginning, from when I heard Lupe the first night, to discovering Chili, to Lupe agreeing to give me lessons, to playing the first three pages of "Für Elise" last night without stopping. Phoebe glances at me every so often as I talk and continues eating her banana with the same bland expression on her face. Finally, when I am finished, she places the empty banana peel neatly aside and folds her hands.

"Okay, let me get this straight. You're telling me that you met some Colombian lady in the shelter who taught you how to magically play the piano?" I take another bite of my mashed potatoes. They taste sour.

"Just forget it," I say quietly. "I don't know why I even told you. I knew you would make fun of it."

"I'm not making fun of it, Hershey!"

"Well, no one *magically* taught me how to play anything. I never said that."

"But all of a sudden, after a few practices, you can play *Bee*thoven? Even though you've never sat at a piano before and you don't know how to read music?"

"Yeah," I say emphatically. "I can."

Phoebe sits back and rests her chin in the middle of her two cupped palms. "How?"

"Because, like I said before, if you were even *lis*tening, Lupe has been *teach*ing me, and I'm learning the notes, and I've been practicing really hard." I take a swig of milk. It's warm. "Lupe said that I'm the fastest-learning student she's ever had. She thinks I have a gift."

Phoebe raises her eyebrows. "Hmm." She's nodding to herself as if considering this last statement of mine. Then she looks straight at me. "What's it really like in there, Hershey?"

"In where? The shelter?" I ask. Phoebe nods. I'm starting to feel uncomfortable with the way she's looking at me. "What do you mean? I've already told you what it's like. It's fine. I mean, considering."

"It's just that, you know, Hershey, sometimes when things get really hard, or really weird, people imagine things. Sort of like when people see mirages in the desert because they're so thirsty. They *want* it to be there so badly that they think they see it. Do you know what I'm talking about?"

I push my tray across the table. "So, what're you saying, Phoebe? You think I'm imagining that I can play the piano? Just because I'm living in a shelter?"

Phoebe shrugs. "I don't know," she says, staring at her bracelets again. She meets my gaze with her big brown eyes, and for a moment neither of us looks away.

Don't you leave me too, I think.

"Listen," she says, poking at the banana peel with her thumb. "I've been thinking about it a lot, and I just don't think we're going to be able to pull this off anymore."

"Pull what off?"

"The . . . talent show, Hersh." Phoebe shakes her head. "I'm not doing this to be mean or anything, but without us being able to practice and everything . . . I . . . I just . . . I mean, I really want to win that money."

"For circus camp," I say. My heart is plunging like a stone down to the center of my belly. "I know, Phoebe. I'm not going to let you down. I know how much it means to you." But she's shaking her head.

"The money isn't for circus camp, Hershey. I just say

that so you and Jack won't ask me any questions." She leans toward me so that the ends of her black hair brush the top of her bracelets. "I'm saving up for something bigger. I don't want to have to keep depending on someone who makes my life miserable." For a second I'm confused. And then all at once I realize what Phoebe is talking about.

"You mean Jack?" I whisper. Phoebe nods. A tear plops down onto the table in front of her. She wipes it away furiously and drops her voice.

"Do you really think I want to live the rest of my life in a mo*tel*, scrounging around every night for loose change so that I can get a Slurpee for dinner? You think it's *fun* to wait for Jack to pass out every night so that I can rearrange the pillow under his head in case he chokes in his sleep?" My mouth drops open. Phoebe's eyes flash. "We've got four more years of school, Hershey, and when we're done, I want to get *out* of here. I want to move as far away from Jack and Sommersville as I can. *That's* what the money's for. I don't care about juggling or circus camp." She pauses. "Not really."

A long silence falls between us as we sit there for a minute, absorbing everything that has just been said. I am too stunned to say anything else. Phoebe picks at her cuticles. The edges of her face are damp and moist.

Of course Andrea takes this opportunity to walk by our table. Her purple and yellow argyle short-sleeve sweater shows off her bony arms, and her legs look a mile long in her khaki shorts. I could probably snap her in half over my knee. She pauses and taps the edge of her pearl ring on the table.

"Three thirty, right, Phoebe?" she asks. Phoebe gives me a sidelong glance and then looks back down at the table.

"Yeah." Her voice is nearly inaudible. "Three thirty, Andrea." Throwing me a look of disgust, Andrea saunters off again, spinning her ring on her finger.

I look back at Phoebe. "What was all that about?" Phoebe doesn't answer. She's picking at the banana peel again. "Why are you meeting Andrea Wicker at three thirty, Phoebe?"

Phoebe gets up and slings her backpack over her shoulder. She makes a big display of looking at the clock on the wall behind me. "Man, we have, like, thirty seconds before the bell rings. And I still have to go to my locker."

"Phoebe," I plead. "Please tell me what's going on." Phoebe shrugs and inhales deeply, as if what she is going to say is no big deal. But she looks like she might cry.

"I . . . just . . . I mean, with everything that's going on right now with you and stuff, I just sorta thought that you wouldn't be the best person to be my assistant anymore. So I asked Andrea if she'd do it. We're meeting today to practice."

Suddenly, I don't remember seeing Andrea in home-room this morning, either.

"*Andrea's* gonna be your assistant?" I ask. Phoebe nods. "That's where you were in homeroom, then? Asking *Andrea?*" She nods again, working her lip with her teeth. I lower my voice. "Is this because of yesterday? Because of everything that happened and me shov—"

"*No.*" Phoebe cuts me off before I can get the whole word out. She stares hard at me with the kind of gaze that people give when they want you to believe they're telling the truth. Except that they're not. I don't know what else to say.

"*Andrea?*" I hear myself repeat. "For real?"

Phoebe puts her hand on her hip. "Yeah, Hershey," she says. "For real." She holds my gaze for another five seconds before turning around. I stare at the back of her black T-shirt as she ducks her head and moves through the crowd.

It's the first time this year that she's walked out of the lunchroom without me.

TWENTY-THREE

I'm so busy cramming bags of junk food into my book bag that I almost miss the afternoon bus. It doesn't help things that the bus is parked all the way behind the school, which means that I have to run a whole block to get to it. Then I stumble getting in and drop my book bag, which I forgot to zip. All my stuff goes flying out, including the junk food from the vending machine. If Andrea had been on the bus and seen me, she would have had a field day. But she's not on the bus. She's with Phoebe. Practicing to be her *assistant* in the talent show. The bus driver helps me gather my notebooks and pencils, but when he hands me my bag of Cheetos and my package of Hostess cupcakes, he frowns.

"You shouldn't be eating this junk," he says. "There's not a single healthy thing in either of them." I snatch the food out of his hand and stuff them deep into my bag.

"I don't eat for my health," I snap, heading for my seat in the back. "And no one asked you anyway."

I start eating immediately, sliding down into my seat

so that no one will see me. One package of cream cheese crackers. Gone. One supersize bag of Cheetos. Gone. Two Hostess cupcakes with the chocolate frosting and little white squiggles on top. Gone. My stomach is starting to hurt. But when I think about Phoebe and Andrea, my whole body hurts. I tear open a bag of peanut butter pretzel nuggets. Ten seconds, gone. I even tip the bag back and pour the salt grains down my throat. On to the bag of cheddar-flavored SunChips. Gone. One partially squished brownie with chopped walnuts on top. Gone. And then, right in the middle of a bag of fire-hot potato straws, I stop chewing.

Why haven't I thought of it before?

I will compete in the talent show! I will practice "Für Elise" until my fingertips bleed, and I will play the Beethoven piece in the Sommersville talent show!

Yes! Why not? Of course! It's one thousand dollars—which I could give right to Mom. She's so worried about money; if I could give her that, maybe it would take some of the pressure off and she wouldn't waver anymore about going back to Slade, which I know she is doing. It means I will be competing against Phoebe, but she's got to understand. I mean, her reasons for wanting that money aren't any more serious than mine. And, with her ditching me the way she did, she hasn't really left me with any choice.

I cram another handful of potato straws into my mouth. They taste horrible. Like salty dirt.

WHY I SHOULD PLAY IN THE TALENT SHOW:

1. So I can win the money for Mom.
2. So that Slade won't ever bother us again.
3. So that Mom will be able to believe in herself.
4. Because I can. (!!!!!!!)

WHY I SHOULDN'T PLAY IN THE TALENT SHOW:

1. Because I'd be competing against Phoebe.
2. Because Phoebe wanted the money first.
3. I might freak out—and make a fool of myself.
4. I won't win anyway.

WHAT I WILL DO IF MOM GOES BACK TO SLADE:

1. Run away.
2. Move in with Phoebe (if she is still talking to me).
3. Stay in the shelter.

REASONS WHY MOM WOULD THINK OF GOING BACK TO SLADE:

1. She loves him. (Barf.)
2. She's scared.
3. She doesn't have any money.
4. She wants Baby Ella to have a dad around.
5. She hates living alone.
6. She doesn't think she can do any better.

THINGS I CAN SAY TO CHANGE HER MIND:

1. He'll probably hit you again. (That's what Naomi said.)
2. What if he hurts Baby Ella?
3. Just think—no more Job Lists.

4. She won't be living alone—she'll have us.
5. Here's one thousand dollars—let's go find a new apartment!
6. It will be scarier living with Slade than it ever will be living without him.
7. I love her more than Slade ever will.
8. We're a family.

After dinner that night I head downstairs in search of Naomi. Things have gotten bad enough between Phoebe and me, and now that I am going to compete against her in the talent show, I have to do something. It's almost seven o'clock, but a slat of light peeks out from under Naomi's door. I knock gently.

"Come in!" Naomi looks up from behind her desk as I push open the door. A pair of glasses with gold rims is balanced on the bridge of her nose, and she is writing on a yellow legal pad. Smoke from her cigarette, resting in a glass ashtray, is unwinding in a delicate column toward the ceiling. "Hershey!" she says, taking her glasses off. "What are you doing down here?"

"I wanted to ask you something." Naomi smiles, and folds in the stems of her glasses.

"Have a seat. You know, I hear Lupe and you in there all the time playing the piano. Is she giving you lessons?"

"Yeah." I pause. "That's okay, isn't it?"

"It's more than okay," Naomi says. "I think it's terrific. You know, your company has done wonders for Lupe. I haven't seen her this relaxed since she arrived. You've done a marvelous thing, becoming her friend. Thank you."

I squirm uncomfortably in my seat. Would Naomi *really* throw Lupe out if she knew about Chili? "Actually," I say, "she's become *my* friend. She's a pretty awesome lady."

Naomi grins and nods. "I agree. So, what did you want to ask me?" she asks, picking up her cigarette. I watch as she exhales and then crushes the butt in the middle of the ashtray.

"I, um, wanted to ask you a favor."

"Anything," Naomi says. Smoke pours from her mouth and nose. "Anything at all."

"It's not really for me," I begin. "It's for a friend of mine."

"Go on," Naomi says.

I start to fidget. "Actually, it's for my friend's dad. Although, if you could do this thing for him, you would be helping her, too."

Naomi looks bemused. "You're gonna have to spill it, Hershey. I'm getting a little lost."

So I sit back and tell her the whole story. I tell her about Phoebe and what it was like meeting her for the first time and how she is the best friend I've ever had in my life. I tell Naomi how much Phoebe has done for me lately, with taking Augustus Gloop and being so supportive about the shelter. Then I tell her about Jack and how I think he is depressed about Phoebe's mother leaving them and that is why he can't stop drinking or getting out of bed and why he doesn't care he is doing something illegal like cheating the workers' comp system, even though I'm still not really sure what that is, exactly. Naomi listens to me with great interest. She doesn't interrupt me once. When I am finished, she sits forward in her chair and refolds her hands.

"Are you asking me if Jack and Phoebe can come live here?" she asks. My mind goes blank for a moment. Then I realize that I have left out the most important part.

"Oh, no!" I cover my mouth so that I don't start laughing. "No, it's not like that at all."

"Okay." Naomi looks slightly relieved. "Because this particular kind of shelter doesn't house men."

"I want you to give Jack a job," I say, taking a deep breath. "He's a carpenter and a pretty good one, from what Phoebe's told me, and you need the rest of your playroom built." Naomi's eyes widen. She tilts her head to the side and studies me for a long minute.

"Well," she says slowly. "I know you want to help your friend, Hershey, but I couldn't hire someone with a drinking problem. And you said he's also cheating the workers' compensation system?" My face gets hot. Why'd I have to tell her *everything*?

"Listen," I say. "Jack's not a bad guy. He just needs a chance. He's been out of work too long and he's depressed. That's all. He just needs someone to give him a job so he can get back to being himself again."

Naomi doodles on her pad for a few moments. I hold my breath. "I'd have to get references," she says slowly. "And see some kind of résumé. I can't just hire someone who doesn't have the qualifications."

I nod my head. "I'll tell Phoebe."

Naomi drums her fingers on top of the desk. "I am dying to get that playroom finished," she says, more to herself than to me. "I want it to be a den, too, for the women. It's been such a madhouse lately that I haven't been able to look for anyone else to do it."

"So you'll call Jack, then?" I ask.

Naomi pauses for a moment. "Yes," she says, sliding a piece of paper across the desk. "Write down his number and I'll call him. We'll see what happens."

My mouth is dry as I dial Phoebe's number a few minutes later. I'm scared for some reason, anticipating the sound of her voice.

I can tell she's been crying when she answers. Her nose is blocked and she keeps clearing her throat.

"Are you okay?" I ask.

"Yeah. I just hab a cold."

"How's Jack?"

"The same."

"How 'bout Augustus Gloop?"

"The same."

I clear my throat. "Listen, Phoebe. Does your dad have references?"

"References?" Phoebe repeats. There's an edge to her voice. "Like names of people he used to work for?"

"Yeah," I say. "Exactly."

"I guess. What do you wanna know *that* for?"

I tell her about the situation with Naomi and the play-room and the impending phone call. Phoebe doesn't answer right away. But when she does, she sounds skeptical.

"So she's really gonna call him?"

"That's what she said," I reply. "She needs someone to finish building this room and she hasn't had time to look for anyone else. But she's gonna need to see his references and stuff."

No answer.

"Phoebe?" I ask. "Are you still there?"

"Yeah," she says. "All right, I'll see what I can find. I know he has things like that around here."

"Okay." I stare at the rug.

"Okay."

"Um, I have to tell you something else," I say, swallowing hard.

"What?"

I take a deep breath. "I'm gonna be in the talent show." My heart is thudding in my ears. The silence on the other end is almost unbearable. I wonder if she's even heard me. "Me, I mean. By myself."

Phoebe blows her nose. "You gonna play the piano?"

"Yeah," I say, surprised. "I am."

More silence.

"Are you mad?" I ask softly.

Phoebe pauses, as if deliberating her answer. "No," she says finally. "You can do whatever you want. It's a free country."

"Yeah. I guess."

She clears her throat. "I'm gonna do the fire sticks, you know." There is an edge to her voice that makes me wince.

"The fire sticks?" I repeat. "You mean, you're gonna juggle with fire?"

"Yup."

"Phoebe. *Don't*. You'll hurt yourself. It takes years to learn how to do something like that."

"I've been practicing." She sounds annoyed.

"Where? I thought you said Jack wouldn't let—"

"Jack doesn't know what I do." Now she sounds *really* annoyed. "Or where I do it."

I think about Mom for a minute. I doubt she knows

anything at all about my trips down to see Lupe or that I am learning how to play the piano. Parents can be really out of it sometimes. "Well . . . ," I say uncertainly. "If that's what you want to do . . ."

"That's what I want to do," Phoebe answers. "Like I said, it's a free country."

Neither of us says anything for a minute.

"So I'll see you around?" I ask finally.

"Yeah," Phoebe says.

"Okay, then."

"Okay."

"Bye, Phoebe."

"Bye."

TWENTY-FOUR

My posture, Lupe says, is worse than an old lady's.

"Sit up straight!" she barks during another late-night practicing session. "You must look proud sitting in front of such an instrument, not like you are about to collapse from exhaustion!" To emphasize her point, she rams her index finger in between the middle vertebrae of my spine.

"Ouch!" I sit up with a jerk.

"That's it!" Lupe says, not moving her finger. "That is how you must sit, Hershey. Chin up! Shoulders back!" I give it my best effort for a few minutes as I replay the middle section of "Für Elise," which is giving me trouble again. It's faster than the first section, and trying to play it while worrying about how straight my back and chin and shoulders are feels kind of like trying to eat steak and mashed potatoes while roller-skating. On ice. I stumble on a section, reset my hands, and plunge in again. But Lupe's finger is starting to feel like a knife in my back. I can't concentrate. Finally I stop and push myself away from the bench.

"I can't do it with your finger digging into my back like that. It's distracting me." Lupe gives me an impatient look.

"Sit down," she says. "Do it again."

I cross my arms. "Not with your finger in my back."

Lupe pulls on her lower lip. "You need discipline, Hershey. It is a must if you are going to be great."

"Lupe," I say with a sigh. "I just need to be great for about three minutes on July fourth. That's it. All I want to do is learn 'Für Elise' and win the Sommersville talent show so that I can get a thousand dollars to give to my mom."

She wrinkles her forehead as I talk. "You are playing the piano to win money for your mother?" I nod my head slowly. I'm embarrassed all of a sudden, but I don't know why. "She does not have any money of her own?" Lupe asks.

I shake my head. "And if I don't get her some, she's going to go back to her boyfriend. I know it."

Lupe looks even more confused. "But why are *you* getting the money? You are only a child."

I cross my arms again. "I'm not a child. I'm thirteen years old."

"Your mother should be worried about getting the money," Lupe says firmly.

"Not the other way around."

I shrug. "Who cares *how* we get it? Just as long as we do. I just want to give Mom the chance to get the heck away from Slade and start over again for real."

Lupe looks at me for a long moment. "So there is a lot riding on this one performance, then, eh?" I nod. "And tell me, Hershey," Lupe says slowly, "what will you do if you don't win?"

I hang my head. "Then I'll lose my mom and my best friend." I pause. "All in one day."

Lupe narrows her eyes. "Let me tell you another story about Beethoven," she says, folding her hands in her lap. I scratch my nose impatiently. I don't really want to hear about Beethoven anymore. The guy was a genius, sure, but he lived a zillion years ago and has been dead for another million. What kind of experience from back then could possibly relate to what I'm going through now? Still, I know better than to interrupt Lupe when she is talking, so I stare at my nails and try hard to pay attention.

"When Beethoven was eighteen years old, he went to Vienna, Austria, to perform for Wolfgang Mozart." I raise my head.

"I've heard of Mozart," I say, thinking back to the time Miss Hardwick told us a little bit about him in third grade. She had a poster of him on the blackboard. He was standing next to a piano and had white powdered hair rolled up in tight curls on either side of his face, blue tights on his legs, and shiny black shoes with silver buckles on his feet. "Didn't he play the piano too?"

"Yes," Lupe answers. "He was even greater than Beethoven at the time he was alive."

"I thought you said Beethoven was the greatest."

Lupe's eyes flash. "I am trying to tell you a story, Hershey. Keep quiet."

"Well, that's what you *said*," I mumble.

"Beethoven was much younger than Mozart," Lupe explains impatiently. "He wrote scores of music for years after Mozart died, which made him the greatest of all time. At least as far as I'm concerned."

"Oh," I say. "Okay. Well, go ahead."

"Thank you." Lupe smoothes the wrinkles in her skirt. "Now, as I was saying, Beethoven went to Vienna when Mozart was still alive to play for him and, hopefully, to become his student. At that time Mozart was considered the best, and Beethoven wanted more than anything to study with him."

"So did he?" I ask. Lupe raises her finger and one eyebrow at the same time. I close my mouth.

"About three weeks after he arrived in Vienna, Beethoven received word that his mother was very sick. His mother, unlike his father, was a very loving and sweet woman. Beethoven could not bear to let her die alone.

So he rushed home to Bonn, which is in Germany, and stayed with his mother until she died. To make things even worse, a short time after his mother died, his baby sister died too."

I shut my eyes at the mention of a baby sister dying. Baby Ella's face floods my head, her beautiful blue eyes and blond curls, her chubby legs and fat fists.

"Also," Lupe continues, "Beethoven's father was drinking even more heavily than ever. The louse. And he still had two young sons at home, Beethoven's younger brothers, Casper and Nikolaus, whom he was neglecting just as he had neglected Beethoven."

Lupe folds and then refolds her hands. She looks at me with a steady gaze. "And so Beethoven did what you are doing now, Hershey."

I make a funny face. "He performed in a talent show to get money?" I ask.

Lupe shakes her head. "He took over responsibility for the family," she says softly. "With a dead mother and a father who might as well have been, Beethoven ran the house, cared for his two younger brothers, and tried to keep his father out of trouble."

"Did it work?"

"For a time. But he couldn't possibly do all of that every day and still continue to practice."

"Well, I won't need to practice after the show is over," I

say, staring at my hands. "I just need to play on July fourth. Just one day."

Lupe takes my hands into her own. "I will help you learn the piece for your show, Hershey. But you cannot throw this away." She pauses. "Look at me, Hershey." I raise my face and stare into Lupe's eyes. They are as dark as her hair. "You will use this gift in the show, yes, pepita, but then you must promise me that you will find a way to keep at it." I don't answer. Lupe squeezes my hands, as if demanding a response.

I shrug. "I guess. Although I don't know how I can, really. We'd never find the money for a piano, let alone be able to afford lessons."

"There is always a way," Lupe says, "if you want it enough. Eventually, Beethoven left his father and his brothers to go back to Vienna and study with another famous musician named Joseph Haydn."

I scratch my head. "And he really left his father and younger brothers behind, huh?"

"He did," Lupe answers. "Because he had to go fulfill his destiny, Hershey. But seven weeks after he left, his father died and the younger boys came to live with him in Vienna."

"Yeah?" I say, my whole face brightening. "They found him again?"

Lupe laughs. "It wasn't all fun and games, Hershey. The

three of them had lots of problems as they got older. But things can work out if you want something badly enough."

I'm not sure if Lupe is telling me this story because she wants me to leave Mom and Baby Ella someday and go practice piano professionally, or if she's telling me this story because she wants me to know that even two hundred years ago some cranky guy who played music like a dream had a life that in some ways was a little like mine. But whatever she's trying to do, it scares me.

"I'm scared," I tell her. "I don't know why you're telling me all this."

"Don't be scared," Lupe says. "I want you to know that there's someone out there, Hershey, who believes in you."

She cups my face in both of her hands and kisses me, first on the right cheek and then on the left. And somehow, although I am still scared, I know that Lupe, more than any other person in my life right now, understands me completely.

TWENTY-FIVE

Josie, Gracie, and Rose are huddled again around the Scrabble board when I come back upstairs from practicing. The light over the table has been dimmed and the floor has been scrubbed clean. The faint scent of Pine-Sol is still in the air. Since Gracie has been doing the dishes, the kitchen is absolutely spotless after every meal. I wonder if she kept her house looking the same way, and if that dork Bernie ever appreciated it. Rose looks tired, but I can tell by the gleam in Josie's eyes that she is still hot in competition with Gracie. Every few minutes Josie reaches inside a half-eaten bowl of Doritos and grabs a few while she scans her letters. Chewing furiously, her eyes dart from her letters to the board and back again.

"Come *on*," Gracie says. "You're already twenty seconds past your time limit." Josie holds up her hand and then begins arranging her tiles neatly on the board. Gracie watches her closely, shaking her head. "I bet you won every spelling bee in grade school."

"Ha *ha*!" Josie yells, jumping up and down in her seat.

"Triple score, *plus* double word! I believe that's . . ." She scribbles a few numbers down on her pad.

"Sixty-three points," Gracie says wearily.

"Holy cow," Rose says. "I didn't even know you could get that many points on one word."

"Ha *ha*!" Josie says again. Just then Gracie notices me standing a little ways behind them.

"What are you doing up so late?" she asks, tightening her bathrobe tie around her waist. A single pink foam curler holds a chunk of hair against her forehead.

"Oh, I couldn't sleep," I say. "I was just downstairs reading."

Josie makes a spitting sound with her lips. "Reading? You're not down there *read*ing."

"What do you mean?" I ask, as if I haven't heard her correctly.

Josie tilts her head ever so slightly to the right. Her T-shirt has a little white bunny on the front. Underneath the bunny's feet it says PSYCHO, BUT CUTE. THINGS EVEN OUT. "It *is* you playing the piano down there with Lupe every night, isn't it?"

I touch the front of my shirt. How does she know? And why would she care, anyway? I thought everyone here had written Lupe off as some crazy loon.

"So what if I am?" Josie raises her eyebrows as Gracie leans back a little.

"She's just asking," Gracie says. "You don't have to get touchy about it."

I'm embarrassed, but feel strangely justified, too. "Sorry."

"You sound really good," Rose says, smiling at me.

I turn to stare at her. "You can hear me?"

"Just when we stay up late to play Scrabble," Josie says, tapping the floor with her slipper. "The broom closet is right underneath the kitchen."

Somehow, I had forgotten that you could hear through the floor. "But how do you know it's me?"

"Lupe plays with more confidence," Josie says boldly. "You're still learning. You can hear it when you play. You're a little all over the place." Gracie shoots Josie a look. "What?" Josie demands, taking her cigarette out of her mouth. "I'm not being mean! I'm just saying it like it is."

"Well, thanks anyway. I'm going to bed." I turn to leave. "See you in the morning." But before I reach our door, Josie pounces again.

"Hey, Hershey?" she says. "We were just wondering if you knew where all our snacks in the kitchen cupboard went." I freeze. "You know, when we play Scrabble, we like to pull out the goodies we went and spent good money on and relax a little." Her voice is fierce. Rose stares at the Scrabble board.

"Hold up, Josie," Gracie murmurs. "We don't know if it

was her yet." There is a pause. "Did you eat all those snacks, Hershey?" I grimace and turn around slowly. There's no point in lying. But I'm so embarrassed I could die.

"Yeah," I say in a whisper. "I'm sorry." Josie makes a *pppfffttt* sound with her lips, but Gracie doesn't say a word. Neither do I. What else is there to say? Instead, I stare at the spot between my shoes, wishing that the floor would open up so I could fall into it.

"We put our names on them for a reason," Gracie says gently. "You shouldn't take them without asking." I nod, too stricken to answer aloud.

"I'll replace them," I say quickly, wondering how I'm going to explain to Mom that I need ten dollars to buy six bags of junk food. "I'll go to Wal-Mart tomorrow. I promise."

"I'll go with you, if you want," Rose says.

"So, what're you practicing on the piano all the time for, anyway?" Josie asks, changing the subject. "You got a recital coming up or something?"

Slowly, gratefully, my brain shifts gears. "I'm going to play in the Sommersville talent show."

Josie sits up a little bit straighter. "Oh *yeah*?" Her right eyebrow is arched high. "Me too. I'm singing 'Blue Bayou' by Linda Ronstadt. It's—"

"I'm *telling* you, Josie," Gracie interrupts, "nobody's ever heard of no Linda Ronstadt. You wanna go country, you'll be better off singing something by Shania Twain or Garth Brooks. Everybody knows them."

Josie sniffs. "Sellouts," she says. "Both of them. Linda Ronstadt is a classic. She's got a real voice, and 'Blue Bayou' is a real country song. You just wait." Josie looks at me again. "You counting on winning that big ol' money prize too, huh?" She's smiling, but her voice has a strange edge to it. I wish I hadn't said anything. But Gracie slaps the table hard with both hands.

"Well, I think it's terrific!" she says, her big mouth open wide. "We got two women from Sunrises Women's Shelter competing in Sommersville's centennial talent show! How *'bout* that?" She looks gleefully at Josie, and then at Rose, and finally at me. Her face is so shiny with joy that I can't help but break into a smile.

"So, what would you do if you won?" Josie asks, tossing her hair over a shoulder. "What would you do with a thousand dollars?" The blue dragon moves under her arm muscles as they tighten. It looks as if it is breathing puffs of real fire from its nose.

I look behind me, worried that Mom is listening. But the door to our room is shut tight. Leaning in, I lower my voice. "Actually, I'm sorta . . . trying to . . . help my mom out. You know, with trying to find us a new place and all. She doesn't really have any money."

Josie snorts. "You're thirteen, Hershey. It's your mother's

job to help *you* out." I shove my hands into my front pockets and grab on to the jeans material with my fingers. Josie is busy lighting another cigarette. Her left hand is trembling slightly.

"What're you worried about, Josie?" Rose asks with a grin. "Think Hershey here might give you a run for your money?" Her grin vanishes as Josie glares at her.

Suddenly I realize why Josie is acting so weird. This competition is about more—much more—than just being in the spotlight. Josie's entering because she needs the money. Desperately. Just like me. And Phoebe. Is it fair of me to be crowding the competition? Is the money Josie needs for a new apartment, maybe even to get food for Macy and Galvin, more important than our needs? And what about Phoebe? Is her reason for wanting to get away from her father any less desperate than Josie's? Or mine?

I close my eyes to stop the room from spinning. And as I do, Slade's face fills my mind's eye. It's just a quick flash, like a snapshot, but it fills my whole body with dread. If I don't do this, Mom will go back to him. There will be another horrible scene as he takes her into his arms and kisses her on the lips. Baby Ella will probably scramble all over him, yelling, *Daddy, Daddy.* I shake my head. She needs me. And if I'm being selfish by doing this, then I'm going to be selfish.

I pull one of my hands out of my pocket and point to my eye. "You see this?"

Rose and Gracie, who have been staring straight ahead at some invisible point in the middle of the table, look up in unison. Josie doesn't move. "This is what my mother's boyfriend did to me. A long time ago. And because she was too scared to live without him, my mother stayed. Even though he hurt me like this. So the way I see it, Josie, I don't have much of a choice about entering the talent show. It's either I win that money so we can get away from him for good, or nothing at all."

The smoke from Josie's cigarette, slithering up toward the ceiling, is the only movement in the room. I've said my piece. I turn to leave.

"Hershey," Josie says, just as I get to the door. I stop, but don't turn around. "I didn't . . . ," she starts. There is a catch in her voice; it breaks on the word "didn't." I turn around. Josie is blinking hard, squeezing back tears. She raises her cigarette and gives me a small grin.

"You know, may the best woman win," she says, her voice quavering. "And all that stuff."

I wish life wasn't so hard sometimes.

"Yeah," I say. "I hope so."

TWENTY-SIX

On the last day of school I run up to Phoebe just as she comes into homeroom, and pull her aside. We haven't talked much all week, except for an awkward "hi" and the occasional "see ya," and I'm still not sure where the heck we stand as far as being friends go, but I need to hear something about Augustus Gloop. It feels like forever since I last saw him.

"He's fine," Phoebe says, gently extricating the sleeve of her cardigan sweater from my fingers. "Still doing the same routine that I told you about." She scuffs the floor with the toe of her shoe. "Oh, he did bring home a dead mole last night. At least I think it was a mole. Maybe it was a really fat mouse. That's all right, isn't it?" She looks up at me. "I mean, if he goes on killing things like that?"

"Yeah, that's okay," I say, staring hard at her, wishing that I could get inside her head.

"How's the piano practice coming?"

"Good," I say. "Harder than I thought it would be."

"Yeah, well most things are, Hershey," Phoebe answers,

rubbing her nose. I feel the back of my throat closing over, because the way she's talking makes me think that, along with eighth grade, our friendship is ending forever. The first bell rings. "I'll see you around," Phoebe says, disappearing slowly among the sea of kids. "Call me if you want."

The last bus ride home is complete mayhem. Balled-up pieces of paper fly as thick as snowballs through the air. Someone has Madonna's *Ray of Light* CD screaming full blast from a portable stereo. The bass is thumping like a maniacal heartbeat, thrumming through my ears like a dull headache. The bus driver bellows at everyone to sit down, but the aisles are full of dancing kids celebrating the end of the school year. Andrea and Rhonda are up front, leering at some poor seventh grader.

"McLean Street!" the bus driver yells. I walk down the aisle toward the door, but Andrea stands up and blocks my path. A paper ball hits me in the back of the head.

"Do you know that when you're overweight, you *smell* more?" she asks, leaning in to make sure I can hear her voice over the music. "Especially in this heat?"

Rhonda cackles and claps her hands together like a seal.

"Get out of my way," I mutter. "Before I crush you like a bug."

Andrea steps aside obligingly, unfazed by my threat.

"I'll see you at the *talent* show, Hershey." She gives me a little salute with two fingers. I push by her and walk down the stairs to the sidewalk.

Hello, summer.

Mom's been assigned to cook dinner this week. She's alone in the kitchen chopping onions when I come in from school, a blue apron tied loosely over her shorts and T-shirt. Her hair is loose around her shoulders, tendrils wisping the sides of her face. The rest of the first floor is empty. Even the TV room down the hall is vacant. Aside from Mom's knife, which makes a dull thudding sound against the chopping block, the only sound in the room is the buzzing of a fly overhead.

I approach Mom cautiously, mostly because she's wielding a large knife so near her fingers, but also because it's been so long since we've spoken that I'm not sure what she'll do when I finally break the silence.

"Hi." My voice sounds weird, a little cloud adrift in an enormous sky.

"Hi," Mom says, not looking up from her onions.

"Last day of school."

"Great. Welcome to summer vacation."

"What are you making?"

"Texas-Chili Casserole." I cringe inwardly. I hate Texas-Chili Casserole, which, aside from its name, is not from

Texas—nor does it resemble chili. It's really just a huge blob of ground beef mixed with black beans, onions, rice, and a can of stewed tomatoes. The whole thing is spread into a big pan and then topped with grated cheese and baked until the cheese melts. Personally, I think it tastes like warm barf. Of course, it was Slade's favorite. He used to eat four or five helpings whenever Mom made it, scraping his plate clean as if he was a starving man. Afterward, he'd sit back in his chair, wipe the tomato juice off his chin with the back of his hand, and drain the last swallow from his third can of Bud Light.

"I'll tell you what, Daisy," he always said, burping loudly into a cupped hand. "You oughta enter that recipe in a contest or something. For real, darlin'. I can't get enough of it." Mom would beam from her end of the table and take a small sip of her first (and only) can of Bud Light. Slade liked it when Mom drank his beer with him.

"It looks good," I volunteer now, watching Mom's knife slice through the onion's translucent skin. In response, Mom brings her shoulder up toward her chin, wiping a trickle of sweat from the side of her face.

"Where's Baby Ella?" I ask as nonchalantly as possible.

"Napping," Mom answers. I drop my backpack. It lands with a thud on the floor.

Mom jumps and puts the knife down on the yellow

countertop. "What do you *want*, Hershey?"

I glare at her. "I want to know when you're going to start talking to me again." Mom's cheeks are pink and her forehead is shiny. Even under her apron, I can see that her T-shirt is damp with sweat.

"I *am* talking to you."

I take a step forward. "No, you're not. Ever since I said I wouldn't go with you if you went back—"

"Why would you ever say such a thing, anyway?" Mom shoots, finally turning to look at me. "Why, with everything going on, Hershey, would you want to make it that much harder for me?"

"Why is it so hard for *you* to choose between me and Slade?" I yell. "Why do you even have to stop and *think* about choosing between us? I'm your daughter, Mom! Your kid! Slade's nothing!" Mom's face turns pale as chalk. She grabs a corner of her apron and wipes her hands. They are shaking.

"I'm not . . . ," she starts, her voice wavering.

"You are! Just admit it, Mom! You love him more than you love me! That's why you went back to him the first time, even after he almost blinded me! That's why you'll go back to him now, even after he's hurt you and will probably do it again!"

"*Stop* it, Hershey!" Mom barks. Her voice is as sharp as glass. The muscles in her jaw twitch as she clenches her teeth. "You are not in charge of this family, and I won't have you acting like you are!"

"Well, somebody has to do it!"

Mom's nostrils flare white. "I'm *try*ing to make the best decisions here that I can," she says, measuring her words carefully. "Don't you understand how much there is to consider, Hershey? I have to find a place to live, a job, money, health insurance, clothes . . ."

"How about considering me?" I ask plainly. My back is stooped and I know that if Lupe was here, she would probably jab her finger into my back right now. I stand up a little straighter.

"Well, of course I'm considering you, Hershey—"

"You're not," I say. "Because you're not listening to anything I've told you. You've never listened to anything I've told you. Remember on the way back from Aunt Kemi's when you almost got into an accident with the car?" Mom looks confused for a split second and then drops her eyes, pretending to study the dirty yellow linoleum. "Remember I asked you not to go back—I *told* you I didn't want to go back, Mom?" Mom's eyes begin to fill with tears at the memory. She wrinkles her nose, presses the knuckle of her index finger under the bridge of it. "You told me back then that it would be different. You promised that things would get better."

"They *did* get better, Hershey!" Mom pleads.

"Look where we're standing, Mom! We're in a battered women's shelter! Just because things were *quiet* for a few years doesn't mean they got any better! They got worse, Mom! Why can't you see that?"

But Mom has no answer for me. She is bent over at the waist, clutching her belly, her nose nearly touching her knees. "Mom?" I rush toward her. She falls into me with her whole weight, and before I know it, we are both in a heap on the floor. "Mom! What's wrong? What is it?" But Mom's eyes are closed, her mouth slack from unconsciousness. For a second I think that she is dead, and my whole body gets cold. I grab her around both shoulders and shake her as hard as I can.

"Mom! Mom, wake up!" Her eyelids flutter as she stirs and a tiny moan escapes from her mouth. The sound is tiny and pitiful, like a baby cow. I sit back in shocked surprise and then yell for help, twisting my head around to look for someone, anyone.

"Help! Someone please help me! My mother's sick!" Mom is clutching at the front of her apron, clawing at the knot in the string. Her face is even whiter than before. The dark circles under her eyes look purple.

"Get—this—off," she pants. "It—hurts." I tear at the knot, struggling to untie it.

"Someone!" I scream again. "Please, help me!" I can hear the pounding of footsteps on the stairs. Kate appears all at once in the kitchen, breathless and frightened-looking. "Where is everyone?" I yell.

"I was downstairs," she says, surveying Mom quickly and dropping to her knees. "Naomi's still at court with the rest of the girls. What is it? Did she fall?"

I shake my head. "I don't know what it is." I am still pulling at the apron strings. "She just sort of sank to the ground all of a sudden. Please, help me get this off her. She says it's hurting her stomach." Kate grabs the string out of my hand and unties it quickly. She cradles Mom's head between her knees and pats her cheeks.

"Daisy!" she says sharply. Mom has closed her eyes again, but her body is still tense and rigid, as if something hurts inside. "Daisy? What happened? What's wrong? Did you faint?" Mom shakes her head the merest bit, but doesn't answer. Kate maneuvers Mom's head out from between her knees and motions to me.

"Stay here, Hershey. I'm going into the office to call 911." I bend my face down close to Mom's when her head is in my lap. She smells like onions and ground beef.

"Mom?" I whisper. "Do you know what's wrong?" She doesn't answer. Kate's voice comes hurtling through the hallway.

"Hershey!"

"Yeah?"

"They want to know if your mom has a history of seizures

or epilepsy!" Mom, who has heard the question, grimaces and moves her head from side to side again.

"No!" I yell back.

"How about high blood pressure?" Mom shakes her head again. She is sweating now and clutching her stomach.

"No!" I scream. "It's hurting worse, though! Tell them to hurry!" I stroke her face, which, despite the sweat, feels cold and clammy.

"It's going to be okay, Mom," I say. "No matter what, it's going to be okay. Just hang in there."

Mom squeezes my hand.

"Stay—with—Ella," she gasps. "She'll—be—scared—without—me."

"Okay," I say, tears starting to stream down my face. "Okay, Mom. I will."

TWENTY-SEVEN

Mom's hospital room is all white, except for the blood pressure machine next to her bed, which is blue. It beeps constantly, like a worried bird. Even the view outside her window, which, on the eighth floor, is nothing but sky, is white as a pearl. A pimply-faced nurse with red hair is blocking Mom from view when Kate, Baby Ella, and I walk in. She has Mom's wrist in her hand and is staring at the clock on the wall. I cough a little to make our presence known. The nurse turns her head, still moving her lips silently to the beat of Mom's pulse, and gives us a curt little nod. Finally, she drops Mom's hand and turns all the way around.

"Here to see Mommy?" she asks, smiling at Baby Ella. She is using that annoyingly fake voice that some adults use when they talk to kids, as if they are all idiots. Her name tag, which is in the shape of a little teddy bear, says RENEE. I squeeze Baby Ella's hand and nod grimly.

"Hershey? Ella?" Mom's voice sounds as weak as a baby's. I barrel past Renee, almost knocking her over, and get as close to Mom as I can without shoving the blood pressure machine across the room.

"Mama!" Baby Ella whimpers, holding out both of her chubby arms. I lift her up quickly, wedging her in tight between Mom and the edge of the bed. Baby Ella looks so small propped up against the wide pillows, like a little doll. Kate stands uncomfortably at the foot of the bed, with her arms crossed, watching us.

"I'm just going to wait outside," she says, taking a step backward. "You guys take your time." I smile gratefully at her. Kate had ordered me to put on my seat belt as she gunned the engine and threw the car into second gear. I started to object, protesting that I hated wearing seat belts, but stopped as my body flattened itself against the seat, compressed by the speed with which Kate began to drive. I snapped the belt around my chest as fast as I could and watched the red lights of the ambulance spinning in front of us. As nerve-racking as the ten-minute ride was, with Kate weaving in and out of traffic like some kind of lightning bug, I was thankful that she was putting forth such an effort for Mom.

I turn back to look at Mom as Kate leaves the room. Her face has regained some of its color, but her lips are dry and chapped. When she blinks, her eyes close for half a second longer than they should. I dig my hand into my pants pocket and pull out my cherry ChapStick.

"Mom," I breathe, dabbing at her lips with the lip balm. "Hi. How are you feeling? What did the doctor say?"

"Oh, she's going to be fine!" Renee exclaims, her voice so loud and overly cheery that I have to grit my teeth to stop myself from saying anything rude. "Your mom just ran out of gas, girls. She's plumb tuckered out! It's what we call heat exhaustion here in the hospital. The weather's been so hot these past few weeks that I'm surprised we don't have more people in here. But it's nothing that a good old rest won't cure." She arches a penciled eyebrow and points a finger at me. "You be sure to help out a little more now, especially with that little one. It's going to take your mother a few days to get back up and running again."

Thank you, Renee, I think. *Now could you please get lost?* Mom clears her throat weakly and nuzzles Baby Ella's hair.

"Well," Renee says, as if she knows exactly what Mom needs, but has decided not to permit it until she is good and ready, "I'll just leave you girls alone for a while to visit." She is rearranging the sheet around Mom while she talks, tucking it so tightly under Mom's arms that she looks like a stuffed sausage. "But like I said, your mother needs her rest right now. Ten minutes, all right? Then I'm going to have to come get you so Mom can get some more sleep." Mom smiles politely at Renee, but I stick my tongue out at her when she turns around again.

"Oh. And, Daisy, those test results will be back shortly, honey," Renee says, her hand on the door. "I'll be in again to let you know how they turned out." She gives Mom a wink. "I'm sure it's nothing to worry about."

"What tests?" I ask as soon as the door clicks shut. Mom shrugs, smoothing Ella's bangs off her forehead.

"Oh, they think I might have an ulcer or something silly like that," she says. "It's not a big deal."

"An ulcer?" I repeat. "Isn't that like a hole in your stomach? Is it serious? Can they fix it?" I watch as Baby Ella leans down, resting her cheek against Mom's chest, and sticks her thumb into her mouth.

"Don't get excited, Hershey," Mom says. "Ulcers aren't a big deal these days. Lots of people get them. They have medicine for them now and everything."

"Well, how did you get one?"

"First of all, honey, we don't even know if I have one yet. But the doctor couldn't find anything else wrong with my stomach, so now they're doing tests to see if that's the problem."

"So, what if you do have one? Where did it come from?"

Mom lets her head fall against one side of the pillow. "Oh, Hershey." She sounds exhausted again. "*I* don't know, honey. The doctor was saying something about being under a lot of stress. He thinks that might be why I fainted in the kitchen, and also why I've been feeling so tired lately."

"You've been feeling tired?" I repeat. "Why didn't you tell me?"

"I didn't want to worry you," Mom answers. "You've got enough going on right now, living where we're living, finishing up school. Besides, it's my problem, not yours." I take Mom's free hand in mine.

"Any problem of yours will always be mine, too, Mom."

I have to tell her, I realize. Right now. I have to tell her everything, all of it. If I don't, I will only be able to watch as the silence drives us farther and farther away from each other. If I don't, the only voice she will be able to hear is Slade's. Especially next week, when she sees him in court, and he comes charging over with my notebook. I watch Mom's hand slip up and down, over and over Baby Ella's soft hair.

"Mom," I say. "I have to tell you something." Her hand stops moving.

"What?" she asks. "What's wrong, Hershey? Did you fail eighth grade?" I look around for a chair. There's a red plastic one in the corner. I grab it and pull it up along the other side of Mom's bed and take her other hand in mine.

"No, I didn't flunk out of school, Mom. But I did something terrible." Mom tries to sit up, but her thin body is trapped between the sheets that Renee pulled so tightly over her. She makes a little whimpering sound and falls back against the pillow.

"Mama?" Baby Ella inquires, trying to sit up.

Mom strokes Baby Ella's head again. "I'm here, angel. I'm okay. Lie down with Mommy." Baby Ella settles herself down again on top of Mom and puts her thumb back into her mouth.

"Hershey," Mom says. "Tell me. Hurry up. Whatever it is, just tell me and get it over with."

I swallow hard. "It's my fault Slade hit you." I ignore the puzzled expression that comes over her face and press on. "It's my fault we're in the shelter and that you have an ulcer. It's all my—"

"Hershey, stop it. What are you even talking about?"

I shake my head. "No, Mom, you don't know. But I'm going to tell you the truth. I'm going to tell you the whole thing." I breathe in once, hard. "I was trying to drive Slade crazy. I kept a notebook and wrote down all the ways I could be as sloppy as possible, just to drive him nuts. I planned it, Mom. I planned it all out, week by week, just to make him mad." Tears are running down my cheeks.

"What do you mean, you *planned* it?" Mom asks.

"I wanted to get him mad. I wanted to get him all riled up again. I just thought . . ."

"What?" Mom whispers. "You thought what? Why would you want to make him mad, Hershey? Things are always so awful when he's . . ." She doesn't finish the sentence, but our eyes meet over Baby Ella's head and that silent communication thing happens between us. "Were you trying to make him hurt you again?" she asks.

"I didn't think he would *hurt* me again," I say, struggling for the truth. I want so much for everything I say right now to be completely accurate. "I was just hoping he would threaten me or say something terrible enough that would make you want to leave again."

"Oh, Hershey!" Mom cries. "Oh, honey!"

I bury my head in her side. "I never thought he would hit *you*!" I sob. "I never thought we'd end up in a shelter! I'm so sorry! I never meant for any of it to happen this way!"

"Oh, honey," Mom says. "Oh, honey, oh my God." She says it over and over again, like a windup doll, and then picks my face up between her hands. "You know how you just said a few minutes ago that any problem of mine will be yours?" I nod, feeling my lips start to quiver. "That's wrong, Hershey," Mom says. "You should never, ever feel like you have to take on my burdens. I am your mother, sweetheart. Your parent. I am the one that should be taking on *your* problems." I lean against her thin frame and let myself go. Great sobs roll up inside of me and then burst out, like waves crashing against the beach. Mom holds me tight. After a while, when I've settled down again, she lifts my tear-streaked face.

"I've treated you more like a sister instead of the mother you needed me to be, Hershey. You've never gotten to be a kid, because you've spent all your life waiting for me to grow up." She looks down at me with runny eyes. "Oh, honey, can you ever forgive me?"

I guess if Renee decides to barge in right about now, she'll have a heart attack, but I don't care what she does, because the only thing I want to do is get as close to my mother as I can. Renee can yell at me the rest of the afternoon if she wants, but I'm not getting out of this bed, or moving my head from under Mom's chin, because everything that I want in my life, everything that I need is right here, where I knew it always was.

The three of us lie there for what seems like a long time, not saying anything. Baby Ella's head is on one side of Mom's chest, and mine is on the other. Mom's arms are stretched around both of us, holding us tight. Baby Ella's slurping noises and the beeping sounds from the blood pressure machine hum in the background. I don't want to ruin the moment, but I have to know.

"Mom?" I say finally, not lifting my head from her chest.

"Hmmm?"

"You're not mad about the notebook?" Mom squeezes me tighter.

"No," she whispers. "I'm not mad about the notebook."

One down, one to go.

"Are you going to go back to Slade?" I can feel Mom's body stiffen under me at the mention of his name, but then it relaxes again.

"Shhhh, Hershey," Mom says. "You let me take care of things from now on."

It's not a yes.

But it's not a no, either.

TWENTY-EIGHT

I have a week left before the talent show. My eyelids snap open in the morning, despite my fatigue from last night's practice, and I don't stop to think about how much my bad eye hurts from staring at the music too long. Late at night, when my neck aches and my back feels as though it might collapse in on itself, I push on, playing "Für Elise" over and over. Tiny calluses bloom like mushroom caps on the pads of my fingertips. Lupe wraps Band-Aids around the ones that split and crack, and tells me to play it through one more time.

I keep my wincing to a minimum on Tuesday night, when, for an entire forty-five minutes, Lupe sticks her finger into my back.

"I wouldn't have to do that," she tells me afterward, "if I could pull a string up through the top of your head."

"I'll take the finger in my back," I reply, rubbing the irritated spot.

I don't object on Wednesday when she tells me to put my right hand behind my waist and play only the second chords with my left. It feels impossible, like trying to learn to write all over again—with my left hand. But Lupe says that the stronger my left hand becomes, the easier the notes will get for me to play. Physically, it's the hardest practice yet, and I leave the room at three in the morning, exhausted.

On Thursday, Lupe ties a soft cloth around my eyes and tells me to play the first two movements of "Für Elise" without stopping. I get through the first one, but stumble like a chicken flapping its wings through the second. She takes the blindfold off and tells me to look at the notes and play the second movement again. I do. Flawlessly. She puts the blindfold back over my eyes.

"Again," she says. I play the two movements again, seeing with my hands this time. I do not miss a single note. When I am done, I pull the blindfold off and turn to Lupe. She is the proudest I have ever seen her.

"You see, you know the music better than you think you do. Now listen to me. If your eye begins to hurt, do not be afraid to shut them both and keep playing. Your heart has eyes too, Hershey. You must trust it."

I float to bed, dreaming of thousand-dollar bills and supersize bags of Cheetos.

But Friday's practice is a mess. When I lay my hands on the keys, they are trembling. I cannot get through the first movement without faltering, and Lupe says that the music sounds "wooden," as if a robot is playing. I am seized with despair and cover my face with my hands.

"I can't play it!" I wail. "I'm not good enough!" Lupe turns my chin with two of her fingers until I am looking directly at her.

"Do you remember what Beethoven said about being the only one?" I shake my head, wiping my nose with the back of my hand.

"You didn't tell me that one."

"'What you are,'" Lupe recites slowly, "'you are by accident of birth; what I am, I am of myself. There are and will be thousands of princes. There is only one Beethoven.'"

"But that was Beethoven talking," I say miserably. "He was allowed to say that. He was great." Lupe shakes her head vigorously.

"You are not listening to the words," she says. "'*What I am, I am of myself.*' Do you know what that means, Hershey?"

"Not exactly."

"It means that there is no one else like you on the entire planet. Not even Beethoven could be what you are, Hershey. He couldn't look like you or act like you, or even play 'Für Elise' exactly the way you do."

"But he could play it pretty well," I point out.

"And so can you, pepita. You just don't believe that you can. You are going to have to find the kind of faith in yourself that will help you believe. Whesn you do, you will realize that you can play 'Für Elise' the only way you know how. With your heart. And when you do that, you will have made it yours."

My shoulders droop. To tell you the truth, I'm getting a little sick of all this talk about faith and believing and playing with your heart. I mean, come on. That stuff is *out* there, floating around with the clouds or something. I'm down here, stuck in the middle of a real predicament. All I need to do is figure out a way to not freak out this weekend so that I can play well enough to win the talent show. That's all. It doesn't have anything to do with my *heart*.

"So, where am I going to find all that faith in two days?" I ask.

Lupe rubs my back. "It's not as far as you think, Hershey." I fight the urge to roll my eyes as she pats my hand. "I want you to go upstairs and take a bath. Or go read a book. Watch some television. But don't think about playing for tonight. Try to be still, Hershey, and see what comes."

When the tub water is as hot as I can stand, I take off my clothes and step in, one foot at a time. My skin turns pink and the steam makes my breath catch in the back of my throat. Still, I sink down under the water, watching it swallow my body like ice melting on a pond. The heat makes it hard to breathe normally for a few minutes, but after a while I settle back and, with the water up to my chin, rest my arms on either side of the blue tile. I can't remember the last time I took a bath. I wonder how long it's been since Mom took one with her Jean Nate bubbles. I wonder how long it's been since she really relaxed at all. She looks much better since she has been on her new ulcer medication, but she is still taking things kind of slow, and Naomi has taken her off the chore chart for the rest of the week. She still doesn't know that I am going to be playing the piano in the talent show. But she's not going to the celebration anyway, in case Slade is there, so I'm not too worried about it. What I *am* worried about is getting up in front of all those people. The thought of people actually staring at me is enough to make me want to forget the whole thing. What if they laugh at me? What if someone points and says something like, *What's that fat girl with the freaky eye doing up there?*

Then there's Phoebe, who, if I know her at all, will most likely stay to watch me perform. I'll feel even worse if I don't win, going up against her. It's not that I want to beat Phoebe; it's that I want her to understand why I had to. I'm still holding on to a little glimmer of hope that when all of this is over, she'll see just how badly I needed to win. But if I get too nervous, I'll lose that chance—and her—forever.

My worrying has curled my toes over and clenched my

fingers into tight fists. I release them both underwater and sit up. At the opposite end of the tub, next to my feet, is a little string sack attached to the wall with a flat white suction cup. When I pull it off the tile, it makes a hollow popping sound. Inside is a blue tugboat with a red smokestack, three yellow rubber ducks (one with a missing beak), a pink starfish with red lips, and a blue porpoise with a large hole in the top of its head. They must be Macy and Galvin's toys. Or maybe Deletha's kids left them behind.

I pull everything out of the sack and lean back against the wall, watching the toys float on top of the water like a little rubber army. Before long I figure out that the smoke-stack on the tugboat makes a tooting sound if I press it, but immersed underwater, it sounds more like a cat drowning. I arrange the three little ducks on the soap dish above me and push each one off. The one who makes the biggest splash wins. Poor Mr. Beakless is at a distinct disadvan-tage. But I have the most fun with the rubber porpoise, filling its submarine-shaped body with water and blow-ing it out again through the dark blowhole. If I push hard enough, the water shoots up like a geyser, almost touch-ing the ceiling. I point the toy at the sliding glass doors and squirt water all over them. Then I turn it around and drench myself. A shriek escapes my lips as water shoots into my nose. Suddenly, there is a heavy knock on the door.

"Hello?" I ask, shrinking back under the water.

"Who's in there?" It's Gracie.

"Um, it's Hershey. I'm almost done."

"What are you *doing*?"

I open my mouth to let some warm water in and then spit it back out. "Just taking a bath." Gracie doesn't answer, but I can hear her walking back down the hall, muttering something under her breath.

I let myself sink all the way under the water so that she won't hear me giggling.

TWENTY-NINE

I toss and turn in bed the night before the talent show. There is no way I am going to be able to fall asleep. Waves of nausea sweep over me every time I think about getting up on that stage. Am I really going to be able to do it?

A tiny tap on my door makes me sit up and prick my ears. I wonder if I am just hearing things.

"Hershey!" someone whispers. I climb down from the top bunk, glancing at the clock on the wall. It's almost eleven p.m. When I open the door, Lupe is standing in the hallway. It's the first time I've ever seen her upstairs. She is wearing a long red and purple scarf over her head, the ends draped loosely around her neck, and a plain black dress.

"Lupe!" I whisper loudly. "What are you doing up here?" That's when I notice the little brown suitcase by her feet. It has a black handle and old-fashioned brass snaps running down the front of it.

"I am here to say good-bye," Lupe says softly. "I am going home. The taxi is coming for me."

"You're going *home*?" I step out of the room and shut the door carefully behind me. "Now? For real? Your papers came?" Lupe nods somberly and leads me over to one of the kitchen chairs. I can barely make out her face in the dark.

"Just this afternoon, pepita. I am taking a midnight flight back to Colombia."

My head is starting to spin. Lupe can't be going anywhere. She is coming to the talent show with me tomorrow. She is going to sit on the bench next to me and turn the pages of my book. She is going to be the one who will lend me the confidence and strength I will need to get through the piece.

"But . . . but . . . ," I say helplessly. "The talent show . . . I can't do it without you. I need you . . ."

Lupe folds my hands into her own, first pressing them to her lips, and then resting her cheek against my palm. After a moment she lifts her head again and looks at me.

"You will be fine tomorrow." Her voice is a fierce whisper. "You do not need me, Hershey. You just think you do. You know the piece perfectly. It is yours." I feel sick to my stomach. I bite my lip and push back the lump in my throat.

"I j-just . . . ," I stammer. "I just feel so much better when you're around. I don't worry about my eye or being—" Lupe brings her finger to her lips.

"Shhh," she says, cupping my face in her small brown hands. "You are perfect just the way you are. You are enough, Hershey, just the way you are."

I stare hard at Lupe's face. She looks different for some reason. Suddenly I realize what it is. The little white Band-Aid across her nose is gone and there are no more bruises around her eyes. She looks beautiful.

Lupe's fingers are moving quietly behind her neck, fiddling with something. The necklace and her medallion slip into her hands. When she takes it and puts it around my neck, I almost stop breathing.

"No, Lupe," I say, touching the silver disc. "I can't. . . . Your mother . . ." But Lupe makes that *tsskk* sound with her mouth and pulls back a little to admire the way the necklace drapes on me. She smiles widely.

"Sí," she says. "It is perfect." I let my fingers trail over the cold, slightly rough silver surface. "Promise me one thing," she says, holding up a finger. I nod mutely.

"Promise me that you won't forget what it means, Hershey."

I blush. "I forget already. Will you tell me again?"

"It is the memory of the heart that eliminates the bad and magnifies the good." Lupe leans over and kisses me hard on both cheeks. "And it is true. You will see."

A loud honk outside interrupts the moment. Kate opens the office door.

"All set, Lupe?" she whispers.

Lupe stands up. "Sí."

"Hi, Hershey," Kate says. "What are you doing up so late?"

I wipe my eyes. "Just saying good-bye."

Kate nods. "I'll wait outside for you, Lupe."

I look back at Lupe. "Where is Chili?" I whisper. She reaches into her pants pocket and withdraws the little chinchilla.

"I had to leave the cage downstairs," she said. "So that no one would see me taking her out." She lets me pet the animal on the back. Chili trembles, her ribs moving in and out as she takes short, shallow breaths. "Thank you for keeping her a secret," Lupe says.

I smile at her. "Can I carry your suitcase?"

She shakes her head and slips Chili back inside her pocket. "You stay inside. Go back to bed. Think about what I told you. And try to get some sleep so that you are fresh for your debut tomorrow."

I cling to Lupe as she hugs me good-bye. Her scarf is soft under my fingers. I don't think I will ever see her again.

"Thank you," I whisper into her ear. "For everything."

"And you," Lupe says, holding me at arm's length. "For being my friend."

I watch as she walks down the hallway, the dim light

overhead making shadows of her small shape on the wall. When she reaches the door, Lupe turns around again.

"Remember!" she calls out. "Keep those hands round and your arch high! And sit up straight, Hershey! Be proud!"

I wave, unable to get any words out around the lump in my throat, as the front door shuts softly behind Lupe. The floor beneath me feels wobbly, like I am standing on a water bed, and my head is as light as a balloon. I sit down quickly, before I fall over, and press my forehead against the floor. The carpet smells like corn chips and dirt. Getting back up, I stagger out of the room and head downstairs.

The broom closet is completely dark. I stand in the middle of it, without turning on the light, and listen for the sound of Chili's feet scraping the bottom of her cage. Nothing. The silence is overwhelming, like being at the bottom of the ocean. I walk over to the piano slowly, sit down on the smooth bench, and close my eyes. *Please let me open my eyes and find out that this was just a dream. Please. Please be here.* I open my eyes slowly, already knowing, but looking around anyway, as if Lupe will emerge from the shadows.

"Dumb . . . Stupid . . ." I flip open the piano lid so hard that it smacks against the back of the instrument. "Stupid . . . Dumb . . ." Something catches my eye. I lean in, squinting at the new words carved roughly underneath the lid.

> *Courage! In spite of all bodily weaknesses*
> *my spirit shall rule.*
> —LUDWIG VAN BEETHOVEN

I whisper the sentence once, and then say it again, louder, my quavering voice gaining strength.

"Courage! Despite all bodily weaknesses, my spirit shall rule!"

It doesn't seem possible that someone like Beethoven— who wrote nine whole symphonies all by himself—needed courage. But what must it have been like for someone like him, someone whose *entire* life revolved around music, to lose his hearing? I remember how panicked I felt waking up from the operation on my eye, and not being able to see. My good eye was still okay, of course, but everything out of it looked lopsided. It was as if the whole world had been cut in half, leaving one side in total darkness. As my eye healed, the blackness faded, and then when I got my glasses, things really improved. But Beethoven never regained his hearing. And he lost it in both ears. Not just one.

"My spirit shall rule," I whisper.

Like the heart, I think, fingering Lupe's medallion.

Maybe these old guys knew something back then that I don't. Maybe it really *is* what's inside that counts.

Or maybe it's just enough to know that even Beethoven was frightened at times. Lupe knew that. Which must be why she left this here, behind, for me to find. She knew I would come back down and play again. She knew that her departure would frighten me. And that I would, more than anything else, need to know that being afraid was all right.

I shut the lid, turn around, and stand up.

"Okay," I whisper. "I think I'm ready."

THIRTY

The sound of sobbing wakes me up early the next morning. I sit up quickly, reaching for my glasses, and look around for Mom. She's still sleeping underneath me. Tiptoeing over to the door, I open it and peek out. Kate and Naomi are sitting at the kitchen table with Rose, who is resting her forehead against her bandaged hands. Kate is rubbing Rose's back, and Naomi is talking in a low voice. Rose keeps shaking her head and crying.

"I should have been there!" she wails. "I didn't want him to die all alone!" I shut the door and climb back into bed. I stare at the ceiling, trying hard to understand Rose's sadness, but it's difficult. Doesn't she understand that she's free now? That she can go and do whatever she wants without having to worry about getting hurt or screamed at? If Slade rolled over and died tomorrow, I'd probably go into the bathroom, lock the door, and do a little jig. *I don't understand adults,* I think. They're just so incredibly complicated.

• • •

Kate, Gracie, Josie, Macy, Galvin, and I board the ten fifteen bus at the corner of McLean Street, which will take us to downtown Sommersville for the centennial celebration. Rose is staying behind with Naomi, to try to figure out what to do next. The talent show doesn't start until three o'clock, but I want to get there early enough so that I have time to sign up, check out the piano they are providing for the show, and get myself ready. I am still shaken by Lupe's departure and need some time to familiarize myself with as much as possible before I play.

"Why isn't your mom coming?" Gracie asks as we settle ourselves into our seats.

"She's worried about running into her boyfriend," I reply.

Gracie snorts and looks over at Josie. "Our boys are in the slammer," she says. "Which is why we're going and *enjoying* ourselves."

"My mom has a job interview at noon at the Wal-Mart too. Ella's staying with Naomi till she gets back."

Gracie raises her eyebrows. "Wouldn't that be great if she got the job?"

I nod. I'm excited about Mom's interview, but I'm too distracted to give it any real kind of consideration. I make a note, though, to ask her about it tonight, after everything is over.

The day is hot and clear, with a blue, cloudless sky shimmering overhead. Josie and I eye each other nervously on the bus, and then look away again. Despite the fact that her nails are bitten down to almost nothing, Josie keeps gnawing on them, as if trying to get to the bone. Macy and Galvin are jumping up and down in their seats, tagging each other and screaming "Got you!" over and over again, until Josie finally yanks them both into sitting positions.

"Be quiet!" she yells. "You're giving me a headache!"

"I'm gonna get me some fried dough," Gracie says, draping her arms over the seat in front of her. "With lots of powdered sugar and honey on top."

"Me too!" Galvin yells.

"Quiet!" Josie barks.

"After that I want a sausage-and-pepper hoagie," Gracie adds. "And maybe some cotton candy and a bowl of fried onions."

"Me too!" screams Macy. Her hair has been pulled up into ponytails on either side of her head.

"I said quiet!" Josie bellows.

"You nervous or something, Josie?" Gracie asks.

Josie rolls her eyes and starts rummaging around in her purse. "I need a peppermint or something. I feel like I'm going to throw up."

Gracie waves her hand. "Oh, stop it. You know you're good, girl. Come on, let's hear a verse or two. It'll be good for you, practicing and all." I look out the window. I don't want to hear the song Josie's going to sing. It will just make me more nervous. Luckily, Josie's not up for it either. She shakes her head, staring into a compact mirror at her eyes, which have been coated thickly with purple liner and violet mascara. The makeup matches her dress, which is also a hideous purple shade.

"I don't want to risk scratching my voice. I shouldn't even be talking to you guys right now." She pulls out a pair of tweezers and starts to pluck her eyebrows.

"Girl, you do anything else to those eyes of yours, they're gonna fall outta your head," Gracie says.

Josie snorts. "Shows how much you know. The eyes are the most expressive part of your face. If the audience can't see mine, they won't be able to understand what it is I'm feeling while I'm singing."

"Oh, they'll see them all right," Gracie says. "But the only thing they're going to be thinking is that you're some kind of kook." Josie stops tweezing, her hand poised upright in the air.

"What, too much?"

"Not if you're trying to look like Tammy Faye Bakker," Gracie replies. Kate laughs, a loud guffawing sound that gets me giggling, even though I don't know who Tammy Faye Bakker is. Josie looks at the three of us, her lacquered eyes blazing.

"You all can just shove it!" She throws her tweezers and compact back into her makeup bag. "None of you know what you're talking about, anyway."

"Gimme!" Macy says, reaching across her mother for the makeup bag.

"Knock it off," Josie says. "God, you kids are going to drive me nuts today."

"Speak for yourself," Gracie says.

I slide my hand into the side pocket of my backpack. I pull Lupe's necklace out of it and hang it around my neck. The silver medallion sits, heavy and proud, against my chest.

Public Square has been transformed into a Sommersville wonderland. There are men, women, teenagers, babies, old people, and toddlers everywhere, walking, sitting, running, or skipping along the newly mowed green grass. Bright bunches of red, pink, and orange zinnias have been planted neatly along the perimeter of the lawn. Every tree trunk has a cluster of red, white, and blue balloons tied around its width; they dance and sway in the breeze like weightless lollipops. HAPPY 100TH BIRTHDAY, SOMMERSVILLE!! signs dangle from every available building, branch, and lamppost. A brass band is playing on the stage, smack-dab in the middle of everything, with an enormous red and white arch over the top, in case of rain. Booths selling potato pancakes, fresh-squeezed lemonade, fried dough, french fries, hoagies, gyros, fruit smoothies, ice cream, deep fried vegetables, and cold beer have been placed all along the square's periphery like fat little deli counters. People stand in long lines, waiting impatiently for their fill. The smell of oil and fat drippings, fried tomatoes, and sugared peanuts makes my stomach growl. But I don't have time to think about food. Not now.

Gracie and Kate and Macy and Galvin stand with their mouths agape, taking it all in, but I don't have time to do that, either. I push past them, angling my way around a sweaty potato pancake booth, and make my way toward the back of the stage, which is where the sign-up sheet for the talent show is posted. If you sign up before noon, you get your entrance fee waived. Josie is a few steps behind me. We eye the relatively long line in front of us with unease.

"Man," Josie says. "Why does there have to be so many contestants? They should have a cutoff number." I don't answer her. Someone in jeans and a red and white T-shirt is waving to me up ahead. I squint so that I can see better. It's Mavis, from Piggy's Place.

"Hey!" I say, as she darts out of line and grabs my hands. "I didn't recognize you without your uniform on! How are you, Mavis?" She looks at me carefully, as if she is searching for something. Her wig has been colored a lemony blond and she is wearing red lipstick that matches her shirt. A white bandanna, tied in a bow, sits neatly atop her hair.

"How are *you*, honey? Where've you been? I haven't seen you in the store in weeks!"

"Oh, you know," I lie. "I had finals and stuff the last few weeks of school. Things have been really busy. I just didn't have a chance to stop in." Mavis points to a spot somewhere behind me.

"Piggy's got a booth here," she says. "Lots of Lemon Meringue Miracles, honey." I grin. "Thanks. I'll swing by."

"You and Phoebe all ready for your big juggling act?" she asks.

Something moves in the pit of my stomach when I hear Phoebe's name. "No, actually, I'm doing my own thing."

"Oh, yeah?" Mavis asks. Her eyebrows meet in the middle of her forehead. "Like what?"

"I'm just playing a little song on the piano. No big deal."

Mavis nods and rubs my arm. "Well, you'll do great, Hershey. Whatever it is. I just know it."

"Thanks, Mavis." I look down at the long black box sitting by her feet. "Is that your saxophone?"

Mavis picks it up. Her body leans a little to the right from the weight of it. "Yes sir! You just wait, little lady. You ain't heard nothing yet!" She gives me a little kiss on the cheek. "I want to see you back in the store again, Hershey. Real soon, okay?"

"You got it," I say, watching her move back into the line. And then, four people ahead of Mavis, I see Phoebe's long black hair, brushed smooth and pulled back off her face with a wide silver clip. Andrea is next to her, leaning in close and whispering something into her ear. She catches my eye just as I start to look away, and jabs Phoebe with her finger. Phoebe lifts her head, glances at me, and then turns back around. My heart sinks. If only Lupe was here with me.

Josie, who is still gnawing on her nails, pulls her fingers out of her mouth for a second so that she can readjust the plunging neckline of her purple dress.

"What do you think, Hershey? You like this dress? You think it does anything for my figure?" I swallow hard. Between her new eye makeup and the dress, with its shiny crinkly material and slashed hem, Josie looks as if she has just wrapped herself up in a bunch of purple tinfoil and let Macy finger paint her face.

"Yeah, you know, it's fine."

"Fine? What does 'fine' mean?" Josie snaps. She yanks the thin straps up around her neck. Her tiny chest, which is embarrassingly exposed, lifts an inch. "I asked you if you thought it looked *good* on me." I scan her shape carelessly. Her collarbones jut out under her neck like wing nubs, and they are so hollow that I could fit a small apple into each one. Her arms are scrawny and needlelike. It's hard to believe that they don't snap under the weight of her kids.

"I'm not really crazy about it," I answer finally, as truthfully as I can.

Josie drops her arms. "What's wrong with it?"

"It just, you know, um, I've never seen you in a dress before. You always wear T-shirts and stuff."

"Not when I'm going to per*form*, Hershey. For crying out loud. You ever see the things Faith Hill wears when she gets up onstage? All those floor-length gowns and dangly diamonds dripping from her ears?" She looks me up and down critically. "You can't go up onstage looking like you just rolled out of bed or something." I hold my white T-shirt slightly away from my body and peer down at my jeans. I hadn't given much thought to any kind of outfit. "And what's with the voodoo medal?" Josie asks, staring at Lupe's medallion hanging in the middle of my chest. "That for good luck or something?"

"Yeah," I say. "Or something."

Josie snorts. "You could've at least ironed your shirt, Hershey."

I look down at it again. "Why, what's wrong with it?"

"Nothing's *wrong* with it. If you're going to be sitting on the sofa, watching TV all day."

"Oh, but going out in public looking like some sort of

demented prom queen is okay?" I'm sorry as soon as the words come out of my mouth, but it is too late.

Josie puts her hands on her hips and licks her dry lips slowly. "That's not very nice. This is the only dress I have, you know."

I press my lips together tightly. "I didn't mean it. I'm sorry. I'm just nervous." Josie tosses her head and laughs lightly.

"Look at us. Picking at each other's outfits like two kids." She tosses her arm around one of my shoulders. "Let's have some fun today, if we can, okay?"

I smile and nod. "Okay."

THIRTY-ONE

I want to wander off and do my own thing, maybe buy a bingo card or play the game where you have to throw a Ping-Pong ball into a goldfish bowl, so that I can win a prize for Baby Ella, but Kate keeps insisting that we all have to stay together in a group.

"I'm not going crazy at the end of the day trying to round everyone up," she says. "We have to be back by nine o'clock sharp, and if we miss the bus, Naomi will kill me." So I put my head down and trudge behind Josie, whose dress makes a crinkling sound every time she moves, and Macy and Galvin, who have not stopped screaming "I want this! I want that!" since we got here. Gracie and Kate are at the front of the group, deep in conversation about what food to try next. We stand in line first at the potato pancake booth, then the sweet-pepper-and-sausage line, and finally the shaved-ice line, none of which have appealed to my stomach. It's not that I'm not hungry, it's that I'm sure if I eat anything, even a cherry-lime ice in a paper cup, I'll throw it up as soon as I get onstage.

Macy and Galvin pull on Josie's arms, screaming to be let into the kid's tent up ahead. It has tables set up with bottles, colored sand, finger painting, an ongoing game of Twister, and three different women dressed as mimes who are painting balloons and monkeys and fat red hearts on the children's cheeks.

Josie turns around to look at Kate. "We'll be in here for a little while," she says apologetically.

Kate claps her hands together. "Let's go!" she says brightly. "It looks fantastic!" Gracie and I head over to sit under an enormous oak tree a few feet away.

"Don't go anywhere without telling me!" Kate says. Gracie waves her hand and rolls her eyes.

"It's nice to have a babysitter when you're fifty years old," she says.

"You're *fifty*?" I ask, stretching out under the tree, trying to get comfortable. But I sit back up suddenly as I spot Phoebe, who has inexplicably appeared from nowhere and is standing in line at the fruit smoothie stand, tapping her foot impatiently. I look around closely, but I can't see Andrea anywhere.

"Yeah, I'm fifty," Gracie sighs, resting her head on the tree trunk next to me. "God help me. Don't get old, honey. It just gets harder." She fans herself with a greasy napkin left over from her potato pancakes. "Lord, it's hot out here." I watch as Phoebe scans the smoothie menu. I already know what she's going to order. "How come you haven't eaten anything yet, Hershey?" Gracie continues. "Your stomach in knots about playing up there onstage?" I smile as the man behind the counter hands Phoebe a banana smoothie. She takes a sip from the red straw sticking out of the top. Then I hear my name being called.

"Hershey, you listening to anything I'm saying?"

"What? I'm sorry. I was thinking about something else."

"I asked you why you weren't eating," Gracie repeats. "Are you nervous about having to play?" I nod, still keeping my eyes on Phoebe as she moves slowly through the crowd. *Look over here*, I say silently. *Over here, Phoebe, three feet past the smoothie stand. Under the big oak tree.* But she's moving away from us. In another moment she'll be gone again. I stand up quickly.

"Listen, if Kate comes back out, tell her I'll be right back," I say, brushing the grass off my pants. "I'm just going over there to talk to someone I know." Gracie looks alarmed.

"Who?" she asks.

I point impatiently toward Phoebe, who is moving farther and farther away by the second. "Right there, straight ahead. That girl with the long black hair. She's just a friend of mine from school. I've got to ask her something." Without waiting for a response, I push through the crowd and catch up breathlessly with Phoebe.

"Hey," I say, grabbing her gently by the elbow. Phoebe's eyes get big above the red straw. I can tell Andrea's done her makeup. All that electric blue eyeliner and mascara does nothing for her.

"Hey." Her voice is soft. "Where'd *you* come from?"

I shrug and point behind me. "I was just sitting under that tree over there when I saw you in the smoothie line."

Phoebe raises her plastic cup. "Still eating my bananas," she says. I smile. Phoebe ducks her head and takes another sip. There must be five hundred people swarming on every side of us, pushing one way and another, jostling us in and out of the crowd, but right now I can only see Phoebe. I stare stupidly at her.

"So, uh, where's Andrea?" I ask after a minute of silence, which has started to get uncomfortable. Phoebe rolls her eyes.

"Oh, she forgot her top hat," she says. "She had to run back to her mom's room at the Mandarin and get it."

"The Mandarin?" I repeat. "Andrea's mom lives at the Mandarin Motel?" Phoebe's cheeks turn pink and then scarlet. She bends her head again over the straw and pulls hard on it.

And then all of a sudden, like one of those telescopes you look through and turn until the picture gets crystal clear, I get it. Now I understand why Andrea suddenly stopped teasing Phoebe. And why she backed down from taunting me whenever Phoebe came into the picture. As if Phoebe knew something about her that she didn't want anyone else to know. Now I understand why it was so easy for Phoebe to ask Andrea—who is literally a few doors down from her at the motel—to take over my spot as her assistant, even if she does hate her guts. And why Andrea said yes.

Phoebe swallows hard.

"Hershey, I swear you can't tell anyone. Andrea would freak if she thought you knew."

"But she's been riding the bus I take at McLean Street," I say. "How . . ."

"Her mom and dad got divorced a few months ago," Phoebe says quickly. "Her dad still lives over there in the part of town you're in now. But her mom had to get a room at the motel. She has no money. Andrea splits her time between both of them."

So *that*'s why Andrea wasn't on the bus some days.

"But I've never seen her at the motel," I press. "All those times I came over to visit . . ."

"She and her mom live all the way at the other end. In number ten. And Andrea always hid whenever she knew you were coming over. After she found out Jack and I were living there, she made me swear that I'd never tell anyone."

"Why would she care if *I* knew?"

Phoebe shrugs. "I don't know. She probably just wanted to keep you scared of her. Just in case you found out. You know, she's pretty popular in that prep crowd. Everyone thinks she's got a ton of money." Phoebe pulls on her straw. "She'd probably lose a lot of them if they knew she was living in a motel."

I want to reach out and hug Phoebe, tell her what an amazing person she is, what a fantastic friend she has been, not only to me, but also, in a way, to someone like Andrea Wicker, whose awful secret she has kept. But I don't move. I can still feel the chasm between us, as wide and deep as the ocean, and I don't know how to cross it.

"Wow," I say finally. "Holy cow."

"Yeah," Phoebe looks steadily at me. "So you won't tell? Even though I know you hate her?"

I shake my head. "I won't tell."

Phoebe drains the last of her smoothie with a hollow gurgling sound. "So, you ready?"

"For what?"

She laughs. "For the show, you goof."

"Oh! The show!" I say, trying to hide my embarrassment. "Yeah, sure. Ready as I'll ever be, I guess. Are you?"

Phoebe nods and looks at her watch. "I will be, if Andrea ever gets back here. She's cutting it pretty close." Her eyes drift behind me, watching someone in the crowd. Suddenly she grabs my arm. "Let's go," she says, steering me with a viselike grip behind the booth for deep fried vegetables. The smell of oily cauliflower and broccoli fills the air around us.

"What's the matter?" I say, finally yanking my arm loose. Phoebe peeks out from behind the stand, keeping me at arm's length. After a moment she ducks back, flattening herself against the wide wooden slats of the food stand.

"It's *Slade!*" She puts her finger to her lips. "I don't think he saw us, but he's walking by right now! Just be quiet!" She peeks out again. "Okay," she says, still watching. "He's gone." She lifts up onto her tiptoes. "I can barely see the top of his head anymore."

"My mom was worried he might be here," I say. "That's why she didn't come."

Phoebe tilts her head. "You mean she's not going to see you play?"

"No. But it doesn't matter." *As long as I win,* I think, a surge of guilt cascading over me.

"Sure it matters!" Phoebe says. "This is going to be your debut!" She throws her empty smoothie cup into a garbage can nearby. "Listen, I've got to go wait for Andrea. I told her I'd meet her by the stage at two."

"Yeah," I say. "Okay." Phoebe sticks her hand out. I take her hand in mine. Her skin is cool from holding the smoothie cup.

"So good luck," she says, staring directly at me. "I'm looking forward to seeing your act, Hershey. For real." I shake Phoebe's hand, hard. I wonder if this is the last time I'll ever see her again.

"You too, Midnight Slim," I say. Phoebe grins and takes a step backward, still looking at me.

"Oh," she says, almost as an afterthought. "That Naomi lady called Jack yesterday."

"And?" I press.

Phoebe shrugs. "Don't know yet. She said she talked to a few of his references, though. And then she offered him the job. It's up to him now, right?" I nod. Phoebe opens her mouth once more, as if she wants to say something else.

But then she turns and, without another word, disappears into the crowd.

THIRTY-TWO

M ayor Sparks, who is tall, bald, and dressed for the occasion in a white tuxedo, looks like an albino penguin up onstage. He drones on and on about the long and boring history of Sommersville. The crowd, worn out from the day's events and full of fried food, listens restlessly. Finally, when it seems as though he will never shut up, Mayor Sparks waves his hand and says, "And now, ladies and gentlemen, what you have all been waiting most anxiously for! Please welcome our town's best and brightest as we begin Sommersville's first ever talent show!" The crowd roars with applause. Mayor Sparks beams and unfolds a piece of paper. "Our first competitor is none other than Mavis Miller, who will be playing the saxophone. Please welcome Mavis, ladies and gentlemen, and let the show begin!" The crowd hollers once more as Mavis steps confidently out onto the stage, carrying her saxophone. Her blue jeans ride up in the back and she has sweat stains under her T-shirt.

"Hey, Mavis!" someone yells out from the crowd. "How 'bout a large coffee, extra cream!"

"Maybe later!" Mavis hollers back. The crowd laughs along with her. She stands next to a three-legged stool, resting a foot on one of its crossbars. Flexing her mouth a few times, she brings the shiny gold instrument to her lips, closes her eyes, and begins to play.

I've never heard a saxophone played before, but I'm pretty sure that even a professional would consider Mavis to be among its better players. The song she plays is deep and low, the notes smooth and fluid, like honey being poured from a jar. She sways her body a little while she plays, as if the rhythm is moving her along, and never once opens her eyes. The crowd is as silent as a winter's day during the tune, but when Mavis finishes, simultaneously opening her eyes and lifting the horn from her lips, a shout erupts like a volcano. Even Mavis seems surprised. Flushed and sweating, she lifts her saxophone into the air and pumps her fist with her other hand.

"Be sure to stop by Piggy's booth!" she screams. "Free doughnut holes for the kids!"

I peek out from behind the curtain, where I have been told to wait with the other piano players. Josie's down behind the other end of the stage with all the other singers, still biting her nails. I scan the crowd nervously, looking for our little group from the shelter.

Instead, on the other side of the metal bleachers, I see Mom and Baby Ella. I blink my eyes and do a double take. *Mom?* Where did *she* come from? I thought she was back at the shelter, too nervous about running into Slade to come! I look out again. Mom's hair has been brushed back into a ponytail and she is wearing a green halter top that I've never seen before. She's just standing there with Baby Ella in her arms, her face as sad as anything I've ever seen. That's when I see Slade, who's almost completely hidden behind the other side of the bleachers, talking to her. Slade's waving his arms up and down while Mom just stands there like a cream puff, listening. Then Baby Ella stretches her arms out for Slade. I can see her little lips moving, saying "Daddy, Daddy." Just as Mom tilts her arms, letting Slade gather Baby Ella to his chest, I drop the curtain. I can't bear to watch. *This is my last chance*, I think. *If I don't win this money, we're toast.*

Storm McNally, dressed in green rubber boots, blue pants, and a red and black checked shirt strides out onto the stage. He's at least eighty years old. A fire hat from his days at the fire station rests atop his white hair like a plastic tomato.

"I'm gonna yodel," he informs the crowd. He stands with his feet spread apart and clears his throat. Something that sounds like a sick goat and screeching tires emanates from his mouth. It goes on and on, until finally he delivers a last, tremulous "ooooo" and throws his fire hat up into the air. The crowd brings their hands down from their ears, clapping politely, and Storm McNally leaves the stage with two thumbs way up in the air.

Next is Anne Randolph, who is six. She's carrying a pair of spoons in her right hand, and when she reaches the middle of the stage, she starts rapping them against each other like castanets. She starts off pretty well, banging the spoons off her thigh and then thrumming them against an outstretched arm, but when she reaches around her neck, she loses her rhythm and, throwing the spoons to the ground, storms offstage in disgust. The crowd claps supportively anyway.

Next the MacDougal brothers from Eastside High School perform a tumbling routine. They look like twins in their matching blue muscle shirts and white stirrup pants, but they are actually three years apart. Their performance includes a series of front tucks, handstands, flying leaps, and back handsprings, all side by side, in nearly perfect alignment. The crowd loves the MacDougal brothers. People jump to their feet, yelling for an encore when the boys leave the stage, and they oblige, reemerging into view with a breathless series of front aerials and side splits.

Next in line is Jenkins Lowry, who works at the Sommersville Library and imitates all kinds of birds. Jenkins is about three sizes larger than I am. Every time he lifts his hands to his mouth, the sweat stains under his blue shirt get bigger and bigger, widening under his arms like a pool filling with water. He imitates everything from a loon to the mating calls of a jungle macaw, but I find myself getting restless. It seems as if he has a hundred of them and that they will never, ever end.

Finally it's time for the singers. A male barbershop quartet, dressed in red vests and straw hats, sings a song I've never heard of. Their harmony is pitch perfect, their mouths open wide and so expressive that I can't help myself but join the crowd, which has begun to clap and yell along. The men finish as one, raising their arms straight up in the air, and the crowd thunders its approval.

Josie is next. I hold my breath as she totters out onto the stage, looking for all the world like a frightened little girl who has been playing in her mother's clothes closet.

"Come on, Josie," I whisper fiercely to myself. "You can do this." There are a few whistles from the crowd, which seem to unsettle Josie. Positioning herself awkwardly on the stool, she starts to fiddle again with the neckline of her dress and pull at her earlobes. When her background music for "Blue Bayou" comes on, she startles, and then raises the microphone to her mouth like an ice-cream cone. Her voice comes out in a whisper.

"Let's go, Mama!" A plaintive cry floats over the crowd. It's Galvin. He's on Gracie's shoulders, waving his arm so hard that it looks like he might dislocate his shoulder. And at the sound of his voice, Josie's whole body relaxes. She stands up in her horrible purple dress, and looks out toward her little boy and sings. She sings to Macy, too, who is on Kate's shoulders, her little hands clasped tightly together.

It's a slow, sad song about a girl who's saving up money so that she can go back to a place called Blue Bayou. "I'm going back someday, come what may, to Blue Bayou," Josie sings, and my heart feels like it is going to break in two, as I realize for the first time that maybe the two of us are performing for exactly the same reason.

The last note of the song is so high and so long that I close my eyes and squeeze them tight, waiting for Josie's voice to crack or squeak. But it does neither, and when she finishes, her head thrown back like a rock star, I leap to my feet with the rest of the crowd and scream until I am hoarse. Josie stands there for a moment, looking stunned. Then she rushes toward me as she descends the back stairs, her mascara gathered in oily little creases at the corners of her eyes. She is speechless, but her eyes are shining.

"You did it!" I yell, grabbing her around the shoulders. "You were fantastic!" She hugs me tight, her dress crinkling and crackling all around her.

"You're next," she says, when she finally pulls away again.

"I'm going to go sit with the kids. Good luck, Hershey." I watch as she snakes her way through the crowd, various people patting her on the back, nodding with pleased looks on their faces. Josie's face is glowing with pride and relief.

Mayor Sparks comes back out onstage and tries to distract the crowd with a horrible joke about a lady with a wooden leg, as three men move the piano behind him. There is a terrible groaning sound as the piano is dragged toward the center of the stage. The crowd boos Mayor Sparks as he delivers the dumb punch line. He blushes and wipes a band of sweat from his forehead. Stepping back with relief, he introduces Dr. Leopold, the town's ophthalmologist, as the next contestant.

Dr. Leopold, who has gray hair and tiny silver spectacles perched on his nose, is wearing a beautiful navy three-piece suit. He strides purposefully onstage and centers himself on the long bench. I make a note to myself to keep my back as straight as his. I try to imagine Lupe's finger in the middle of my spine. Dr. Leopold tells the crowd that he is going to be playing a piece by Mozart, called Fugue Something or Other. My hearing is going, I realize, as I watch his broad hands descend upon the keys and start to move up and down the ivory bars. It is a very fast piece, full of drama and excitement, but I don't hear a note of it. I am far back in my own head, trying to remember the things Lupe taught me: fingers round, arch high, back straight, feel the music, try to love it. I think of the things Beethoven said: There is only one Beethoven. What I am, I am of myself. *I can do this,* I think, as a smattering of applause ripples across the crowd, signaling the end of Dr. Leopold's performance.

"Next," Mayor Sparks says, his shoulders sagging ever so slightly under his white tuxedo jacket, "we have Miss Hershey Hollenback, also on piano. She will be playing 'Für Elise,' written by Ludwig van Beethoven." The crowd claps politely, nothing like the roars for Josie or the MacDougal brothers. I look out at the crowd as I come out onstage, instantly wishing that I hadn't. My breath catches in my throat as I stare at the sea of them, a field of strange faces that are now looking directly at me. I would give anything to hide the way my legs wobble back and forth, or my jiggling stomach . . . *Stop it,* I tell myself fiercely. *I am not playing for the crowd. I am playing to win one thousand dollars so that Mom and Baby Ella and I can get a place of our own and leave Slade behind forever.* Arranging myself on the piano bench, I close my eyes and touch the medallion briefly, trying to center myself.

Please, I whisper, hoping no one can see my lips moving from where they are sitting. *Please, Beethoven, help me to get behind the music. Help me to feel it the way you did— even just a little bit.*

My bad eye twitches. I push my glasses up along my

ears and rest my fingers lightly on the keys. The crowd is quiet, waiting.

I begin, pressing the slow, lovely melody out from the keys as nimbly and confidently as I ever have. I am overwhelmed by how beautiful the music is, as I am every time I sit down to play it. My body moves back and forth as my fingers segue seamlessly into the second segment. This part is slightly faster, and a different melody, but I know it well. I close my eyes, feeling it fill my chest like water.

And then, like a glass being smashed in a silent room, a yell bursts out from the crowd. My ears fly open again as the horrible words shoot over six hundred heads and plunge like an arrow into the center of my heart:

"Give it up, you cow!"

I know it's Slade even before I open my eyes, and in that split second I tell myself that I don't care, that the money means more than anything he can ever say to me, but my hands are stumbling over the keys, and before I know it, I have stopped playing and am sitting there like a big dumb walrus in front of the whole crowd.

For a full two seconds the crowd is silent, Slade's words reverberating over the whole of them like a terrible echo. And then, as if everyone is stuck together at the hip, men and women, children and old ladies rise as one and boo Slade with a deafening bellow.

"Get him out of here!" one woman screams.

"You loser!" someone else yells. "What's the matter with you?"

So many people are standing up and screaming at him, in fact, that a policeman comes rushing forward and pulls Slade away from their pointed, menacing fingers. As the policeman leads Slade, who, obviously drunk, is pointing back at the crowd and yelling his own favorite curse words at the top of his lungs, to his patrol car, the crowd cheers wildly. After a few more minutes things settle down for good and Mayor Sparks hurries back out onstage.

"Well," he says nervously. "That was an unfortunate incident." He looks over at me with a desperate expression. "Are you all right, young lady?" I just stare down at the keys. Mayor Sparks nods and blots his forehead again. "I would like to point out that despite such a singular example of ugliness, our town's sense of unity has just been expressed. I personally have never seen so many people take a stand like you just did." The crowd claps frantically.

"Play some more, Hershey!" comes a shout from the crowd. It's Mavis. She's in the front row, blotting her forehead with her bandanna. "You can do it, sweetheart!" "Yes, keep going!" comes another voice. I recognize Kate. And then Gracie. Mayor Sparks grins stupidly at me. He has huge teeth, like a horse.

"Well now, it looks like the fine citizens of Sommersville

would like to hear you finish your piece," he announces. "Is that right?" The rest of the crowd roars their answer. Overwhelmed, I nod weakly at Mayor Sparks, turn back to the piano, and try again.

But I can't get back to the place I was before. Try as I might, no pictures of Beethoven come to my head, no sadness fills my chest, and the only thing I can feel inside is just a horrible numbness. I stare at the slender keys under my calloused fingers as they begin to blur through my tears. There is no way I am going to cry. Especially not in front of hundreds of people. And so I just sit there, holding my breath.

And then I remember what Lupe said about trying to have faith in myself. That if I can believe in my heart, somehow the rest will come. I close my eyes.

"It is the memory of the heart that eliminates the bad and magnifies the good."

I will forget about the part that hurts right now and magnify the good instead. I will play the piano because I can and because I have practiced until my fingers have swelled and because I will never forgive myself if I do not. I close my eyes and see the notes in my head. My heart. I open my hands and place them back on the keys. And I play.

I know I have played as well as I ever have when I finish the piece. I rise as the crowd begins to applaud, and I take a bow. The medallion swings under me as I lower my head. Today, against the sun, the beautiful Spanish words etched in silver look like tiny wings.

Mayor Sparks's voice crackles over the intercom.

"And now, ladies and gentlemen, we're going to end our show with an amazing juggling duo."

I walk around to the left side of the stage to watch for Phoebe and Andrea's grand entrance. My heart sinks a little as Andrea emerges first, wearing one of the outfits Phoebe and I picked out months earlier: a black leotard, black leggings, a top hat, and a little silk cape tied loosely around her shoulders. She strides nervously toward the other end of the stage, pulling Phoebe's little red box, which is on wheels now, behind her. Untying the sash from her cape, Andrea rips it off her shoulders and cracks it in the air.

"And now!" she announces, throwing her cape to the ground and flinging her arm up into the air. (*My flourish would have killed her flourish,* I say to myself.) "May I introduce to you the one and only, the first and foremost, the dazzling and dizzying *Phoebe Millright!*" What happened to Midnight Slim? Why isn't Phoebe using her stage name?

Phoebe cartwheels out onstage, landing on one knee and opens her arms to embrace the crowd. Andrea, in turn, throws open the trunk, and one by one tosses

Phoebe four lightbulbs. Phoebe, still on one knee, juggles the lightbulbs so quickly, first forward and then backward, inverting them and then reversing them, that the crowd begins to applaud before she is finished. Next, Andrea tosses her six rolls of toilet paper. The crowd laughs when they see what it is and cheer again as Phoebe juggles them two at a time, three at a time, and finally all six at once. At one point, the rolls are spinning so rapidly in a circle above her head that they look like a cloud. Phoebe is sweating by the time Andrea throws her the bowling pins. Her forehead has knotted itself into one big line, and her legs are staggering beneath her. Six small saucepans are next, followed by two sets of tea cups (with the saucers), and then four large picture frames, their edges slicing the air with a hollow whistling sound. Phoebe doesn't drop a single thing. By now the crowd is up on its feet, shouting her name.

"Phoe-be! Phoe-be! Phoe-be!" Andrea puts the last of the picture frames away in the box and raises her hand for quiet.

"And now," she says in an ominous tone, "the great and glorious Phoebe Millright will attempt to juggle not one, not two, but three fire sticks with her own two hands." The crowd gasps as Andrea pulls three black sticks out of the box and holds a lighter to one end of one of them. It ignites in a whoosh of flame.

My chest tightens, watching her. There's no way Phoebe can really be doing this. There can't possibly have been enough time for her to practice. She's going to burn herself, all for a stupid show. I step forward, my fist in my mouth, ready to jump onstage should Phoebe falter the slightest bit, as Andrea finishes lighting the second and then the third stake. She holds them all in one hand over her head, like an enormous burning flower. And then, one by one, she tosses them to Phoebe. I don't take a single breath the entire time Phoebe has the sticks in the air, nor do I take my eyes off her fists, which somehow, miraculously, manage to grab the unlit end of every stick that comes around. I don't think the crowd does, either. It is a glorious thing, watching her juggle. The fire twists and whirls above her, a wheel of flame, a spinning sun in its own orbit. Phoebe finishes by catching each stick one last time as it descends past her head, holding the bouquet of fire victoriously aloft as the crowd screams with delight.

I sink to my knees and hang on to the edge of the stage, overcome with relief that she has not been hurt. Andrea lifts Phoebe's arm, and side by side the two girls leave the stage. It has been a thunderous show, and the crowd, exhausted and happy, cheers Mayor Sparks one last time as he comes back onstage.

The winner, he says, will be announced shortly.

THIRTY-THREE

"Hershey?" The voice is behind me. "Are you okay?" Mom's face is red and swollen, her eyes a hazy purple color. Baby Ella holds out her arms.

"Shee!" she yells. "Shee onstage!" I hold my sister tightly, afraid to let go. She has blue cotton candy in her hair. Mom is crying new tears, watching us together.

"Why are you crying?" I ask. Mom laughs a little, embarrassed.

"Why am I *crying*?" she repeats. "Hershey *Hollen*back! When did you learn to play a piano like that? And how did you learn 'Für Elise'? The whole thing, baby! The whole thing!" I stare at Baby Ella's cheek, which is also covered with cotton candy, and shrug.

"I made friends with the lady we met the first night at the shelter. Lupe. She taught me."

Mom shakes her head, still crying. "That was you?" she asks. "All those nights when I heard the piano through the floor? That was *you* playing?" I nod. Mom reaches out and touches my cheek. "Rose told me when I got back from my job interview that you were going to play. She asked me if I was nervous for you. I didn't know what she was talking about! But she insisted that you had been playing the piano and that you were going to perform today, which is why we came. But, honey, how did you learn to play something like Beethoven in two weeks? It's like a miracle, honey!"

"Mir-cle!" Baby Ella shouts, clapping her hands on either side of my face.

"I wasn't so good," I say, extricating Baby Ella's sticky hands from my cheeks. "I lost my concentration after Slade—" Mom steps forward.

"Hershey," she says. "I had Slade arrested."

I look up. "What do you mean?"

"I mean I had him arrested and taken to jail," she repeats. "He violated the protection order by talking to me here, and when I told him to get lost, he wouldn't. Then, after he yelled at you and the policeman took him to his car, he started hollering horrible things at me. I told the policeman I wanted to press charges."

"But I saw you talking to him," I say. "I *saw* you give Baby Ella to him."

Mom takes my free hand. "Honey," she says. "Ella is Slade's daughter. Whenever we work out a custody agreement with the courts, he's going to be given permission to see her, probably once a week. I can't prevent that." She squeezes my hand. "And Ella loves him, Hershey. He's her daddy. She wanted to give him a hug when she saw him, and I let her."

"And then what?" I ask suspiciously.

"And then he wanted me to go for a walk with him and talk and blah, blah, blah," Mom says. "That's when I told him to get lost. He was so angry, Hershey. That's why I think he yelled out to you when he did. He just didn't have anything else left. And you've always been the one . . . " She stops, heaving with sobs. "The one he takes it out on when he can't have me."

"So what was different this time?"

"Me," Mom says, her eyes getting wet again. "I was different this time. I realized that I wanted my girls more than I ever thought I wanted Slade West."

"For real?" I ask, hope surging over the edges of my voice.

"For real," Mom says. "For real, Hershey. You've got to believe me, honey. Please."

"Will you stay away from him even if I don't win the money today?" I ask.

"What money?" Mom asks.

I nod toward the stage. "The talent show money. First prize is a thousand dollars."

Mom looks uncertainly at me for a second and then closes her fingers around her mouth. "That's why you played, Hershey? To win the money? For me?"

"For us," I say. "I thought if I could give you a thousand dollars and we could find a new place and start over, you wouldn't go . . . " But I can't finish the sentence. My voice is cracking, thinking about the lost money, how I failed myself, my mother, my family. But Mom has gathered me in her arms anyway; she is crying so hard against my neck that I can feel her body trembling against mine.

"Mama!" Baby Ella says, pulling at Mom's hair, trying to get her to right herself again. "Mama, up! No sad!" Mom pulls herself back up and smiles broadly through her tears for Baby Ella.

"No sad," she says, brushing her tears away. "No sad, Ella. Look." Baby Ella grins and claps her hands.

"Hap-pee! Hap-pee!" Mom and I start to laugh as Baby Ella's face lights up, and then Mom puts her arms around me again.

"I just had no idea, Hershey. You overwhelm me."

"Don't get too excited," I say softly. "I know I didn't win."

"No, Hershey," Mom says, cupping my face in her palms. "You did win. Maybe not the money, maybe not the prize, but you won." She strokes my cheek with the back of her finger. "Oh, my love, did you ever win."

"Ladies and gentleman!" Mayor Sparks's voice booms over the intercom. "May I have your attention please!"

I pull Mom toward the bleachers. "Let's sit over here."

It's so hot out that I feel like I might throw up. As we wind our way through the crowd, I catch sight of Phoebe and Andrea on the other side of the stands. They have been piling Phoebe's juggling items into her suitcase, but at the sound of Mayor Sparks's voice, they both stand up straight and look toward the stage. Phoebe turns her head as Mom and I climb up the bleachers. I give her a thumbs up. *You were amazing*, I mouth. She grins and winks at me. Behind her, Andrea is watching us. I press my lips together and give her a little wave. And when I do that, her whole face breaks open into a smile. It's a real one too, not one of those horrible fake kinds that people give you when they're trying to be nice. It makes her look really, really pretty. She puts her hand over her mouth suddenly, as if she has been caught doing something forbidden, and turns back around.

"We have the winners!" Mayor Sparks says. A ripple of excitement charges through the crowd. Even Baby Ella strains forward, clapping her hands. "Third place goes to . . ." A drumroll sounds as Mayor Sparks opens a sheet of paper. "Mavis Miller!" The crowd roars as Mavis rushes to the stage, pumping her fist in the air again. I leap to my feet, clapping like crazy. My hands are hot and the back of my shirt is sticking to me. The drum sounds once more. "Second place . . ." The drum gets louder. "The MacDougal brothers!" The young gymnasts appear from behind the curtain, accepting their (slightly larger) trophy with smiles and nods of their heads. Then, in unison, they do a backflip, right there, in front of Mayor Sparks. The crowd cheers.

"And now," Mayor Sparks says, clearing his throat. A hush descends as he unfolds the last piece of paper. "For the one-thousand-dollar prize." I can feel Phoebe looking over at me, but I can't move. I can't even breathe. The drum beats a final time as Mayor Sparks's eyes flit over the paper. He raises his head. "First prize goes to . . ."

THIRTY-FOUR

"I'm telling you, those judges were completely biased," Josie says the next morning as we all gather around the kitchen table for breakfast. She's wearing one of her old T-shirts that says I GOT UP FOR THIS? in puffy blue letters. "I was watching them the whole time, and they barely even looked up when the singers came out. Actually, the only time they ever looked really interested was when the MacDougal brothers started flipping themselves around like a pair of circus freaks."

"Would you stop?" Gracie asks. "You didn't win, Josie, and no amount of sore-loser griping is going to change that. Now get over it."

Mom's sitting a few feet away from the table, feeding Baby Ella. It's Gracie's week to cook. She hands me a plate stacked high with thick slices of corn bread, pats of butter wedged in between each slice, and tells me to pass it around. There are also scrambled eggs with cheddar cheese, big chunks of fried ham, and orange juice. I take two pieces of corn bread and pass the plate to Josie, who is sitting next to me.

"Well, I know you're bummed out, Josie," Kate says, an apron tied around her waist. She's helping Gracie serve the meal. "But I think she deserved to win. She was really good."

"Good, shmood," Josie pouts. "Were you even *lis*tening when I sang? Did you *hear* that last note?" She stabs two pieces of ham with her fork and plops them onto her plate. "I got robbed."

"I had no idea you could sing like that," Mom says, looking at Josie. "I thought you were terrific."

"Darn right," Josie says. She points her fork at everyone. "And you're all going to see me on TV one day. Just you wait."

Gracie sighs heavily. "Oh, we'll wait, girl. We'll wait." She takes a big bite of corn bread and chews noisily. "Betcha Rose woulda liked this breakfast," she says. Gracie still hasn't gotten over coming back from the talent show last night to find Rose packed and gone. Kate told us that her grandfather had left everything to her. Money, the house, everything. She was going back to arrange his funeral, and then she thought she might take off. Maybe go back and finish college. It was another example of something being sad and beautiful at the same time, I thought. Life is so weird.

"You know, that girl's gonna be fine," Kate says, taking off her oven mitts. "She doesn't even *know* how good she's gonna be."

"Well, I'ma miss her," Gracie says.

Kate spears a piece of ham. "We all will."

The sound of a hammer pounding makes me turn around. "What's that?"

Gracie points backward with her thumb. "Some guy's out there working on the playroom. Guess Naomi finally found someone to finish the job."

I stand up quickly and wipe my mouth with a napkin. "I'll be right back."

The morning sun is warm on my face as I step outside. It's another beautiful blue day. Over the fence I can see Jack's top half. He is perched up on a ladder, hammering nails into a wide piece of wood. A tool belt hangs heavily around his waist.

"Hi, Mr. Millright." The sun is right behind his head and I have to squint when I look up. Jack stops hammering and looks over the fence at me. He has two nails in his mouth.

"Hey, Hershey! How you doing?"

"I'm good." I can't stop smiling. "It's good to see you up there." He nods and takes the nails out of his mouth. He's gotten a haircut and shaved.

"It feels good to be up here."

"How long do you think it will take you to finish?"

Jack shrugs. "A month. Maybe more. Naomi says she has another project for me, though, when I finish. Looks like I might be busy for a while."

"That's great." I point toward the door. "We're, um, still eating breakfast. I have to go back inside."

Jack nods. "Of course." He picks up his hammer and studies it. "You know, Phoebe told me what you did, Hershey. Talking to Naomi for me and all. I just want you to know how much I appreciate it."

I blush and shove my hands into the back pockets of my jeans. "I'm just really glad it worked out."

Jack waves his hammer toward the empty frame. "And I hope you like the room when I'm through with it. You know, if you're still here by then, I mean."

"Oh, yeah," I answer softly. "I'm sure I will."

"And I'm gonna miss that cat of yours!" he yells. "He's a cuddler, that one!"

I grin, thinking about Augustus Gloop. "I can't wait to see him again."

The women are still talking about the show when I walk back in, but as I sit down, Gracie turns to Mom.

"So, Daisy, what do you think of this girl of yours playing Beethoven up on the stage?" Mom smiles again and shifts in her seat. She looks over at me and I drop my eyes, pretending to be immersed in my corn bread.

"I told her yesterday, but I'll say it again," Mom says. "She overwhelms me. I just had no idea she had a gift like that." I keep my head low, as everyone's eyes shift in my direction.

Gracie nods slowly. "Well, I think it's gotta be some kind of gift. I've never seen no one play the piano in so short a time like Hershey here did."

"You guys got a piano?" Kate asks. Mom shakes her head. "Oh, that's too bad. 'Cause you gotta keep playing, Hershey. You gotta find a way. You know that, don't you?"

"Maybe I'll ask around at school," I say halfheartedly. "You know, in the music department." I know I'll never step foot in the music department, or talk to Mrs. Risk, the high school music director, who is always screaming at everyone to take the gum out of their mouths and "e-*nun*-ci-ate."

"I wish you would, Hershey," Mom says. "I think Kate's right. It's important that you keep playing. Not too many people are blessed in this life with a talent like that." I shoot Mom a look that says, *Please don't say any more*. Gracie, of course, catches it. Gracie catches everything.

"Oh, but she's right, Hershey. You might not think too much of it now, being that you used it yesterday to serve a specific purpose, but you've got a bigger purpose now, girl. Bigger, probably, than you can ever imagine."

Oh, man. Now they're all going to get deep on me. I just know it. Why can't they stop? Please, someone put a napkin in Gracie's mouth. Or better yet, a couple more pieces of corn bread. Gracie raises her hands in front of her chest.

"Look, I'm not going to start preaching to you or nothing here, girl. But you better believe . . . " She stops here to point a cherry red fingernail at me. "You better believe God's given you something special. And the only thing he asks for when he gives you something is for you to use it."

"I thought you said you weren't going to start preaching," Josie says.

Gracie glowers at her. "Zip it," she says. "I just want Hershey here to know that throwing something like that away would be a mistake." Mom is nodding, hanging on to Gracie's every word.

"Take it from us," Kate chimes in, a fresh pan of corn bread in her oven-mittened hands. "There's a whole bunch of mistakes just waiting for you out there to make. And you're going to make them. That's life. But don't let this be one of them, Hershey."

"It's just . . . ," I say, struggling for the words. "Well, we've got so much else to worry about right now. We've got to find a place to live. Me playing the piano doesn't really fit in right now, you know? It just doesn't make any sense."

"Hershey," Mom says. "Remember what I told you when I was in the hospital? I want you to let me worry about things from now on. You don't have to do it anymore. Playing the piano does make sense. For you, honey, it makes all the sense in the world."

A knock at the door interrupts the conversation. Kate

rushes from the room. Gracie looks over at Josie. "Is that new girl Kate told us about coming today?"

Josie nods and sighs deeply. "With four kids."

Everyone turns as Kate strides into the room. She's holding a red, white, and blue envelope from the post office. It says PRIORITY MAIL across the top in white letters.

"Where's the new girl?" Gracie asks, looking behind Kate.

"That wasn't her," Kate answers. "That was the mailman. He had a special delivery for a Miss Hershey Hollenback." Kate hands the envelope to me "*Priority* mail, no less." I look at the flat package as all the women watch and wait. There is no return address, no sender information. I turn it over to see if I can decipher anything from the back. Nothing.

"Well, come on," Josie says. "You gonna open it or what? We don't have all day, you know." Pulling open the paper zipper across the top of the envelope, I glance at Mom quizzically. She looks a little scared. For a second I think maybe it's something from Slade. Some other kind of sick joke just to twist the knife a little bit more.

But when I see the money, everything around me freezes, as if someone just pressed pause on the TV. I withdraw five crisp brand-new one-hundred-dollar bills slowly, to the gasps of everyone around me.

"Sweet Jesus!" Gracie yelps. "Where'd that come from?"

"Five hundred dollars!" Kate breathes.

"*Give* me that," Josie says, snatching a bill out of my hand. She holds it up to the light, peering closely at one side and then the other. "It's real," she says, tossing it back in my direction.

"Hershey," Mom says quietly. "Who is it from?" I look in the cardboard pocket again, but it's empty. I turn it upside down and shake it, just in case. A tiny piece of yellow paper flutters out like a butterfly. I pick it up.

Friends forever
Love, Midnight Slim

"Midnight Slim?" Josie asks, reading over my shoulder. "Who the heck is Midnight Slim? Some kind of cowboy?" Even Mom is looking at me with a bewildered expression.

"It's the girl who won the talent show," I answer. "Phoebe Millright." Everyone stares at me for a moment.

"You mean, she did that whole juggling routine with the flaming sticks, and won all that money, and then shipped half of it off to *you*?" Josie looks incredulous.

"I have to go make a phone call," I say, getting up once more. "I'll be right back."

I dial Phoebe's number with trembling fingers.

"Hello?" she asks sleepily.

"Phoebe." It's hard to get her name out around the lump in my throat.

"Hey!" she says. "Did you see Jack? Is he there? Is he working?" I glance outside, stare at Jack's arms as he pounds another nail into the frame.

"I'm looking at him right now. He's up on a ladder, hammering nails into the wall." I swear I can feel Phoebe grinning through the phone. "Phoebe," I start again. "I got the package."

"You did? *Already?*"

"Yeah, I did." There is a dense silence. "Phoebe, I can't take your money. It's too much. Besides, you won it, fair and square."

"Of course you can take it. It's to help for your new place."

"No, Phoebe. You need it more. And you earned it. I mean, throwing those fire sticks around like you did . . . "

"Well, I only decided to do those at the last minute, after Slade yelled out at you. I figured if they weren't going to give you first prize because of that, then I sure as heck was going to get it. You're the one who earned it, Hershey, not me."

"Oh, Phoebe . . . "

"No, it's true, Hershey. Slade's taken a lot from you for a long time. I didn't want him to take that, too."

"But I finished playing," I protest. "He didn't ruin it completely."

"I know," Phoebe says softly. "I was watching you on

that bench, trying so hard to pull it back together again. And you did it, Hershey. I could tell when you started playing again that you had dug deep and found something inside that even Slade hadn't touched."

"You saw that?" I whisper.

"Yeah," Phoebe says. "I did."

The two of us sit for a moment, huddled over our phones, just breathing.

"You're the best friend I've ever had," I say finally, trying hard not to cry.

"And you," Phoebe says, "are not so bad yourself."

THIRTY-FIVE

THE BEST THINGS ABOUT OUR NEW PLACE:

1. Slade isn't here.
2. Augustus Gloop loves it!
3. I can have Phoebe over to visit.
4. I got to paint my bedroom yellow and hang my necklace from Lupe over my bed.
5. I don't have to hide my notebooks.
6. My piano.

Despite all my begging and pleading, Mom wouldn't take the talent show money from Phoebe. She said it was mine to keep, that I deserved it more than anyone else she knew. I spent twenty-five dollars on new snacks for the shelter kitchen, and then kept the rest of it under my pillow for a few days, just thinking about stuff I could buy. Maybe I could get Augustus Gloop a new bed. Or shoes for Baby Ella, who would be starting nursery school in the fall. Maybe I would open a savings account, like Phoebe had done with her half, and keep adding to it. But then, a few days after Mom found a new apartment and signed the lease, she took me and Ella downtown.

"Where're we going?" I asked, looking uneasily around the familiar neighborhood.

"Over to Sally's," Mom said, taking my hand. "I want to show you something." Her chin was set, her shoulders squared. If she wasn't worried about running into Slade, I thought, then I wouldn't worry about it either. "Look," she said, pointing toward the corner as we walked inside. The old piano she had played for me all those years ago was still sitting there, covered with dust and clothes. "How much?" she asked Sally. It was three hundred and fifty dollars. Mom looked at me and raised her eyebrows. I stared at her for a minute, hardly daring to let myself breathe. It was as if everything had finally come together, all at the same time, for both of us. I didn't know whether to laugh or shout, cry or yell, whoop or scream.

"Can I?" I asked.

"*Can* you?" Mom burst out, crying now. "I'll buy it myself, Hershey Hollenback, if you don't!"

A whole month has gone by since we left the shelter. I am sitting at our new kitchen table on a Saturday morning in August, thinking about Gracie and Josie. I think about them a lot, mostly just to wonder how they're doing. Gracie left just before us, after getting an invitation from her sister, who lives in South Carolina, to move in with her. Josie got a brand-new place on the other side of Sommersville, and was scheduled to leave the day after us. Saying good-bye was harder than I thought. Not as hard as saying good-bye to Lupe, but hard enough. I hadn't realized how much I had grown to like having them around, even if it was just listening to them talk outside my bedroom door. Gracie hugged me hard before she left.

"You keep playing that piano," she said to me, tweaking me on the nose. "And don't be stubborn about it. Just do it, girl." She hugged Mom, too, and whispered something in her ear before she pulled away. Mom still won't tell me what she said.

Josie punched me in the arm the day we left, which, for her I guess, was the equivalent of giving me a big ol' good-bye kiss.

"It was great hanging with you, Hershey," she said.

I nodded and grinned. "You too, Josie. Good luck with everything."

I looked down when I felt a tug on my shorts.

"Bye, Hershey," Macy said. Her nose was still running, but Josie had pinned her hair back neatly with a pink barrette. She was holding her little brother's hand.

"Hoi-shey baw!" Galvin said. "Bye, bye, Hoi-shey baw!"

I hugged them both. Tight. I thought about telling Josie

right then, right at that minute, that as small as Galvin was, he understood too. The same as Macy. But I didn't. I have a feeling that deep down she already knows.

"Bye, guys," I whispered. "Take care."

Now I look down at Augustus Gloop, who is in my lap, sleeping. Ever since I picked him up at the motel on that last day, he's been attached to me like glue. And I'm glad. I carry him around the house all day, just like I used to do with Baby Ella. And when he curls up around my feet in bed and tucks his little head under his paw for the night, there's nothing better in the world.

A knock on the door interrupts my thoughts. I hold my tongue between my teeth and go over to open it.

"Hey, Hershey," Slade says. He runs a hand nervously over his clean-shaven face.

"Hey," I say. He's much thinner than the last time I saw him in court, when Mom and I went to get the custody order for Baby Ella. The protection order was modified too, so that he and Mom could have contact just in regards to Baby Ella. Otherwise, he's not allowed to be around us. At all. He's been pretty good about it too. The last time he came for Baby Ella, he even told Mom that he had stopped drinking.

"The baby ready?" he asks.

I turn on my heel and sit back down in my place at the table. "Mom! Slade's here for Baby Ella!" Slade stares at his shoes.

Mom emerges from Baby Ella's bedroom, holding her hand. When Baby Ella sees Slade, she rushes to him, her chubby arms out wide.

"Daddy!" she shrieks. "Daddy!" He scoops her up and kisses her fat cheek. Mom bites her lip and looks at the floor.

"I'll have her home by five," Slade says. He looks over my way. "See you, Hershey." I lift my hand but don't look up. Slade disappears behind the door. Mom walks over to where I am and puts her arms around me.

"So it's Saturday. What are you doing today?" As if in response, Phoebe appears at the front door.

"You ready, Hersh?" she calls out.

I grab my jacket. "Just going downtown with Phoebe." I look at Mom over my shoulder. "She wants to look for new hair stuff. You have work?"

She nods. "I'll be at Wal-Mart until four. I was thinking maybe we could all go see a movie tomorrow. Me, you, and Ella. You wanna go?"

"Yeah." I grin. "That'd be great, Mom."

She smiles. "Be home in time for dinner, okay? Have fun."

"Thanks, Mom. I will."

It's going to be a great rest of the summer.

THIRTY-SIX

It's after midnight, but I'm still wide awake. I feel restless and hungry. Leaning over the side of my bed, I stare at the orange bag of Cheetos sitting on the floor next to my tennis shoes. It's a supersize bag, which means it will take a nice long time to eat. But then I remember how eating them over the last few months hasn't really filled anything inside of me. At least not the stuff that needs to be filled, anyway. I think about the new music book Mom bought me a few days ago. It's all Mozart. I already love him. Beethoven will probably always be my favorite, but Mozart is a little lighter, a little happier, which is how I've been feeling these days. I get up and walk out to the living room. The black and white piano keys gleam like tiny lily pads in the moonlight.

I sit down at the bench and open the piano. Before I start, I whisper the sentence I engraved under the lid:

Courage! In spite of all bodily weaknesses
my spirit shall rule.
—LUDWIG VAN BEETHOVEN

I say it out loud at least once a day.

It makes me feel strong inside, like I can do anything.

And that maybe Lupe is never really that far away, after all.

I start to play.

And I don't stop until I am full.